PRAISE FOR *NEW YOR[K]* *USA TODAY* BESTSELL[ING] ANNE FRASIER

"Frasier has perfected the art of making a reader's skin crawl."

—*Publishers Weekly*

"A master."

—*Minneapolis Star Tribune*

"Anne Frasier delivers thoroughly engrossing, completely riveting suspense."

—Lisa Gardner

"Frasier's writing is fast and furious."

—Jayne Ann Krentz

PRAISE FOR *FIND ME*

An Amazon Charts number 1 bestseller.

Number 26 Amazon bestseller of 2020.

"An exquisitely crafted thriller. Frasier has outdone herself with this shocker."

—*Publishers Weekly* (starred review)

"For thriller fans who appreciate intricate and unconventional plots, with shocking twists."

—*Library Journal*

PRAISE FOR *THE BODY READER*

Winner of the International Thriller Writers 2017 Thriller Award for Best Paperback Original.

"Absorbing."

—*Publishers Weekly*

"This is an electrifying murder mystery—one of the best of the year."

—Mysterious Reviews

"I see the name Anne Frasier on a book and I know I am in for a treat . . . I thought it was a very unique premise and coupled with the good characters, made for an almost nonstop read for me. I highly recommend this."

—Pure Textuality

"*The Body Reader* earned its five stars, a rarity for me, even for books I like. Kudos to Anne Frasier."

—The Wyrdd and the Bazaar

"A must-read for mystery suspense fans."

—*Babbling About Books*

PRAISE FOR *PLAY DEAD*

"This is a truly creepy and thrilling book. Frasier's skill at exposing the dark emotions and motivations of individuals gives it a gripping edge."

—RT Book Reviews

"*Play Dead* is a compelling and memorable police procedural, made even better by the way the characters interact with one another. Anne Frasier will be appreciated by fans who like Kay Hooper, Iris Johansen, and Lisa Gardner."

—Blether: The Book Review Site

"A nicely constructed combination of mystery and thriller. Frasier is a talented writer whose forte is probing into the psyches of her characters, and she produces a fast-paced novel with a finale containing many surprises."

—I Love a Mystery

"Has all the essentials of an edge-of-your-seat story. There is suspense, believable characters, an interesting setting, and just the right amount of details to keep the reader's eyes always moving forward . . . I recommend *Play Dead* as a great addition to any mystery library."

—Roundtable Reviews

PRAISE FOR *PRETTY DEAD*

"Besides being beautifully written and tightly plotted, this book was that sort of great read you need on a regular basis to restore your faith in a genre."

—Lynn Viehl, *Paperback Writer* (Book of the Month)

"By far the best of the three books. I couldn't put my Kindle down till I'd read every last page."

—NetGalley

PRAISE FOR *HUSH*

"This is by far and away the best serial-killer story I've read in a long time . . . strong characters, with a truly twisted bad guy."
—Jayne Ann Krentz

"I couldn't put it down. Engrossing . . . scary . . . I loved it."
—Linda Howard

"A deeply engrossing read, *Hush* delivers a creepy villain, a chilling plot, and two remarkable investigators whose personal struggles are only equaled by their compelling need to stop a madman before he kills again. Warning: don't read this book if you are home alone."
—Lisa Gardner

"A wealth of procedural detail, a heart-thumping finale, and two scarred but indelible protagonists make this a first-rate read."
—*Publishers Weekly*

"Anne Frasier has crafted a taut and suspenseful thriller."
—Kay Hooper

"Well-realized characters and taut, suspenseful plotting."
—*Minneapolis Star Tribune*

PRAISE FOR *SLEEP TIGHT*

"Guaranteed to keep you awake at night."
—Lisa Jackson

"There'll be no sleeping after reading this one. Laced with forensic detail and psychological twists."

—Andrea Kane

"Gripping and intense . . . Along with a fine plot, Frasier delivers her characters as whole people, each trying to cope in the face of violence and jealousies."

—*Minneapolis Star Tribune*

"Enthralling. There's a lot more to this clever intrigue than graphic police procedures. Indeed, one of Frasier's many strengths is her ability to create characters and relationships that are as compelling as the mystery itself. Will linger with the reader after the killer is caught."

—*Publishers Weekly*

PRAISE FOR *THE ORCHARD*
(writing as Theresa Weir)

"Eerie and atmospheric, this is an indie movie in print. You'll read and read to see where it is going, although it's clear early on that the future is not going to be kind to anyone involved. Weir's story is more proof that only love can break your heart."

—*Library Journal*

"A gripping account of divided loyalties, the real cost of farming, and the shattered people on the front lines. Not since Jane Smiley's *A Thousand Acres* has there been so enrapturing a family drama percolating out from the back forty."

—*Maclean's*

"This poignant memoir of love, labor, and dangerous pesticides reveals the terrible true price."

—*O, the Oprah Magazine* (Fall Book Pick)

"Equal parts moving love story and environmental warning."

—*Entertainment Weekly* (B+)

"While reading this extraordinarily moving memoir, I kept remembering the last two lines of Muriel Rukeyser's poem 'Käthe Kollwitz' ('What would happen if one woman told the truth about her life? / The world would split open'), for Weir proffers a worldview that is at once eloquent, sincere, and searing."

—*Library Journal* (Librarians' Best Books of 2011)

"She tells her story with grace, unflinching honesty, and compassion all the while establishing a sense of place and time with a master storyteller's perspective so engaging you forget it is a memoir."

—Calvin Crosby, Books Inc. (Berkeley, CA)

"One of my favorite reads of 2011, *The Orchard* is easily mistakable as a novel for its engaging, page-turning flow and its seemingly imaginative plot."

—Susan McBeth, founder and owner of Adventures by the Book, San Diego, CA

"Moving and surprising."

—The Next Chapter (Fall 2011 Top 20 Best Books)

"Searing . . . the past is artfully juxtaposed with the present in this finely wrought work. Its haunting passages will linger long after the last page is turned."

—*Boston Globe* (Pick of the Week)

"If a writing instructor wanted an excellent example of voice in a piece of writing, this would be a five-star choice!"

—*San Diego Union-Tribune* (Recommended Read)

"This book produced a string of emotions that had my hand flying up to my mouth time and again, and not only made me realize, 'This woman can write!' but also made me appreciate the importance of this book, and how it reaches far beyond Weir's own story."

—Linda Grana, Diesel, a Bookstore

"*The Orchard* is a lovely book in all the ways that really matter, one of those rare and wonderful memoirs in which people you've never met become your friends."

—Nicholas Sparks

"A hypnotic tale of place, people, and of Midwestern family roots that run deep, stubbornly hidden, and equally menacing."

—Jamie Ford, *New York Times* bestselling author of *Hotel on the Corner of Bitter and Sweet*

FOUND
OBJECT

FOUND OBJECT

ANNE FRASIER

Text copyright © 2022 by Theresa Weir
All rights reserved.

Published by Thomas & Mercer, Seattle

www.apub.com

Amazon, the Amazon logo, and Thomas & Mercer are trademarks of Amazon.com, Inc., or its affiliates.

ISBN-13: 9781542036405
ISBN-10: 1542036402

Cover design by Damon Freeman

Printed in the United States of America

FOUND
OBJECT

1

I looked down at the release form on the desk, my main focus being the empty line awaiting my signature. They couldn't hold me longer than seventy-two hours, but I still had to sign the paperwork to get out. I picked up the pen, leaned over, and, with a dramatic flourish, wrote *Found Object*.

It made sense once you knew the story. My mother's name was Marie Nova Bellarose, but she'd gone by Marie Nova. The press sometimes called her Supernova or Supernova Superstar. It ended up being prophetic. Her star shined bright, then exploded—both in the acting world and in real life. But long before my mother's murder, she used to tell the story of how she and my father, Max, found me on a country road in Georgia, not far from Savannah, where my mother was originally from. Whenever she'd relate the event, she'd throw back her head and laugh with this loud and joyous sound that could be heard a block away, and she'd call me her found object. My father, even though she was his sun and air and the earth under his feet, would protest, saying the story was mean.

I'd always liked it.

There were various versions, with various embellishments, but the core tale remained the same. She and my father had been driving home late at night after one of her movie premieres, the event having taken place just a few hours from Savannah, in Charleston, South Carolina, when the headlights illuminated an infant seat in the middle of the road, positioned exactly on the yellow lines like something just begging for a photo. My father had been prepared to go around it, thinking it was trash some jerk had tossed out rather than thrown away properly.

My mother made him stop.

While he sat behind the wheel, tapping his fingers in impatient annoyance, she danced in front of the headlights, finally pausing to lean over the seat. Then she looked up, her face frozen in shock. As the story went, my father thought it was all an act, because that was what she did—act—but she picked up the carrier and hurried back to the car and showed it to my father.

Inside was a baby girl, maybe a few weeks old. Not just any baby—me.

They took me home to raise and love and call their own.

I'm not sure when I stopped believing the story. I think it was gradual, like Santa Claus and the Easter Bunny. It was just fun, silly nonsense, and just the kind of thing my mother loved to indulge in. They found a child and took her home. It was a wonderful fairy tale.

Throughout the years and at seemingly every age of my life, I'd beg her to tell it to me again and again. I couldn't get enough. It would be no stretch to say I'd heard it thousands of times. In grade school, when we were forced to stand and announce where we were from, I'd proudly say *the road* while glancing at the baffled faces around me, a zing of glee shooting up my spine. With prodding from the teacher, I'd go on to explain, as if it should have been common knowledge. The story made me special and different in a good way.

Always stand out, my mother had said.

I think that was why I loved it so much. It would have been excruciating to be ordinary people with ordinary lives. Instead I'd been given an origin story and thus decreed unique. I would always be a "found object."

And yet that day, that horrible day when our world ended, started out as a boring Saturday. Maybe that was why I seemed to remember the mundane things about it. The way my dad had smelled, like coconut soap and coffee. The clothes I was wearing, the braids and the bracelets and my dress and tights and black boots. The earrings I'd put on that morning, and how I was thinking about secretly getting a tattoo even though I was too young. I'd heard about a guy who didn't check IDs. All of those stupid, stupid things that become the focus when the pain of being alive is too much to bear.

I knew my mother and father's relationship wasn't perfect. I knew she saw other men. My dad called it cheating; she said it was natural, that monogamy was smothering her. They fought about it. I'd even heard my dad crying because he loved her so much. He said he was already sharing her with the entire world until there seemed very little left for him . . . or for me.

But on that day, a most ordinary day of sunshine and seventy degrees and birds singing and a breeze coming in off the faraway ocean, on that day we were just a father and daughter, going to visit a wife and mother.

Marie hated when anybody dropped in on her, even us. Sometimes I think the idea of surprising her was mine. Other times I remember it differently. Maybe it was my father's. He might have been trying to catch her with somebody. It was an odd time for our visit—early on a Saturday morning; she liked to sleep late if she wasn't on set.

Marie Nova was in the biggest show on television. *Divination* had been running for three years and was expected to keep going for many more to come. Viewers couldn't get enough. The show was one of the reasons we'd moved from Los Angeles to Savannah, Georgia, so we could be close to where she was filming, the shoot location an hour away on the South Carolina coast. Being in Savannah also put her closer to Luminescent. She'd already been the face of the famous skin-care company for years, and having a real Georgia beauty in their campaigns was a major selling point.

Her house was close enough for us to drive and see her whenever her schedule allowed. I'd watched her struggle over the years, losing roles to others. *Divination* had been the break she'd worked so hard for. The break she deserved. I was proud of her.

On set, the actors had their own trailers. Off set, some of the cast stayed in a motel the production company rented. A whole motel. But my mother and a few other important people had their own homes. It didn't seem that strange to me that my father and I lived twenty miles away in what was almost a suburb of Savannah. She immersed herself in her work and couldn't be distracted by friends or family. The schools were better in the suburbs, she said. Only later did I realize her home was a place for her to entertain her lovers.

I was old enough to know that things weren't right between my parents, but I was also young enough to hope that I could keep them together. That I could help to make the relationship stronger. So when Max and I got in the car to drive from our home in Richmond Hill to Savannah, we left on an ordinary day and drove into a most un-ordinary day.

I had my learner's permit. In Georgia we had something called Joshua's Law, named after a teen who died in a car accident. Joshua's Law made getting a license a lot harder than it was in most other states and required forty hours of driving with a parent. You couldn't even get a real license until you were seventeen, and only then with classroom and driving hours, night and day, fulfilled. I knew kids who hadn't been able to get their license until they were eighteen.

"I could have sworn the tank was full," my father said as we drove toward the city. He glanced at my wrist and the pedometer I always wore. Almost always. "Did you wear that last night?"

"Not with my corsage. And besides, I haven't sleepwalked for a long time."

We took Highway 17 all the way in, avoiding the interstate. We crossed and drove beside coastal inlets and waterways that seemed to go every direction. I was feeling pretty smug about the good job I was doing until I heard a siren behind me. I freaked and screamed, "What do I do?"

My father stiffened and looked over his shoulder. I checked my mirror and saw lights flashing and a police car behind us, coming fast. I slammed on the brakes, changed my mind, and stepped on the gas, almost putting us in a ditch. My father grabbed the wheel, steering us back into our lane.

"You're fine," he said calmly. "Take your time. Reduce your speed, turn on your blinker, and watch the shoulder. Don't pull off the road until you reach an open spot." He pointed. "That looks good. Just angle your way over."

I was shaking, but I listened to his calm directions and finally stopped at the side of the road. I looked in the rearview mirror and watched the flashing red lights getting closer. My heart was slamming. Did I have my permit with me? What else? Registration. Where was that?

The squad car flew past.

It took me a minute to understand that they weren't after me. They were going somewhere else, to some emergency far ahead of us. "Oh my God." My voice was shaking. My body was shaking. "Oh my God."

"You did great." Dad reached over and turned on the hazard lights. "And next time you'll know just what to do."

We sat there a little bit, until I calmed down. Then I laughed. And laughed some more. That was how relieved I was.

Another cop flew past, and we waited a little longer. "Maybe you should drive," I said.

"You can do it. Take a deep breath. When you're ready, turn off the hazards, turn on your blinker, check your mirrors, and pull back on the road."

I did what he said. The deep breathing alone was helpful.

Another ten miles, and we were turning onto the one-way street in a busy downtown square that led to the house where my mother lived. The world seemed to have gotten boring again, when, with my peripheral vision, I saw my father tense and sit up straighter, leaning closer to the windshield like somebody with poor eyesight. Then I saw it. More flashing red lights. A lot of them.

"I hope the street isn't blocked," I said. "I hope we can get to her place."

Bad things didn't happen to people I knew, much less to people I loved. But beside me, my father seemed to have received some inner alert.

"Stop the car," he said. His voice held an odd tone I'd never heard before. Flat, emotionless, but also sinister. It scared me.

"But we're not—"

"Stop the car."

Her house was still half a block away. I could see it now, a cute little Victorian painted in several shades of purple, three stories with a turret.

I rolled to the curb.

"Stay here." Without looking at me, my father got out, slammed the door, and ran toward the flashing lights.

He must have thought this had something to do with my mother. I let out a whimper that came from nowhere. I cupped my hands over my mouth and nose to stop any other unwelcome sounds. *This could be anybody, anything,* I told myself.

I waited for him to come back, tell me it was her neighbor, or maybe someone had broken into their house. Maybe someone had broken into my mother's house. A crime, but not serious. Not tragic. And as I sat there, I became aware of my mother's signature scent inside the car. It was a perfume made just for her by Luminescent. Woodsy, almost masculine. The smell of it brought me comfort, along with a new wave of unease.

I had no idea how much time passed, but when my father didn't come back, I got out. Slammed the door. Walked in long strides down the sidewalk, looking like I belonged there, and I did. I cut past cars, avoided cops who were huddled together.

People stood in their front yards, their whispers carrying to my ears. They wondered what was going on. A woman said she'd heard someone had been killed. Someone had heard it was murder. Someone said it was Marie Nova.

I ran toward my mother's house, arms pumping, feet flying over the sidewalk, faces around me a blur of gaping mouths. Someone, a cop maybe, shouted at me. Or was it someone I knew? They told me to stop.

I didn't.

Finally, I got close enough to see a cluster of people in uniforms in the front yard, some of the uniformed people unrolling yellow crime-scene tape, looping it around trees and light poles. *At my mother's house.*

The sirens were silent now, but the lights were still on, red ones, blue ones too. I heard an occasional squelch from a police car, followed by a disembodied voice quacking through a radio. Other than those things, it was like someone had turned off all the sound in the world. The people gathering on the sidewalk were silent. Even the birds were quiet. The police weren't even talking to one another.

But then an awful noise split the air. A sobbing, a keening, followed by a wail of raw despair. "Marie!"

It was like my dad's voice, but different. It came from the backyard.

I ducked under the yellow tape, following the direction of my father's cry. The side gate hung open, and I walked through. Nobody stopped me. A few people noticed but seemed too shocked to care. Like they were unable to think or process my presence. I passed faces that had the same expression, all equally hard to describe. I guess it was stunned, but also like they might throw up or cry or both. Men, women, some in uniform, some not.

I wondered if it wouldn't have embedded so deeply into my brain if it hadn't been for how bright the sun was shining, creating a light that blew out all shadows and made everything look fake and staged, that made me question what all the variations of washed-out images actually were. Like looking at a photo that had been underdeveloped.

The film comparison led to another thought, and I latched on to the idea that this was a scene from her show. Yeah, that was totally it. Didn't my dad understand that? Didn't everybody else get it, or were they all actors? Had we all stepped into the middle of a shot? Were cameras rolling?

They didn't always film on set, so they'd probably staged this here, at her house. They had amazing special effects and makeup departments that could do anything. And actually, as I looked, I thought they hadn't done a very good job this time. They could have done better. There was really too much blood. And the missing head was so overdone. And the intestines. But they'd gotten the details right. Like the bird tattoo on the torso's shoulder. The other one on the thigh. Even the small line on the inner wrist that was my name.

They'd gotten all of those things right. And what about the flies? How had they done that? Cover the body parts with honey, and let a bunch of flies loose? Was the cicada noise part of it? Was the audio department behind that particularly annoying and invasive sound?

It just kept getting louder, almost like it was in my head, but it wasn't. A high-pitched buzz that intensified by the second. Was it just one, or a bunch of cicadas? Finally something else cut through the insect noise. The *whip, whip* of blades.

I looked up and saw a helicopter hovering above the backyard, blowing leaves around, creating mini tornadoes that rose and dissipated. Hard leaves smacked into the house and skittered across the brick walk. Tree branches trembled and Spanish moss snapped, broke, swirled, fell to the ground like chopped-off hair. A guy in a suit gestured toward the aircraft and shouted something about restricted air space. It seemed like a lot of activity for a single scene. And where were the cameras?

"Jupiter!"

I spotted my dad's face in the crowd. He was shouting, waving his arms, telling me to go back.

"Get out of here! Get her out of here!"

I started laughing like I'd laughed in the car once I'd realized the cop hadn't been after me. Dad didn't get it. Or he was just that good an actor. Marie always said he was a much better actor than she was, but he didn't have a camera face. I finally turned and ran toward the house, aiming for the back door. She was probably inside laughing too, watching us. She loved a good prank.

Just part of the show.

An arm reached out and blocked me. Hands grabbed me. I shoved and ripped myself free. I ran for the house again, pushing people out of the way. Up the steps, in the door, into the kitchen.

Surprised faces. "Hey, you can't be here."

More cops.

"I want to see my mother." I put my palms together as if I were diving into water. I tried to part the people, shoving, trying to move through and past them. This time I couldn't do it. Someone gripped my arm too tightly. I turned and looked. A male cop who looked horribly miscast, but his acting was decent. He had a good mixture of sympathy and horror on his face.

"You're too young," I said. "For the part," I added, in case he wasn't following. "Nobody will believe it." My mother often explained about viewer commitment, and she'd fought a few times over actors who didn't deliver the right amount of realism because they didn't look the part.

He didn't understand what I was trying to tell him. He didn't get it. Nobody got it.

"That's not my mother out there." I gave my words a firm nod. "It's really not even that good."

He frowned.

"The makeup. FX. I can't believe you fell for it." I spun around and shouted at the room of people. "I can't believe any of you fell for it!"

My dad was suddenly there in the house. Just seemed to materialize out of the walls. Crying, calling my name, telling me to get out.

I wanted to, but how?

The path to the front door was blocked. The back door? Even though I seemed to be the only one in on the joke, I still didn't want to exit the way I'd just come.

I looked at the cop. Just eyes. He was just eyes. I whispered in the lowest whisper on earth, my voice shaking, my body shaking, tears rolling down my face: "Get me out of here."

He seemed to understand my dilemma, the dilemma of the backyard. He pulled me through a sea of people, heading through the living room toward the foyer. People weren't happy about it.

"Crime scene!" someone shouted. "You have to leave!"

"No, it's not!" I shouted back.

The wooden floor had the same bounce as always. I even heard it creak in all the places it had always creaked. Some part of me seemed to understand that this might be real. This might have really happened. My mother had been murdered, her body cut up and scattered around the yard.

Had I seen her head? Was her head there? Would anybody live in this house again? Would someone buy it and give tours? Would it become another Hollywood murder story?

Out the front door. Out on the lawn. I could smell the camellias. My mother loved that about the house. All the flowers. And then my father was there again. He looked at me. His mouth dropped open, and I thought he was going to let out a roar of laughter. I felt the start of an echoing smile. But then, instead of the laugh I was anticipating, his hands went to his face. He wailed and fell to his knees. Forehead to the ground, he sobbed, his shoulders shaking. He moaned both my mother's name and mine.

The young cop was still hanging on to me. He said something. I don't know what. I was too caught up in the horror of the moment.

2

Like my mother, I could be a pretty good actress. Her acting had been the real deal, whereas mine was the kind that came in handy in undercover work and even day-to-day life. The kind that had gotten me into trouble in my last assignment and had landed me here in the mental health wing of the Hennepin County Medical Center in Minneapolis, not a place I felt I needed to be. That said, unlike some who were hospitalized against their will, I didn't mind it. Just a little vacation, with meals and drugs.

I blamed what had happened on my job. Some of my gigs required a depth that could get confusing, and the person you were playing and the people you were deceiving could begin to seem more important than your real life. But this last one had been different. I still woke up in the middle of the night thinking I was in the bed of the guy I'd ratted out.

I had no idea why, but I said, "Life does not consist mainly, or even largely, of facts and happenings. It consists mainly of the storm of thoughts that is forever blowing through one's head."

The psychiatrist across the desk from me seemed impressed. "Did you write that?"

He had a thin face and a vacation tan, commonly seen this time of year in the Land of 10,000 Lakes. If you had the money, escaping the snow and cold was one of the ways to make living in Minnesota tolerable. And if you were to visit the local airport during winter, most departing travelers would be pale and dressed in black, shoulders hunched, expressions pinched, eyes blank. The returning were tan and dressed in bright clothing, expressions open, their strides—in flip-flop happy feet—long and springy. Like returning from a soul spa.

I passed the signed sheet of paper across the desk to him. "Nope. Mark Twain."

He made an *ah* face and nodded in possible memory. "I suppose you have a lot of author quotes in your head. A quote for every occasion."

He smiled in a friendly way, but when he looked at the *Found Object* signature, the smile vanished. He heaved a sigh that involved both his shoulders, then turned around in his swivel chair. Without getting up, he rummaged in a filing cabinet.

The doctor placed a clean sheet of paper in front of me, asked that I sign again, with my real name this time. A do-over, which I could use right now. Or maybe I was just stalling. Maybe I didn't want to leave the safe cocoon, where nothing was expected of me, and every single thing was out of my control. Or better, under the control of someone else. I wasn't responsible for anything. I could do no harm here, and nobody— the people I'd hurt, family, friends if I had any left, reporters—could try to find me, talk to me, ask me questions.

He seemed bored.

I understood.

It had to be unrewarding for these emergency doctors of any specialty to spend time wading through files of people they didn't know and would never know and would never see again. Not their patients. We must all run together after a point. So many people who were hurt and lost and damaged. I wouldn't have blamed him for resisting a deep dive into me even though most people found my story interesting. But my life had been fodder for too many years, and I didn't want to talk about the recent event that had led to my hospital stay.

"Sorry," I mumbled.

"No problem," he said. "You've got some strong drugs in your system."

I kept forgetting about that. Drugs explained the heaviness in my arms and the thickness of my tongue. My slower thinking and even slower moving. To be honest, I wanted to put my head down on the desk and take a quick nap, but I forced myself to sign the form instead, correctly this time, with my *full* name, which I never used, but it seemed another amusing thing to do right now.

Jupiter Edwina Delilah Bellarose

I'd gone through a lot of nicknames in my thirty-six years because most people didn't seem inclined to call me Jupiter. I actually *liked* the name. But it was true, as I'd been told, it didn't suit me. Too flamboyant, too whimsical. Not me at all, which might explain why I liked it. I know the name Jupiter said more about my parents. It was a certain kind of person who'd name their kid after a planet.

Over the years, my name has been many things: JuJu, Bad JuJu, Good JuJu, Jujubes, Juno, Jupe, June. People who knew nothing about me immediately assumed my folks were hippies or off-gridders. I liked when that happened.

I passed the paper back.

"Jupiter," the doctor said. "Don't think I've ever met a Jupiter."

I didn't respond. It seemed like too much work.

Maybe he understood, because he moved forward. "We need to go over a few additional things before I can release you. Your occupation says you're an investigative journalist."

He was sitting in front of a large window that framed a blue winter sky, the kind of deceptive brilliance that fooled you into thinking it was warm out and not below zero. The reality was that it was often so cold cars wouldn't start, and even the interior metal door handle in the entryway of my condo became covered in frost. Touching it with a bare hand could rip the skin right off your fingers. The sun didn't fool me.

"Have I read anything you've written?"

I moved my gaze from the window back to him. I thought about some of the stories I'd broken over the years and some of the disturbing journeys I'd taken into dark lives and darker deeds, but few people noted bylines anymore. Most journalists were invisible worker bees, cogs in a machine, doing their jobs. I was more than okay with that. Invisible was good. By being invisible, I'd managed to get a few very bad men arrested and incarcerated. I'd saved kidnapped children, and I once rescued a woman who'd been imprisoned as a sex slave.

I always joked that my middle name was *Toiling in Obscurity*, and I preferred it that way. I'd seen what notoriety could do. I didn't need fame or attention. I didn't need him to know I'd saved lives but been unable to save the most important life of all, that of my mother.

I also hadn't been able to save my fake boyfriend.

I smiled a little, deliberately diverting my mind from old pain and new pain. "I broke the story about Prince's doctor."

"Really?" His interest grew, and he leaned forward, hoping for more, maybe hoping for something juicy. With the lifting and opening of his expression, I could see he wasn't quite as old as I'd first thought. He was probably in his midforties.

"I'm kidding," I confessed. People rarely wanted to hear the truth. That was what I'd learned over the years. They were much more interested in my telling them I'd known a celebrity than hearing I'd saved some kidnapped kids. I'm not sure the doctor had been that interested in the first place. He simply needed to ask all the questions and check all the release boxes. I'd seen the form before. There were a lot of evaluations that needed evaluating.

He adjusted his monitor and read more of my patient profile, then glanced up. "This photo doesn't look like you." He turned the screen long enough for me to see the image but not long enough for me to absorb any other info in case I was using someone else's insurance.

"Oh, that's me." It had been taken just before I'd gone undercover, before I'd designed myself to be the person Salvador Cassavetes would fall for. In my research, I'd noted that every single woman on Salvador's arm had been some form of blonde, from platinum to gold.

My expensive salon color had long since begun to fade. The manicured nails were already gone, bitten or clipped off. I bent forward and showed the doctor my dark roots. They were almost an inch long, stopping abruptly where the gold began. I smoothed my shoulder-length, blunt-cut hair, which had been trimmed with scissors that cost as much as my van. The hair, plus a wardrobe like something I'd never wear in my real life, had taken me way over budget, and my boss had almost cried when he'd seen the credit card statement. I'd assured him the look was everything. He mumbled something about being glad I hadn't gotten Botox and a boob job.

I'd considered it. That was how committed I'd been.

Now it all seemed so stupid and un-gloriously unnoble. It hadn't been to save a person's life. Salvador hadn't really been hurting anybody, not really. But for some reason, art forgery had felt especially loathsome to me. I'd seen it as a challenge, and I'd felt he should be exposed.

"I've been working undercover," I explained.

"I knew I recognized your name. I read about the forger." He looked at me with kind eyes, that kindness enough to bring on a fresh wave of guilt over the signature.

"That couldn't have been easy for you," he said. "But good job. Excellent work."

I wouldn't mention the regret I had over the "good job" I'd done. I wouldn't mention it was the very reason I'd fallen into a deep depression, so shut down that someone had called 911 for a wellness check.

I suspected my boss had requested it. And I suspected it wasn't really out of concern for me, but more about the paper. He'd tried to reach me several times before I'd finally turned off my phone. And he'd come to my condo. I'd seen his car from my second-story window. He'd even slipped in and made it all the way to my door. I hadn't answered his knock.

It wasn't easy being a snitch, a mole, a liar, not if you had any conscience at all. Lines got blurry, really blurry, when you were in the middle of it. And it was especially sick and tragic if you fell in love with the very person you were supposed to be exposing. I mean, it was laughable, really. And so unlike me that I often wanted to kick my own ass. But love tripped me up and was still tripping me up.

That train of inquiry exhausted, the doctor went back to my profile, read a little more. "Do you still sleepwalk?" he asked.

The first time had been in Georgia as a teen. Before my mother's murder. I woke up far from home, just standing in the middle of a sidewalk. Another time I was found trying to get into someone's house. Once I even drove my parents' car around. Maybe more than once. There had always been some dispute about that. My parents bought me a pedometer and made me wear it so they could monitor my movements. Sometimes I'd wake up in bed with no memory of walking miles that night.

"I was a kid," I said. "A teenager, and I was taking something to help me sleep. We suspect that caused it. It doesn't happen anymore."

"It can be a childhood problem," he said. "But keep in mind that stress and trauma and even new medication can retrigger it in people who have a history."

In my adult life, I'd graduated from a pedometer to a tracker, worn it off and on, and finally quit after no sign of nocturnal movement.

"Here's an interesting thing," he said. "Supposedly some people have committed crimes while sleepwalking."

I'd heard of that defense. "Do you actually believe someone can kill when they're sleepwalking?"

"I don't know. Seems like a stretch to me."

"Me too."

As if I'd willed an escape from the conversation, I felt a heaviness overtake my body, and my mind returned to Salvador. It felt like a year since the night it happened, but it also felt closer than that, like just yesterday. The calendar and my roots told me a month had passed. I'd turned in my story, and the plan had been to spend the evening with him. He'd sent his jet to pick me up, and I flew to the Keys, where he had a private home on a private island. I wanted to tell him before the story ran. I didn't want him to find out by reading it.

There was a weather delay, grounding the plane for much of the day at some tiny airport. When the rain finally abated, we circled a storm and finally set down on the island. In retrospect, I should have noticed that he'd been subdued, but I thought maybe it had been me, maybe I was creating tension waiting to reveal my deceit.

I put it off. I wanted one more evening, one more stroll, one more sunset. And so, at his suggestion, we'd walked hand in hand on his private beach the way we often did, and as the sun went down, he called me his golden goddess. I loved it.

But I should have known I'd never deceived him.

He had people who scrutinized new contacts. They would have looked into my backstory and found it flimsy. Someone could have run my face to find my true identity. It wasn't hard these days. It had been foolish of me to think I'd carried it off.

I always knew who you were, he'd said.

Of course he had.

3

The doctor gave me a giant bag of my belongings, along with enough drugs to get me through a couple of days. Antidepressants that I was familiar with and a sedative to be taken as needed.

"You can get the rest of your prescription filled before leaving the building," he said.

I'd wait. Maybe I wouldn't fill it at all. I deserved to suffer more.

"Is someone picking you up?" he asked. "Would you like my assistant to call a cab?"

I pulled my winter coat from the bag and put it on, tugging the hood with the fake fur over my head. The jacket was old and would gross most people out, but it was soft and familiar to me, and it smelled like the condo I'd inherited from my aunt. Like old walls, and old wood, and old books, and the broken hearts of all the men my aunt had never married. "I'll get an Uber."

He seemed relieved to be able to wrap up.

I wondered if I'd been there a long time. Or not long at all.

"Here's my card. Call me if you need anything. Don't be afraid to reach out. Also included are some numbers that might be helpful."

I looked at the card. Suicide hotline. Depression hotline. "If I get an extra ticket to Paisley Park, I'll give you a call."

He looked confused.

"Bad joke," I said. "We were talking about Prince earlier?"

"Oh yes."

Now I was just annoying him. I would leave. "Don't worry. I'll rate you five stars." I always felt the need to exit on a joke.

I left.

Outside the hospital, the temperature close to zero according to the app on my phone, I breathed deep, exhaling the stale sadness of the hospital. For all my negative thoughts about Minnesota winters, I had to admit there was nothing like the air this time of year. Even mixed with exhaust fumes, it seemed like primo stuff. And even after the heat of the building, the sunshine on my face still felt almost warm. The wide sidewalk was clear, with deep snow on each side, but I could feel the promise of warmer weather even though it was February. I became aware of myself just standing on the walk, in this city, in this country, on this earth. I was wearing the winter coat, unzipped, army green with the fake fur hood and a plaid cloth lining. No gloves.

I should do something.

I looped the plastic bag over one wrist and shoved my hands in my pockets, thankful to feel the metal edge of my condo key. I wasn't wearing winter boots but instead the wool slippers from home. I guess I hadn't changed when the cops showed up at my door. People were glancing at me. Some shot me looks of exasperation while others smiled.

I realized I was blocking the path to the front doors. "I can take a hint." I moved.

And then I spotted something that penetrated the fog in my brain . . .

A black Cadillac Escalade waiting at the end of the long sidewalk in a no-parking zone. I managed to veer to the left as the back door was flung wide by some unknown and unseen person in the dark interior.

I heard my name.

My heart clenched in my chest, and the world seemed to tip so much I thought I might slide right off.

The voice repeated the summons.

Some ancient warning that harkened back to my cave-gal ancestors told me to run. Fast. But there was enough awareness not obliterated by drugs for me to keep my cool a few seconds longer.

I shuffled forward and acted as if I planned to get inside the vehicle. I ducked my head. I saw the driver, and I saw the person in the back seat, both people who'd once looked at me with kindness, their faces now hostile. It was two worlds colliding, because they belonged to warm places with beaches and sun.

I spun away, my feet smacking the sidewalk, arms pumping, strides as long as I could make them without losing my slippers. Behind me, the car door slammed, and tires squealed. I could not possibly outrun a vehicle. My escape was blocked by boulevards of deep snow turned black from exhaust fumes. Muted sunlight ricocheting off tall buildings of glass.

The SUV lurched to a stop, blocking my path. The door flew open again, this time revealing long legs and expensive clothing and big dark glasses. Salvador's sister, Ferdie.

Like Sal, she was mostly Italian mixed with a little Greek, both of those qualities giving her that take-no-prisoners persona.

I had so many questions. How had she gotten to Minnesota? She lived in Miami. She'd probably taken her brother's private jet, the same one I'd taken the day he swam away. How long had she been in town? Had she come just to confront me? Seemed likely. What did she think of the weather? That question was probably due to the drugs in my system, but I was also curious about how a sunshine-and-warm-weather person could tolerate the shock. But she had a lot more on her mind than weather.

"Are those your real clothes?" she asked with disdain. She had shiny black hair and lips that were a perfect shade of red. Eyes, with their expertly applied liner, a blue green.

I looked down at my unzipped coat, spotting a black T-shirt advertising a local bar. Below that, jeans, leather belt, and boots. Nothing like the clothes I'd worn to seduce her brother.

Seduce.

The idea was laughable. I was no seductress. But now I wondered if I'd been pretending to be my mother. My mother could seduce the hell out of any guy. Like the boy who'd escorted me to homecoming. Marie Nova had always been the attractive one in the family, and whenever someone complimented my looks, it was because of some small thing, maybe the dimple in one cheek, that reminded them of my mother's blinding magnificence. It had been nice to be considered beautiful on my own even if it had required a disguise.

"You're more fake than any of his paintings ever were," Ferdie said. "He was an artist. He was an old soul, connected to the past. He was channeling the masters. You didn't understand that."

I wanted to say she was fooling herself. I wanted to say it was all lies. But in my drugged state I instead focused on the February sun, watching as it became big and orange and indistinct, and I felt myself warm with the memory of that last day with Salvador. The sun had hovered in the sky so long that I'd thought maybe it wasn't the sun at all. But then the orange glow sank ever so slowly to finally dip below the horizon and vanish.

With no conversation, Salvador removed his clothes, even his gold watch, which he placed on top of his leather shoes.

"What are you doing?" I asked.

"Going for a swim."

"It's almost dark. Wait until morning." Undertows had killed in this spot.

"Tomorrow will be too late."

With his fingers through my hair, he pulled my face to his and kissed me.

"Did you feel loved?" he asked.

I didn't even know what to say to that. He'd never talked of love before.

"I hope so," he said.

21

"I don't understand."

"I want you to know I would have loved you, regardless. It was *you* I fell for. Your sense of humor, especially. You made me laugh so many times. I needed that in my life. I always knew who you were. I thought I could win you over. And I think I did, didn't I?"

I felt the cold Minnesota air on my face, realizing I was here in the now, facing the sister of a man I'd killed.

"He loved you," his sister said. A gentle man who'd had, at least as far as I knew, the perfect childhood. A man who'd loved not just the girl with the golden hair, but apparently the deep-down Jupiter me.

"*I* loved you," she continued.

So many times, I'd almost deleted my computer files. I wished I had. It hadn't been the money or the lifestyle. Although, to be honest, I'd tried to imagine him without all of that, and it was impossible, so I wasn't sure. I think that was part of his magic. But he'd also brought a sense of security to my world.

"I'm sorry." I licked my lips. They were dry and chapped. Then I stupidly said, "I'm stoned."

She opened her purse and reached inside. I flinched, expecting her to pull out the gun I knew she kept there. Instead, much more shocking than a gun, she held a framed piece of artwork. Eight by ten. It was one of Van Gogh's lesser-known seascapes of dark and tumultuous waves, the raw prescience of it sharply painful.

My mouth went even drier. I thought about the night Sal had painted it, and how in love I'd been.

She tossed it out the door, and it fell to my feet, the frame splintering and the glass shattering.

He could imitate anything. Any piece of art you put in front of him. I'd issued the challenge to reproduce a Van Gogh. He'd done it while we were drinking wine, probably a bottle that had cost hundreds of dollars. He'd finished the piece in less than two hours.

Let's not call it a forgery, he'd said. *Because it's just for you.* Then he'd gone on to explain how his imitations were more accurate than the originals.

He knew about such things because he was the person museums hired when buying art, an authenticator. His was the eye they wanted, and his was the advice they took. He'd sold them some of his own art, pointing out the little mistakes the artist had made. He would draw attention to things in originals that he could say were forgeries. Flaws from an unskilled hand. Paint colors that didn't match. His forgeries were perfectly flawed.

My nose was running from the cold. My fingers were numb. I wiped at my face with the back of my hand, bent over, and began picking up the glass. I cut myself. I saw the blood, saw the slice on my finger, but didn't feel anything. And all the while I was aware of Ferdie sitting in the car watching me.

I threw away the glass and the frame in a nearby trash can, but I kept the fake Van Gogh, careful not to get blood on it. I would reframe it.

I stared at the image.

"I came here to kill you," Ferdie said.

I nodded. I deserved to die.

"But then I realized he wouldn't have wanted me to do that."

She was probably right. But that didn't stop the aching feeling that I probably deserved death.

Ferdie started crying.

He'd paid for her education. He'd taken care of her and taken care of his entire family, even second and third cousins. He'd paid their medical bills, bought them cars, made sure they didn't want for anything. And they'd all welcomed me into their midst. A liar. And I'd taken their North Star from them.

I thought back to when my own star was extinguished. The entire world seemed to stop the day my mother was murdered. It had been weird to see the outpouring of grief from around the globe and know it was all for her. Not that others didn't deserve to grieve in their own way, but I kept thinking about how strange it was and how it somehow diminished the importance of my own grief, as if I had no more right to it than strangers.

They didn't know her. How did someone possibly grieve for someone they didn't even know? But their sorrow had been real even though they would never experience the true her. Just a shadow of her, or just the persona of her. They would never know the person who threw back her head and roared in laughter after telling the story of finding me in the middle of the road in the middle of the night.

As I stood on the sidewalk, clutching my small bag of drugs, standing under the blinding midwestern sun, my panting breath a cloud in front of my face, I missed him with an ache that went all the way to my bones, with a physical pain even the drugs couldn't dull. I missed the feel of his cool, dry hand against mine. I missed how he said my name, with the hint of a southern drawl even though he'd never lived in the South. He'd loved to mimic my accent.

"You killed him," she said.

"I did." And there were times I wondered if I'd had anything to do with my mother's murder. That was survivor's guilt for you. We always wished we'd done or not done something.

A horn honked. I looked across traffic to see a white Jetta at a red light. The window was lowered, and a gloved hand motioned me to come. "Jupe! Hurry! Before the light changes."

The guy behind the wheel was my boss, Bennett Roth, the person who'd betrayed me. The person behind this entire clusterfuck. Under other circumstances, I would have thrown him the finger and marched off, never speaking to him again. But I was high, could use a ride, and desperately needed to get away from Ferdie.

Clutching my fake Van Gogh and my hospital bag, I scuttled across the street, slipping through cars. The light turned green. Horns honked. I opened the back door of the Jetta and dove inside. "Take me home."

4

Bennett tromped down on the gas. Tires squealed, and we pulled away.

"Did you call for the wellness check?" I asked from the cramped back seat.

He glanced at me in the rearview mirror. "No."

"Liar."

"Okay, yeah. Stay in the car, though."

Like he thought I might jump out once I knew the truth.

Most of the time he wore contacts, but today he was wearing glasses with heavy black frames that matched the black stocking cap on his head. His brown hair with streaks of gray was pulled into a ponytail, and he was several months into his winter beard, which he'd shave come spring.

I called it the Minnesota lumberjack look. I liked when wealth and social status, for lack of a better description, were ignored. Bennett had remained under the radar, driving his own little beater, dressing in clothes he'd probably had for ten years, going up north to camp and canoe in the Boundary Waters like many middle-aged dudes in the area. It also made me more aware of the difference between him and Sal. And made me wonder how I could have fallen for someone who embraced a lavish lifestyle. It really was like the old Jupiter had gone far away to be replaced by Sal's golden girl. And now who was left? I didn't know.

"You weren't answering your phone or the door." Eyes on the road, he took a well-executed turn, heading toward my condo. He smelled like coffee and Bryant Lake Bowl, the grill where he could often be found conducting business from a corner booth. He had an office in Saint Paul, but he liked the bustle of the café. "I was worried about you."

"Worried because all of this is on you."

He made a choking sound but didn't reply. The rest of the ride was silent.

At my place, I put the fake Van Gogh on a shelf in the living room. I distantly noted that my hand was no longer bleeding.

The living space was old Minneapolis, four condos, two up and two down. Mine was on the second floor of the brick building, overlooking a street with big trees and Victorian-style light posts. I'd come here as a teen, after my mother's murder. Over the years I'd left and returned, but it always felt like a sanctuary. The interior was dark by choice. A scattering of lamps on bookcases and end tables, and no rude overhead lights. The long curtains that hung ceiling to floor were still open, framing the deep blue of the world outside, that very specific blue you saw only in a cold climate after the sun went down.

I hadn't changed much of the condo since my aunt's death. She'd lived in the building for forty years, a professor at the University of Minnesota, surrounded by her books and antiques. I could never let it go, since it was the last I had of her. And through her, the last of my mother.

My aunt Stella had died of cancer three years earlier, hadn't suffered long, and I should have been thankful for that. But I'd wanted one more day, one more hour, one more minute. I had Bennett, but our relationship was complicated. He thought he knew what was best for me. Sometimes he was wrong. Sometimes he was right. My aunt had been my last real family other than my father. Both sides, mother and father, had been an unreproductive bunch.

Bennett kicked off his boots and shrugged out of his coat but left his stocking cap on his head. "That does look realistic," he said, standing in front of the painting. "I mean, I wouldn't really know, but . . ."

I tossed my jacket on a chair and dropped to the couch, lay down, and waited for Bennett to leave.

Instead, he ordered food from a nearby Thai place.

I tried to stay awake, a down comforter over me. My mind drifted in and out. I drowsed yet was aware of him moving around, straightening up, picking up trash. At one point I heard water running and realized he was doing dishes. The normalcy of it, along with being taken care of, was soothing and made me even sleepier.

It was fully dark by the time the food arrived. He tipped the delivery person. Must have been a generous amount, because she gave him an enthusiastic thanks.

"I wanted to talk to you about your plans," Bennett said once the girl was gone and he was unpacking our order.

"I don't have any."

"That's what I mean. I think you should make some. It would be good for you."

"I'll never work for you again. You betrayed me."

"Tell me this. If I hadn't run the piece when I did, where would you be right now? You were going to warn him. And he would have vanished in a totally different way."

"But he would have still been alive. You . . . and *I* wouldn't be responsible for killing him."

"They haven't found a body yet."

"And they might never. I was there. Unless he was part fish, and I'm pretty sure he wasn't, he's dead."

"You need a job. You need income. But more than that, you need to work. I know you."

I'd never mentioned falling for Sal to anybody, but Bennett had known. Maybe he'd spotted the unmistakable glow in our video meetings.

Lack of money was a real concern. I wondered if I'd paid my taxes and utilities. I should have had some kind of bonus coming, but I'd have to look at my contract. I recalled something about losing it if I quit. "I could do some talk shows," I said. They typically compensated well. Some of them.

"You in front of the camera? I doubt it."

He was right. I hated that kind of thing, and it was risky. People always wanted to question me about my mother. "I'll write a memoir."

"That takes time. And honestly, I can't see you being satisfied. You like to dig for the truth. That's what you're good at. Listen, Jupiter, I'm sorry. I was trying to protect the paper, protect the story, protect you. I made a tough decision. I hate that he's dead. Of course I hate that. I hate what you went through, but, okay, here's the truth. I was afraid you'd run off with him and end up in prison yourself. And I'd never hear from you again."

"I wish I'd done that. Run."

"No, you don't. Time would come when you'd start to regret that choice."

"You're trying to frame this like you were thinking about me, but you were thinking about you."

"Of course! The story would lose impact if he ran and nobody knew where he was," Bennett said. "But I wanted to see him arrested. Not dead. Definitely not dead. And"—he pressed a finger against the table-top as if he were pressing an unseen alert button—"I did not want to see you go down with him. I do regret how it all played out, but I don't think I'd choose to do things differently. And he was a criminal. No telling what he was capable of. You might have been the one to end up dead."

Salvador would never have hurt me. I was sure of that.

We sat down to eat.

Wordlessly, we passed the white takeout containers back and forth, putting items on our plates. I preferred spring rolls; Bennett, pad Thai. I looked across the table into his kind eyes, and I felt my anger lessen, my heart soften. He *had* been watching out for me, just like right now, just like his call to the cops to check on me. He hadn't wanted me to vanish with Sal. Or die.

"Feels like old times, right?" he asked, retrieving the plastic forks that had come with the carryout.

What I wished for Bennett was a soul mate, someone he would spend the rest of his life with. "That person you were married to was a bitch," I said bluntly.

He laughed. A big laugh. I liked to make people laugh.

"No," he said. "She was just kind of messed up. It wasn't her fault."

"Okay, but I think you're being too kind."

"A person can never be too kind."

Even the plates we used had belonged to my aunt. I don't know what that said about me. That I didn't want to let her go, not even her plates and glasses and lamps with orange shades, or that I didn't want to find my true self.

Bennett took a bite of food, chewed, then, elbows on the table—also my aunt's—asked a startling question. "Was Cassavetes the first guy you ever really loved?"

"That's a little personal, especially coming from you."

"I'm in the truth business."

"Okay, how about this? I had a bad crush on a guy in high school. His name was Quint Dupont."

"Does everybody in the South have an exotic, romantic name? Because it sure seems that way."

The teapot on the stove began to whistle. He moved to get to his feet. I put up my hand, stopping him. "I'm closer." I brought the kettle to the table and filled two cups with hot water, then sat back down. And reluctantly allowed myself to think about the night before my mother died and the last time I saw her. "Dupont and I went to homecoming together."

"Wow. And we know what can happen on homecoming night."

"No. Not that. My mother made sure of it." I didn't want to talk about that day, or the day that followed. "He even got me home early. But he was probably my first real crush." Uncomfortable, I changed the subject. "You don't think I loved my ex?"

"I think he was convenient."

"I disagree."

"Maybe you loved him for a little while. Maybe you loved him with half your heart and not your whole heart." He looked at me from across the table. "I think you loved Cassavetes completely, but from the perspective of the person you were pretending to be, so much that his personality devoured yours."

I wasn't going to tell him I'd had similar thoughts. I searched through the tea bags, found something with fruit in it. "You seem to think you know an awful lot about me."

"I do know a lot about you. Maybe more than you know yourself. Cassavetes was so opposite everything you'd experienced in your life, from the island setting to the extravagance, that it made it easier to leave yourself behind and embrace something entirely new and removed from all the bad things."

I let that sit in my brain a moment. "You could very well be right."

He looked pleased.

"But the love was real." The pain I was experiencing was definitely real.

"I don't think it was. I don't think you've ever really been in love. At least the real Jupiter hasn't."

I was too tired to argue with him about whether I'd been in love or not.

He put down his fork and looked at me. I'd seen that expression before, and it involved trying to convince me to do something I didn't want to do.

"How about writing something happy?" he said. "From somewhere other than here. Somewhere warmer."

"Happy? I think I should jump right back into investigative work," I told him.

"Maybe just give happy stuff a try. Consider it a little vacation."

"I don't do happy stuff. Although I wouldn't mind being elsewhere." The last thing I needed was a vacation, but he was right about getting out of town. And he was right about needing to work, immerse myself in something completely new. But as far as happy stories went, I had no interest in writing fluff pieces about the newest cupcake shop in town or someone who made bags from old signs.

"Do you have a missing persons case?" I asked. Something I might actually solve. "Or a possible homicide? I'd really love a juicy homicide. Some mystery I can really sink into."

"I'm thinking you could write a story about the history of the Luminescent empire."

I froze with my cup halfway to my mouth. To go home, to even think of going home, made my heart race in a terrible way.

"The company is turning one hundred this year."

"Fluff." Skin products famous around the world. Skin products tied to something I didn't want to discuss. I took a sip of tea while I tried to steady my pulse. "And does anybody really care about Luminescent anymore?" It was easy to forget that Luminescent wasn't the family surname. We'd all called them that for so long, the Luminescents or the Luminescent family, but the name was Lumet. Quite handy, and something I suspected had been changed when the first Lumets migrated from France in the late 1800s and arrived in New York penniless. What they achieved was truly admirable and astounding.

"I'll bet more than you think," he said. "I know your father lives near their estate. You could go home. See him. Rest. Write the story. Conduct a few interviews. A little research. No need to even mention her in the article unless you want to."

Her. My mother. It would be hard to avoid referencing her, since before her death she'd been the face of their product. "This sounds like a pity job to me." Or guilt.

"Go visit your dad."

So much baggage went with going home. I didn't remember a day when my mother's death hadn't been a part of every breath I took. It was just there, ever present. But all would be amplified in Georgia.

"Maybe the thing to do is quit avoiding Savannah and just go there," Bennett said. "I know it won't be easy, but maybe try. It's the land of great writers," he offered. "Flannery O'Connor. Pat Conroy. John Berendt. Might find some inspiration."

He was working hard to convince me. It was a weak pitch. "I think I'm done searching for inspiration." People did not want great literature now; they wanted a quick sound bite. I knew how to deliver those.

He suddenly looked surprised and reached across the table, grabbed my hand, and turned it to expose my inner wrist, revealing my tattoo.

Salvador

He'd gotten my name on his wrist at the same time. An artist had come to his beach home, the one south of Miami. It had felt real. Now, though, knowing he was onto me even back then, I wonder if it had been a test to see if I'd go through with it. It had been his first and only tattoo, but he'd always been intrigued by mine, of which I had many. Southern flowers, trees, and birds. On my back, a dark road where I imagined my parents had found me.

"I'm always telling you that you never need to do anything you don't want to do."

"The tattoo was nothing."

"It is now."

True.

"I'll pay to get it removed."

"That's okay. It will always remind me to make better decisions."

He checked my meds. Filled a glass with water. Watched me swallow a pill. Fifteen minutes later, I was having a hard time keeping my eyes open. I stumbled to the bedroom and fell across the mattress. He followed and pulled a blanket over me. I felt the bed dip, felt him lie down beside me.

"Sleeping with my boss," I mumbled with a weak giggle.

He took my hand and rubbed my knuckles the way he used to. "You know I worry about you, don't you?"

"I do."

"You know I love you, right?"

"I do."

"You know I'll never marry you again, right?"

"I do."

I fell asleep and slept that kind of deep, dead sleep that comes only with medication, and yet I still managed to dream of Salvador. When I awoke, it was light out and Bennett was gone.

I shuffled to the living room and found a note on the table letting me know he'd made reservations for me at an Airbnb in Savannah. He'd also bought a plane ticket, but I didn't want to fly. I'd drive and sleep in my van. Maude, the minivan, was my house on wheels. A few years back, I'd taken the car-camping plunge and removed the seats, put in a bed, a dresser, even a solar battery. I loved being able to basically bring my home with me. It would be there for me if I needed to hide, and it would be there for me when I needed to leave. After all, the open road was part of my origin story.

I got my prescriptions filled, shopped for groceries and supplies, paid my bills, mapped out my trip, and planned my stops. I packed and arranged for my neighbor to keep watching my place. I dyed my hair back to its original shade of deep brown, and I got rid of every remnant of the person I'd been with Salvador except for the tattoo. I dropped off all the phony clothes at Goodwill, but my own clothes felt just as alien. My jeans and boots and T-shirts felt like another impersonation.

I had zero interest in visiting the Lumet family, but there were other reasons to make the trip to Georgia. Bennett's plan was all about taking it easy, not stepping back into something dark and disturbing and potentially dangerous, but it might be time to finally face my past, face my father, face myself.

5

Three days after Bennett picked me up near the hospital, I drove south out of Minneapolis, leaving town before a winter blizzard hit. It was good to be on the move, good to be heading to a place where people didn't slip on ice and break bones just walking to the car. But each night of travel involved me lying awake, wondering if I should be doing this, if I could do this, telling myself it was time. And once I hit Georgia, I felt myself winding tighter. Occasionally I'd pull over, heart hammering, breathing fast, and think about turning around. Going back to the sanctuary of my condo. Maybe getting a cat. But then I'd put the van in gear and drive until the next wave of nerves hit.

It wasn't like I'd never been back since the murder. I had. Twice, but not for years. And I'd driven this very highway a million times in my dreams and in my imaginings, so many times it felt like I'd been here just yesterday, but it also felt like a million years ago, lifetimes ago. As well as someone else's life. Foreign and familiar at the same time. Driving past forests of planted trees, past areas where the flatness of the marsh met the flatness of the ocean. Vast sky and vast land. Signs that warned of tidal flooding, roadside stands selling boiled peanuts and Vidalia onions. The onslaught of nostalgia was a contrast of unsettling and comforting, a battle between my emotions, something I was going to have to sit with awhile and let flow over and around me.

As I drew closer to Savannah, I had to face the fact that this final day of driving was not going to be like any other one. It would be worse. The final day was wrapped in a long-unvisited dread, a dread that was suddenly transformed when I spotted a sign that told me the city where my mother had lived and died was only five miles away.

I called it the stomach clench of unexpected memories. The physical reaction was distinctive, different from regular memory terror or anticipated horror. Not like going to a funeral or seeing an ex or visiting a dying loved one or saying goodbye to a beloved pet. All of those things were equally bad in different ways, but there was something about being taken by surprise and feeling that jolt, that clench and twist deep in the gut that was especially horrendous. I'd had over thirteen hundred miles to prepare, but a million miles wouldn't have been enough.

I'd braced myself for the town itself. For the buildings that would soon appear. The streets lined with live-oak trees, their branches draped in Spanish moss. The way the shadows fell differently in the Lowcountry, as if designed by a fan of baroque and languid beauty. I'd also been prepared for the scent, that wonderful woodsy smell that I'd never experienced anywhere else, certainly not in Minneapolis, although Minnesota could have pretty spectacular air in the deep, dark heart of winter. I'd prepared for all the things I'd thought I should prepare for, but I hadn't prepared myself for the most obvious. A sign. Just a stupid green mileage sign.

The shakes came fast; the spasms traveled up my arms. I gripped the steering wheel tighter, gritted my teeth, focused on the road and the painted yellow lines flying at me and under me.

And then a cop. Just like that other time.

I wasn't sure how long he'd been behind me. Could have been seconds or minutes, but I suddenly spotted the lights in my rearview mirror and caught the faint siren buried under the music I was blasting to distract me from any possible mental anguish. Hadn't helped.

I turned down the volume. I looked for a place to pull over.

Late afternoon. The road was narrow, windy, lined with forest on each side, evergreen trees that pierced the blue sky. No other cars, just me and the cop.

I briefly considered trying to outrun him. I didn't even know why. Just overload, just too much going on in my brain. I didn't want to talk to anybody. I didn't want anybody to see me or intrude on my panic, on a situation that was already more than I could handle. Also, I probably looked like I had something to hide.

But I didn't run.

Instead, like my dad had taught me, I eyeballed a safe-looking spot and a patch of earth that hopefully wasn't too soft, and I got all four tires off the road and stopped.

The squad car pulled up behind me. Black SUV with gold letters. *Chatham County Sheriff.*

I put the van in park and lowered my window while watching in the mirror. Male cop. Long stride. Not the chest-out, cocky stride of some officers. Just a lanky kind of lazy stroll. Could have been walking anywhere.

He got to the van. Bent down. Looked in. Age, probably in his early to mid forties. He introduced himself. *Officer Griffin.* The name seemed familiar, but I couldn't place it. Not a common or uncommon name. He was wearing a body cam. I managed to resist the urge to smile and wave and give the camera a thumbs-up.

Now that he was out of his car, I couldn't believe I was once again considering driving away. Just slamming my foot down on the gas pedal and spraying him with Georgia dirt and leaving him standing there in a cloud of dust.

"Do you realize you were going fifteen miles over the speed limit?" he asked.

"I did not." I'd been too caught up in my own panic, and my speed had probably accelerated along with my heart.

"We've had some serious accidents on this stretch of road." Thumbs in his belt. Mace. A Smith & Wesson. He went into a typical spiel I'd always felt was intrusive. "Where you going?"

"Savannah."

"Why?"

I wanted to say, *None of your business.* "A job. I'm a journalist."

"So you're not moving there."

"Oh, hell no. I mean, no."

It looked like he might have been trying to hide a smile. "That's good."

What a weird reaction. "Why?"

"I don't think it's the best place to live, I guess. Good place to visit, though."

"I've seen it on lists of retirement towns. And you must live there, right?"

"I've always lived in the area."

I could see myself in his reflective lenses.

"What's the assignment?" he asked.

I sighed to myself. He hadn't gone full-on cop, but I didn't want to test him. "I'm doing an article on the Lumet family." In case he hadn't heard of them, which seemed impossible, I expanded on that. "Their company, Luminescent, is turning one hundred this year."

"Ah." He nodded. "I heard about that. A hundred years is impressive. It's a milestone, that's for sure."

One thing about people in the South? They loved their history, yet they had an understandably awkward relationship with that history they loved. But nobody in any part of the United States embraced stories of the past the way southern people did. A business started in the Lowcountry a hundred years ago was a very big deal.

It was strange to think the company's start reached way back, to a time before air-conditioning, when people sat on their porches and waited for the heat of the day to pass and the night to come. Waited for the frogs to sing and the jasmine to open and spread fragrance on the soft damp breeze that moved slowly across bare skin. In a place where the live-oak leaves rustled and softly pattered to the ground like a gentle rain. Where the Spanish moss moved gently, as if stirring the air rather than the other way around.

He asked for my driver's license.

Without making any sudden movements, I dug it out, handed it to him, and told him I'd been on the road three days. "From Minneapolis," I said. "It's over thirteen hundred miles." Not that distance was an excuse for speeding. I was just nervous-talking, hoping he'd have a little mercy and not write a ticket, but cops tended to have less mercy on out-of-state drivers.

Using his thumb and forefinger, he held the driver's license up to his face and adjusted his glasses.

We were at the point of the stop when any other officer would have told me to wait there, he'd be right back. Then he'd walk to his vehicle and run a check on me.

Most of life seemed to be made up of little scripted scenes of learned behavior. When Officer Griffin went off script by not returning to his car, something in my head sounded an alert. A person being pulled over was always supposed to behave in a certain way too. I wasn't prepared.

"Are you okay?" I asked.

He was pale. Perspiration trickled down the side of his face as if it were crawling from under his black cap.

Most of us were struggling with something. Could be as small as a toothache or as big as the loss of a loved one. I'd known a few people in my life who never seemed to have a bad day, and I'd found them untrustworthy, just as living, breathing beings on this earth. At the same time, I wanted to know their secret.

He made a gurgling noise, dropped my license, turned, and ran. Not back to his car, but into the woods.

Into the woods.

I actually looked in the visor mirror to see if there was anything weird going on with my face. It didn't look any different. Two eyes, a nose, a mouth. I closed the mirror and pushed the visor up. I sat there for a few more beats, staring at the place he'd vanished. I actually considered driving away. Again. I didn't. I shut off the van, got out, and picked up the license he'd dropped.

Behind my van, his SUV revved the way vehicles did when the AC kicked on.

I examined the license in my hand, wondering if something about it had freaked him out. Nothing weird that I could detect. The photo was the typical unflattering shot. You'd think when the people at the DMV took photos all day, they'd get better at it. Not the case. The image was distorted, taken from a low angle, giving me a broad jawline and a big forehead. But if I squinted, I could see my mother and maybe even my aunt. Without squinting, I saw my dad.

I didn't have my mother's beauty. Few people did. She'd had the kind of thing Marilyn Monroe and Elizabeth Taylor had. The startling splendor that caused strangers to stop in their tracks and gape. I had her dark hair and my dad's blue-green eyes. I was tall like him. People used to comment on how tall my mother was. But she only seemed tall. She was statuesque and held herself with confidence. *Bigger than life* would always apply to her.

Beyond those things, I was what I considered normal weight. I didn't need glasses to drive. Looked like I hadn't checked the donor box, but a cop wouldn't run off because I hadn't checked the donor box, would he? Maybe he'd recognized my name and knew about my mother's murder. But still . . .

I slipped the license into the back pocket of my jeans and peered toward the stand of trees that marked the edge of the pine forest. I could smell the greenery from the road. *Guess I should go check on him.* It hit me that I was no longer shaking. I'd totally forgotten about the mileage sign.

I pulled in a deep breath, sucked that woodsy whatever deep into my lungs, and let it out. Then I headed in the direction the cop had gone, still wondering if I'd stepped into some alternate universe just as easily as I was now stepping into dense undergrowth. I didn't need to go deep before I spotted him lying on the ground in heavy brush, facedown, unmoving, his cap a few feet away as if the impact of his fall had tossed it from his head. His sunglasses were also nearby.

"Hey," I called softly at first, then louder. "Hey!"

No movement.

I glanced around, looking for what? People? Snipers? I didn't know. Then I ran for him, dropped to my knees. With a grunt and shove, I rolled him to his back. His eyes were closed. His face had a scratch on it, probably from a branch.

I glanced down his body, looking for a gunshot wound, because that was all I could think of. No blood. I knew how to do CPR, but I hoped to hell I didn't have to. The thought of putting my lips on a stranger's was enough to make me shudder.

I observed him closely. His mouth was slack, but he was breathing. No need for CPR. Chest rising and falling. His dark hair was so soaked with sweat it looked like he'd gotten out of a swimming pool.

"Hey." I shook his arm. I'd give him a few seconds before calling 911. "Hey."

He groaned.

Promising.

I checked his wrists for a medical-alert bracelet. Didn't find anything. "Are you diabetic?" I asked.

"What?" His eyes opened slightly. He tried to focus, failed, his eyes rolling. "Huh?"

"Are you diabetic?" I repeated.

"Why do you keep asking me that?"

"Because you were unconscious."

Some of the fog left his eyes.

I watched as awareness of me and the situation slowly blossomed until he reached full-blown shame, and color flushed his cheeks. At least he wasn't ashen any longer.

Without moving anything but his mouth, he said, "You were speeding."

He was obviously feeling better.

"Do you want to write me a ticket?" I said, offering him a prompt. "That's usually what happens after you pull someone over."

"A warning. I think a warning is fine."

Without looking, he reached up and shut off his body cam.

I'd forgotten about it. "Should you do that?" His shutting it off made me nervous, but if I was being honest, I preferred not to be recorded.

He mumbled something I didn't catch.

While I waited for him to recover, the journalist in me dialed into the situation.

"Why don't you move away?" I asked him. "If you don't like it here?"

"I think I might be addicted to the bittersweet pain of familiar places."

Nice. So much better than my stomach-clench thing. He was kind of breaking my heart a little. Something about him seemed almost too sweet for this world. There were a lot of unexpected things happening all at once. Maybe this actually was a dream. Maybe I was still in the hospital.

"I tried to move to the desert once for a change," he said, "but the lack of seasons got to me."

"I totally understand. I was on assignment in the Mojave for several months," I told him. "It was during a drought, so I get what you mean. I called it the mind-numbing monotony of a landscape untouched and unchanged by weather." The desert could be undeniably breathtaking at times, but not a good place for people who liked weather.

The Lowcountry, an area that included parts of Georgia and South Carolina, had big weather and amazing storms. It would have been a drastic change for him.

"You nailed it." He eased into a sitting position, then remained where he was as if waiting to stabilize. "What was the assignment?"

"I helped expose a child-trafficking ring."

"But now you're doing a piece about a skin-care company?"

I blinked. Astute. The odd circumstances, his seeming vulnerability—at odds with his occupation—had lulled me into sharing more than I normally would. I had to be careful. He might have been more cunning than his actions and words led me to believe. Maybe he was playing me. "I needed a break." I picked up his sunglasses and handed them to him.

He put on the glasses. "They say a short nap can be very refreshing. But a long one is a bad idea."

"You're funny." That surprised me.

"That's what my mom said when the doctor handed me to her."

I groaned at the bad joke. "An officer with a sense of humor is rare."

He looked a little miffed by that comment. "Not *that* rare."

Maybe it was who you knew. I wasn't going to argue, so I just said, "I can always appreciate humor. I can't imagine going through life without it."

"It would be tough." As he struggled to his feet, I picked up his cap, slapped it against my thigh to get the dirt off, like somebody in a western, then handed it to him. Seeming to lock into my interpretation of the scene, he settled the hat on his head like a cowboy getting ready to ride a bull.

"Have you ever seen a fainting goat?" he asked.

Was he really a cop? People were known to masquerade as cops. Some had killed their victims by impersonating an officer. I memorized his badge number. I'd check him out once this weirdness was over. If he didn't kill me or take me to his shack as his forever bride.

"I've seen videos of them," I said. "It always seemed sad to me. To be so scared you faint."

"Always seemed sad to me too."

"Is that what just happened? So scared or shocked that you fainted?"

He let out a defensive snort. "No."

"You're the one who brought up fainting goats."

"I don't know why I did that."

"Should I call someone for you?" I wasn't sure he should be driving.

"I'm fine." He began walking back the way we'd come, like someone who'd just taken a little nap.

"Does this happen a lot?" I asked.

He stopped and turned back. "What?"

"Fainting."

"Oh, that." He waved a hand as if to say the past ten minutes hadn't been at all weird. But then he seemed to think about my question. "It doesn't happen very often anymore. But it was bad when it first started years ago."

"Do you know what caused it?"

He frowned. "I don't want to talk about it. And you wouldn't want to hear about it either, believe me."

That sounded good to me. I didn't need the additional burden of a stranger's pain.

Bennett would have begged to hear it.

We'd made it back to the road and the vehicles. His black SUV with the gold letters was still running. It looked like the real deal, but I couldn't be sure. I stood there waiting for him to do something cop-like. When he didn't, I said, "Aren't you supposed to at least give me a warning ticket?"

"Nah." He turned away and walked toward his ride.

"Well . . . thanks."

"No problem."

"Are you sure I can't call someone?"

43

He touched the scrape on his face and looked at the blood on his fingers, then back at me. "I'm fine."

"Okay. Then have a good day. Drive carefully," I added. That was kind of a joke too, the *drive carefully*, because he was the one who was supposed to say that to *me*. "And check yourself for ticks."

"Always."

I got in my van, opened the note app on my phone, and entered his name and badge number. I saw I had a couple of texts from Bennett. I let him know I was almost to Savannah, but didn't mention the cop. For some reason, maybe because it had seemed almost like a dream, I wanted to keep it to myself for now. After hitting send, I dropped the phone beside me and drove away, watching Officer Griffin's vehicle shrink in the rearview mirror.

6

In his squad car, Ian Griffin watched Jupiter Bellarose's blue van pull back onto the highway heading toward Savannah. Her Minnesota plates had some kind of bird on them. He liked that. Once she was out of sight, he removed his body cam and reviewed the recent footage. He sped through the stop and his walking to the car. He slowed it down during the time he looked at her driver's license.

He could hear himself breathing hard, like someone hyperventilating and in need of a paper bag. Then there was the terrified run through the woods and finally Ms. Bellarose leaning over him, asking if he was okay. Not one of his better moments. At least she didn't seem to recognize him.

But why'd he run?

Good question. He guessed he'd sensed what was coming. Not in thought, but emotionally. He hadn't wanted to faint in front of someone.

Ian had seen his first fainting goats when he was in grade school. Someone brought them for education day. All the kids in Ian's class filed outside to stand in the bright sun while a woman led two goats across the fenced schoolyard. At one point, she stopped and unsnapped their leashes and the goats began playing, bouncing around as if they were on springs. The children, Ian included, giggled at the sheer cuteness of it all. Then the owner of the goats clapped her hands together very hard, very loud. It sounded almost like a series of gunshots. The goats staggered, then dropped to the ground on their sides. And they just remained there, looking dead.

The students stood in shocked silence at what they'd witnessed. Like a reaction to a terrible crime. One girl, Sarah, started crying. The teacher shushed her, and the owner of the goats reassured them that everything was okay.

"They're fine!" the owner said. "They're just fine." She went on to explain that it was a protective response.

Even as a child, Ian couldn't figure out how that kind of behavior could protect anybody. It rendered the goats powerless to predators. That was what it did.

"Won't something eat them when they're like that?" he'd asked even though he'd been relieved to see that the goats were waking up, finally bounding to their feet. "Like a coyote?"

"Not if they're in a pen," the woman told them. "They're safe."

The class bully clapped his hands. A few others did the same. Some children shrieked. Ian gestured frantically, trying to get them to stop, to be quiet.

"You're scaring them," Ian said. "Stop scaring them!"

The goats dropped again.

"They do it all day long," the owner told him with irritation in her voice. "They're used to it. It's part of their life."

"How do you know how they feel?" he asked. "You don't know. I don't think I'd like to do that all day long."

Years later, years after the goats had visited his school, he was diagnosed with myotonia congenita, which was basically a fainting disorder, the human equivalent to the goat syndrome.

Ian had always wondered if his fainting was psychosomatic. He'd spent a lot of years worrying about those goats. But maybe that day on the schoolyard had been Ian's horrified glimpse of his own future, a sense of something disturbing to come, and the day his own life shifted, went from innocent and yes, naive, to damaged.

Why was she in town? She said she was working on the Luminescent story. Was she? Really? He'd seen the forger piece when it broke. That couldn't have been easy for her, but he didn't think returning to Savannah would be easy either. Would writing a piece on the Lumets be important enough for her to come back to a place she'd surely prefer to forget?

He didn't like the idea that she might be digging around. He'd been hiding a dark secret for twenty years, living with crippling guilt, and he hoped to hell she wasn't here to uncover the truth about her mother's murder.

7

A half hour after being pulled over by the cop, I rolled into Savannah and located the Airbnb Bennett had arranged for me to stay in. It was on Oglethorpe Square, about five blocks from the Savannah River. Curious fact: James Oglethorpe, a British general with a family history dating back to William the Conqueror, had been the mastermind behind the Oglethorpe Plan of the city's squares, the idea being that every house, which typically perched practically on the narrow streets, had a communal front yard. And yet Oglethorpe had been honored by a statue in another square altogether.

The founder of Savannah had appeared to be against slavery, but anybody could dig a little and find he'd once worked for a British slave-trading company. Labeled malcontented, idealistic, and impractical, Oglethorpe was basically run out of the colony. He sailed back to his homeland of England, never to return to Georgia. But his plan had been brilliant, the design making Savannah a beautiful and unique city. It had originally been twenty-four squares, but there were only twenty-two today. Most of the traffic around the squares was one-way. Parking was tough because, of course, the plan hadn't included cars. I was happy to find that my lodging, a narrow, three-story Victorian, had an off-street area where I was able to unload.

I let myself into the Airbnb with a keypad code.

I much preferred places where I didn't have to have any human contact, especially when road weary and dealing with too many emotions to participate in a casual conversation, a get-to-know-you chat while being shown around. Hopefully, I wouldn't run into anybody coming or going.

My private apartment was on the third floor, up two tight flights of stairs, most likely a servants' passage in the past. It turned out to be the only lodging on that level. I was glad about that too, and glad to be above everyone rather than under them.

Another keypad, and I was inside.

It was cute, and it didn't smell like air freshener. Perfect for one person, with the living room featuring the requisite print of *Bird Girl*, the famous cemetery sculpture featured on the cover of John Berendt's book *Midnight in the Garden of Good and Evil*, the actual sculpture now residing in the Telfair Museum for safekeeping, although there was a small replica statue displayed on an end table in the rental. A bit of overkill, I thought. Off the kitchen, a narrow brick hallway led to a bedroom. The bathroom had been updated with spa tiles and a porcelain vessel sink.

Back in the living room after my quick perusal, I opened the balcony doors to sounds of traffic and the scent of exhaust, along with something faintly floral. I could see tourists milling about, and someone with an easel was sketching portraits. The beauty of the city drowned out the pain of being there, and I suddenly felt close to comforting tears.

I'd heard it took the average person a year to quit seeing the beauty of their surroundings. And some people never saw it to begin with. I felt sorry for those people. It was no secret that you had to go away and come back in order to reawaken that heart swell in a way that was painful and beautiful all at the same time. I was experiencing that right now.

Throughout much of my life after my mother's death, every word I spoke had been sifted through a strainer that removed anything that remotely resembled emotion, especially when I talked to my father. But more recently I'd made an effort to change. I lived closer to my own tears today, which could explain how I'd become too vulnerable, too attached to Sal. Not to mention that he'd reminded me of my mother. That same raw, charged spirit. But previously I'd lived a guarded life. Wounded people did. Because of that, I had regrets, and I now allowed the pain of living to reside right below the surface of my skin, where the nerve endings clustered. I tried to tell myself that some pain was better than no pain, but honestly, I wasn't sure about that. I was still experimenting.

And then there were those people who compartmentalized the bad things, the horrible things. It was a skill. They pushed those memories aside as if they belonged to someone else. Another person, another story, not their story. Those people moved on as if nothing had happened, even though the deed, the crime, the pain lingered like shards of broken glass.

I unpacked, putting my toothbrush and toothpaste in a mug I found in the kitchen. Then I showered, washed my hair, dried it with a towel, and set up a workstation next to the bed, against the brick wall, near a fireplace that was just decorative now. I logged on to the Wi-Fi. The connection wasn't fast but didn't seem awful. I wasn't going to be uploading or downloading big files. I just needed to keep in touch with Bennett and do research.

I let him know I'd arrived. I checked my email and saw he hadn't wasted any time and had already arranged for me to meet with the Lumet family tomorrow at the estate, about fifteen miles away.

So you can get the interview off your plate and focus on fun and research, Bennett's email said.

That could have been his plan, or it might have been the only date they had open. I told him I would be there.

Then I looked up Officer Griffin's badge number. It didn't take long for me to realize why he'd freaked out upon seeing my license. He'd been there the day my mother's body had been found. He was the guy who'd seemed too young and fragile to play the part of a cop.

8

I should have recognized him. I might have said something, though my stomach ached with an old sick feeling, an old unnamed dread, the basis being that I couldn't accept that everything was solved, yet at the same time I knew my reaction could just be me being unable to acknowledge such an easy explanation. That some creep killed my mother. I had an unhealthy desire to keep the narrative going, no matter how off base it might be. I needed it to make more sense, but murder didn't make sense.

Now that I knew who Griffin was, I had an odd and overwhelming urge to reach out. Maybe send him flowers. Sympathy flowers. I perused bouquets in one browser window, and searched for more information on him in another. He was no longer a city officer. Must have moved to county after my mother's death. I figured out the precinct where he worked. Had the flowers in my shopping cart. I stared at the screen for a long time, the cursor over the purchase button. Then I clicked away.

How silly. I didn't want him to get the wrong idea, and it was foolish of me to send flowers to someone for something that happened twenty years ago. He wouldn't understand why. I didn't even understand.

I was hungry and thought about ordering something, but in the end decided to go out. I closed my laptop and tucked it under a pillow, probably the first place a thief would look. For a while it was said the kitchen was the best location to hide electronics, like behind pots and pans or even in an oven. The oven had always seemed like a bad idea, and now the word was out on kitchen cupboards—proven by a lot of security camera footage of criminals rifling through them.

I put on a little mascara and a pair of earrings, ran my fingers through hair that was still damp and beginning to frizz from the humidity, and headed out, on foot, to find a low-key place to get something quick.

I vaguely remembered a spot from one of the times I'd come back. The last visit was to help my father after a minor surgery, and even then I hadn't stayed at his house and hadn't remained in town but a couple of nights, mainly just driving him to and from the hospital and being nearby in case anything happened. He'd been nervous about going under. I think he had a fear of not waking up, but I'd wondered if he was afraid of saying things he shouldn't say when he was out of it.

The café was still there. Different name, different owners, same wood-plank floor that creaked and gave a little as I walked on it. Like so much in the South, and especially in the historical district of Savannah, the buildings emitted a sense of warmth and history. This place was no different.

I ordered at the counter, deliberately choosing southern fare, Savannah red rice and crab cakes, and was given a cold glass of sweet tea and a number attached to a metal stand. I found a table near the front so I could look at the street and square.

I'm sure the food was good, but I was understandably distracted. At least the tea was refreshing. A young man in a white apron asked if I wanted a to-go cup. Here, you took your drink, alcoholic or otherwise, with you. I smiled, shook my head, and said, "No thanks."

Upon leaving, I paused near the door to look over the array of advertisements in the entryway. A familiar musician's face looked back at me from one of the flyers tacked to the wall. I made note of the address.

It was dark now, and the air was heavy, the humidity intensifying the aroma of flowers, the scent wrapping around me. I imagined the perfume as an invisible cloud I moved in and through. It felt comforting, a reminder of why it could be good to go home. Home might not be all bad.

I heard the soft patter of leaves hitting the brick walk. Antique streetlamps and ornate benches added to the dark and compelling charm. It was a weekday in Savannah, so things weren't crowded the way they could be in a tourist town. Some people were out, strolling toward lights or away. From the far distance, I heard water lapping and saw moving reflections on the surface of the Savannah River, a waterway that was a major channel for some of the biggest container ships from all over the world.

I moved down the street, going several blocks, missing the bar, backtracking to find a steep cobblestone lane leading to an alley. A hinged sidewalk sign announced the evening's entertainment and a special on beer from a local brewery.

I was surprised I'd never had a drinking problem, all things considered. I enjoyed an occasional beer, but I'd gotten severely drunk only a handful of times in my life, and I'd hated it. I guess I liked being in control. Or maybe it was the fear of having something bad happen when I was vulnerable. Like sleepwalking. Losing my own narrative that I clung so tightly to.

Nobody was taking money or checking ID at the bar door, so I slipped inside. At the far end was a small stage. Closer, a jukebox played, and it felt like I'd stepped into a world within a world. The darkness was protective, hiding me.

I ordered a glass of the local beer from a heavily tattooed girl behind the bar. I drank too fast, but I was nervous. When I was halfway through the glass, a man walked onto the stage, picked up an acoustic guitar, and sat down on a stool.

He played with the beauty I remembered, and he sang with a voice that was still strong even though he hit some off notes and had lost some of his range. That could be part of his charm. After a few songs, he put the guitar aside, stood up, and removed the microphone from the stand.

And he started his monologue.

My father liked to call himself a jack-of-all-trades and master of none. It wouldn't have been so sad if it wasn't the truth. Actor, musician, mechanic, bartender, and now, apparently stand-up comic.

I didn't know if his jokes were any good. People laughed, but I was just watching him, the content sinking in only peripherally. He talked about everyday life. Like ordering at a drive-thru, or grocery shopping. But things that were probably funny. At one point he seemed to lose his train of thought. He stopped altogether and squinted past the stage lights. I got the idea he was trying to find someone, me perhaps. Could he somehow feel my presence in the room? He finally zoomed in and smiled. It wasn't until that moment I realized the audience was holding a collective breath. Dead air was no performer's friend.

"I have a surprise visitor I'd like to introduce," Max said from the stage.

I shook my head and waved my hand in a big negative. He ignored me.

"My daughter is here. Come on up, sweetheart."

Every damn person in the bar turned to look at me. And kept looking. I wasn't a pushover, but it seemed the easiest and quickest way to end the humiliation was to walk the gauntlet through the tables up to the stage. Once I made it there, he reached out and hugged me with one arm, kissed me on top of my head, and then spoke back into the mic.

"Hi, Jujubes."

It was an old nickname. A gumdrop candy that went along with watching movies. Came in a box you opened at one end and shook to get the fruit-flavored snack into your palm. It might have been a cute name for a kid, but not for an adult.

I leaned close and gave him a quick hug. He smelled familiar, like coconut and, faintly, cigarettes, even though he liked to say he'd quit smoking years ago. His eyes were shining, his longish hair turning gray, his flannel shirt and jeans faded, his leather sandals well worn. Comfortable in who he was.

"Hi, Dad." I pulled away, but he kept a grip on my elbow.

My dad was still good looking. Not movie star good looking, which was probably why he hadn't risen to the level of fame my mother had achieved, or maybe it was because music had always been more his thing. Or maybe he hadn't cared enough to be a movie star. Most people didn't make it. Most people gave up.

I wondered if he was embarrassed to be found playing such a small gig.

He addressed the crowd. "We have a routine we used to do." He turned to me. "Remember that, Eddie?"

Oh, it was Eddie now, short for Edwina. "No." But I did. We'd practiced it nightly for a year. But I'd been about six then, not thirty-six.

The jokes he launched into required riffing from me to keep them going. At first I didn't respond; I just glared at him while he smiled back. He seemed genuinely glad to see me, so there was that, anyway.

I think the laughter was what I'd missed the most after my mother's death. It wasn't something you really thought about once it was gone, because you were too immersed in grief, and eventually that low-level sorrow became a part of your daily existence. But the two of us, the three of us, had always laughed. Every day had been filled with laughter.

I took a deep breath and dove in, and we did our five-minute set. Most jokes elicited groans, as they very well should have, and when we were done, people clapped, probably glad it was over. Someone turned the jukebox back on, and it was like Max and I had our own soundtrack, a Leonard Cohen song, as we walked to the bar, where he ordered drinks.

Sweet tea for him. I was glad he wasn't drinking.

I flashed on an old memory. My dad sitting at his desk in the house we'd shared together, his back to me. He was looking at something. I stepped closer and saw an eight-by-ten photo in his hand—of my mother's mutilated body. I let out a gasp. He shoved the photo, along with others which my brief glance told me were similar, into a manila envelope and stuffed it in his desk, then spun around in the chair.

"Hey, sweetie." His eyes were red and bloodshot. He was very drunk.

What had he been doing with photos of my mother's body? Where were those photos now? Killers took pictures of their victims to save and salivate over later. I couldn't imagine the man sitting next to me in that way. But wasn't that adulthood? Realizing all the things you didn't think could be true about your parents?

I pushed my unfinished beer aside. "I'll have sweet tea too," I told the bartender. "Also, sorry you had to witness that."

She laughed. "It was cute. Refreshing."

Once she was out of earshot, my dad asked, "What are you doing here? It's not your birthday. Or my birthday. Or Father's Day." Not that I came around then, but he was trying to figure it out. "Or any other anniversary." Discomfort and sorrow flashed in his face. Now I could see he meant the anniversary of her death, which was thankfully months away.

"You should have told me you were coming." He looked me over, seeming genuinely glad to see me. And I think he was. I think he loved me. I know he did. I had to be careful of that love. I couldn't allow it to trick me into trusting him, believing him.

"I would have gotten a room ready for you."

"The paper is paying for my lodging," I said. But he knew why I didn't want to stay with him. He lived there. In the place where it had happened. Why would anybody move into the house where his dead wife had been murdered? His explanation? It was paid for—a cash purchase made by my mother, and available at a time when he'd been too beset by grief to work.

I didn't know what his excuse was now. I felt sure my mother had left him in a good financial situation, so I suspected there was more to it than that. Maybe he wanted to feel closer to her, staying in the house where she died. Death could make loved ones do weird things that looked strange from the outside, and comfort came from many places. But his living in what I called the death house threw more doubt on him. I'd never been able to stay there, but maybe I should. Maybe it was time. But if I turned up something, if he'd been in some way connected to her death, could I live with what I found?

"It would be nice to wake up in the same house and have breakfast together," he said.

I didn't know how to respond to that, because we'd had the same conversation numerous times over the years.

I did worry about him. He was my father, after all. But I didn't know if I'd ever get over the resentment I felt toward him for sending me away when I'd most needed him. Sometimes that resentment flared at the most uncomfortable of times. And I was also aware of clinging tightly to that resentment in order to drown out any other thoughts, any other suspicions that might arise. I had to protect myself, protect my narrative, because there was only a certain amount of truth a person could bear. So I clung to my bitterness like a child clutching a favorite stuffed toy.

After my mother was murdered, my father disappeared into his own thoughts and almost seemed to forget I existed. I'd drive to the grocery store and buy food even though I wasn't supposed to drive by myself. I cooked meals, while he would just stare at nothing. Sometimes he'd cry so hard it seemed like his bones might break. I'd find myself thinking about the cops asking him questions, and about how he and my mother had fought that day, and he'd said he wished she were dead. And I'd wonder if he was crying because she was dead or because he'd killed her. As soon as I had that thought, I'd pushed it down, pushed it away. I couldn't lose both of my parents.

My aunt, my mother's younger sister, showed up one day and told me she was taking me to live with her. I didn't want to go.

"Just for a while," Stella said as she hugged me and rubbed my shoulders.

"Who'll take care of Dad?" He obviously couldn't take care of himself.

"We're making arrangements," she told me.

I'd met her only a few times. She was tall, with short dark hair and a way about her that made me feel safe just being in the same room. Like she could handle anything. But I hardly knew her. She was a college professor living in some cold place in the north. Minneapolis? Milwaukee? I got those cold northern cities mixed up. She was single, maybe had a cat, at least that was what I guessed. She seemed like somebody who wouldn't want to put up with anybody's stupidity, even though she exuded a quiet kindness toward me.

"Someone is going to come and stay with him during the day," she said. "Cook his meals and clean. He'll also be seeing a therapist. I think he needs to be alone right now to work through this."

"Can he? Work through it?" I wanted to say, *But what about me? Don't I need to work through it too? Shouldn't we work through it together? Why is he sending me away?* Was there something else? Something I didn't know?

"He will. He's strong. But it'll take time. And he can't be a parent right now. I'm sorry, Jupiter. Just for a little while."

Sometimes people think they're doing the right thing when they really aren't. Because they don't want to admit that there is no answer and there is nothing they can do. So they act; they plan. They do the series of things they think should be done and react the way a human should react. I had the feeling this was one of those times. But Stella and my dad were breaking up two people who needed each other.

"I don't think I should go."

"Come with me," she said. "Let's just try it. If you don't like it, you can come back. I promise."

Would they really let me? I wondered.

I agreed to go, but it was because I had no choice. My choice would have been to stay.

In the time since my mother's murder, I hadn't been back to school, and I'd been dreading it. Everybody would look at me. Or not look at me. I wondered if I could change my name if I went to a new school.

"Maybe nobody has to know," I said. At her puzzled look, I explained. "At another school."

"I'll talk to the principal about that."

She helped me pack, just two big bags: one my dad's, one that had belonged to my mom. I kept thinking about my mother's trailer. Somebody needed to go through her things. "What will happen to her stuff?" I asked. "On the set?"

"From what I understand, most of it has been collected as evidence. They'll eventually release it, I believe."

"To my dad?"

"Yes."

"All of it?" I thought about things like her special lotion. And her perfume. The products that had been given to her by the Lumet family. I suddenly realized they'd lost the face of their brand. She'd been their famous beauty for a long time—years. When people thought of Luminescent, they thought of her.

"I'm not sure. If it has nothing to do with the case, then probably so."

I stared at her. She looked a little like my mother, but it was like when you tried to draw something and the first attempt wasn't so great. She was pretty, but not beautiful like Marie. Of course, she didn't try, as my mother used to say.

If Stella would only try a little.

We found my dad sitting in a chair, staring out the window. I crossed the room to stand behind him as I put my hands on his shoulders. I leaned a cheek against the top of his head. At first, he didn't respond. He finally noticed me, reached up, and touched my hand, giving it an absentminded pat.

He smelled like liquor. Years before, he'd had a drinking problem. Some people said it was the reason he couldn't get any acting jobs anymore. *He's an angry drunk. He loses it when he drinks.* But until recently I'd hardly ever seen him drunk or even drink more than a glass of beer or wine.

"I'll make sure he never sees the light of day again," he said about the guy who'd confessed to killing her. A man I'd met a few times, someone who ran errands for my mother and took care of the house.

I didn't understand why that mattered. She was gone. "You don't have to."

"I do."

"I don't want to go." I started crying.

My aunt stepped into the room. She and my dad passed a look between them the way people who don't need words do. Like they could read each other's minds. Like they knew something they didn't want me to know. They both nodded. He gave my hand another pat. "Go with Stella."

"When will I see you again?"

"You'll either come home or I'll fly there for Christmas."

Christmas. I didn't even know what month it was or what season. I let my mind move backward to the day I saw the body. The weather hadn't been hot, so not summer. "What month is it?" I asked.

"November," Stella said gently.

"Oh, that's right." My mother had died shortly before Halloween.

Suddenly, we were outside, just me and Stella.

I glanced back toward the house. My father was where we'd left him, sitting in front of a window, staring out.

He didn't see me anymore.

It was unusually windy. Like the day of my mother's death, it blew oak leaves off the trees and tumbled them down the street, the movement sounding like a million things running away fast, reminding me of the backyard again and the blood in the grass, the blood on the tree trunks, intestines strung across branches like Christmas lights. I didn't think I wanted to celebrate Christmas or New Year's, or any other holiday, ever again.

I wanted to go back to that Saturday when we'd gone to Savannah to see her. I wanted to go back to the drive from that back road to the place my mother had been killed. Maybe if we did it again, it would end differently this time. Just go back. Change a few things. Go see her earlier in the day, pick her up, take her out to eat. If we'd just gone earlier. If we'd just been more aware, more careful.

In the rental car, as we drove to the airport, my aunt said, "I didn't want to tell you this, but I think you should know. He's worried that you might also be in danger. This was his idea, sweetie."

That actually made me feel a little better, to know I wasn't leaving because he could no longer be a parent. He'd made a parental decision. And he might have been right, but what about him? Was he in danger too? I didn't understand, because the killer had been arrested.

At the airport, before we went through security, my aunt pulled out a heavy black coat, black gloves, and a black hat, and handed them to me. What was I supposed to do with them?

"It's cold in Minnesota," she said.

I guessed everybody dressed like ravens there.

And maybe my aunt was right. Maybe it was the best thing.

I didn't see my dad that Christmas. I didn't see him much at all. Distance became our thing and ended up being the best for both of us. Or so I told myself.

"Good job with the art forger," my dad said from his seat beside me at the bar, pulling me out of the deep memory of the day he'd sent me away. "I know you're always up for any kind of challenge, but that couldn't have been an easy assignment. I tried to call you. Left a few messages. I finally reached out to Bennett and told him to check on you."

It made sense that he knew about it. The news was everywhere. "It was just my job."

He nodded and seemed relieved by my forced nonchalance. "I've auditioned for a few shows," he said. "Two sitcoms and one drama. Can you believe I'm no longer trying out for the handsome lead?" He laughed. "Maybe that was always a stretch."

"I hope you land something." But I'd heard it before, and I was never sure if the auditions were real or just something he injected into the conversation to make it look like he was searching for something beyond a bar gig or living on my mother's money. I didn't see a reason for him to be ashamed of either, but work, any work, wasn't a bad thing. I was always mentally better when involved in an investigation. Bennett had been right about that. Although what had happened with Sal was not a shining moment.

I gathered up my things and saw panic flare in his eyes.

"Don't go," he said. "I've missed you."

"I know, Dad."

"I'll see you again, right? You won't leave town without getting together?"

I'd done it before, calling him as I sped down the highway as if a flock of gargoyles were after me. "I'll see you again before I go."

"Good. And honey? Don't dig too deep. We don't always need to know the truth. Some things are better left settled and undisturbed."

What was that supposed to mean? I didn't ask. Instead, I headed back to the Airbnb.

The temperature had dropped now that it was getting late. People were bundled up, some shivering, but having come from Minnesota, it still felt almost balmy to me. I didn't encounter anybody on the stairs of the rental, and soon I was crawling into a bed with a mattress the Airbnb listing said would provide a luxurious night's rest. I hadn't slept that great on the way to Georgia, not because Maude wasn't comfortable—she was—but because I'd been worried about going home.

I didn't think I'd fall asleep, but I must have, because at some point in the night I woke up and lay there in the dark, staring up at the ceiling. I'd been dreaming about the cop, Ian Griffin. In the dream, we were standing outside my mother's house. I looked down and saw that the hand gripping my arm was stained with blood. The dream had seemed so real. Maybe it was an actual memory, brought to me by my subconscious. But how did that make sense? There would never be a reason for a cop to have blood on his hands in that type of situation.

I got out of bed, opened my laptop, and searched his name once again. The most recent address that came up was on Whitemarsh Island, outside Savannah. He must have been married, because a female was also listed at the same place, someone just a couple of years younger, same last name.

I entered the location in my phone. I needed to talk to him about the dream, but I had to visit the Lumet estate first.

9

Although I'd been there only a few times with my mother, I felt I could sense the Lumet estate, romantically named Camellia Manor, long before I arrived. Ten miles from the place, the highway changed, and the two-lane became lined with flowering pink camellias, planted over a hundred years ago by the Lumet family, from what I'd heard. The only thing marring the otherwise perfect scene was massive electrical towers. Those must have been new.

Camellias were everywhere in Georgia, yet there seemed to be a specific purpose in the miles of plantings, a way of letting visitors know they were heading toward something grand, something special. And yet reaching the destination required a turn off the highway to wind down narrow roads, the exact location a secret, part of a deliberately calculated mystique, according to my mother. Today, with social media, a secret location was impossible.

As I'd mentioned to Bennett, I made the sad assumption that nobody really cared much about the Lumet family anymore. The company and its products had dropped drastically in popularity and value, and many younger people had never even heard of Luminescent, although at one time it had been the most popular beauty line in the world. But that was back when pretty much anything could be put in skin products. It was rumored that the best Luminescent had to offer, when the company was at its peak, were potions made with human fat.

Later, in the thirties, before it was known that radium caused cancer, the night creams and day creams had been infused with a magical radio-active ingredient that "assisted blood circulation and toned the skin." Those products had been a hard act to follow.

I had done the boring homework and knew the estate covered two hundred acres and even had a helipad for the Lumet helicopter, visible on Google Earth. The property ran from a spur to Ossabaw Sound, one section meeting the Intracoastal Waterway. Inlets wound around, dividing areas of ground, creating an island for the plantation house to sit on, not high on a hill, but back behind trees, hidden from the eyes of anybody who wasn't looking for it. I passed over two small bridges and drove down a curving road. Because of marshes and narrow inlets, there was only one way in and one way out. It truly was a world of its own.

The Lumet family had been known for extravagant parties, and the events at Camellia Manor had once been the talk—and envy—of Savannah high society. The curated guest list always changed, with people being demoted and removed, to their shame, and others added, to their delight. My mother was invited because she was the face of their product, but she claimed to *loathe* the events. But such things were the obligations of the business, and she could say no only so many times without pissing somebody off. My father hated the parties, and they certainly weren't the right place for anybody's underage daughter.

"We never know how long this ride will last," she liked to say. "This could all be over in a year or two. I might not be around as much as I should be, Jupiter, but I'm doing this for us."

Even as a kid, I knew better than to believe that.

On one particular visit of memory, we arrived in the late afternoon. The event was mostly women and was supposed to create a comfortable environment for them to sample new products. They mingled, filling champagne glasses from a fountain, but also grabbing mixed cocktails from trays, drinks with names like mint julep and gin fizz. Someone mentioned one called a hurricane, and I thought I'd like to try that.

Everybody looked beautiful, dressed in fancy gowns, gliding around while servers in crisp white shirts and black pants offered oysters and drinks outside under shade canopies. There were display tables with serious and sober cosmeticians in white smocks helping to demonstrate new facial products.

My mother called it a soft launch, an event where the chosen few tried out new products. The guests included some of the most influential women in the area, and also people who would be selling the product in the upscale markets in town. I think some attendees had even been flown in from Florida, New York, and California. I hadn't wanted to go, but my mother insisted. I don't even know why, because once there, I didn't see her again until it was time to leave. Maybe she wasn't the strong person she wanted people to think she was.

She liked to have somebody around her, even if they weren't *with* her. A driver, an assistant. She hated solitude, and yet she often told me and my father she needed to be alone and that we needed to stay away. Later, I came to realize she'd lived another life separate from ours, one of which my father hadn't approved.

It was hard to know where my mother had ended and the real Marie Nova Bellarose began. She probably hadn't even known. After a time, after creating a fake persona for the public to consume, actors, people in the public eye started to become the fake person, the facade, while the real core person faded.

I reached the security booth, where the guard checked my ID and then passed it back, saying, "Have a good afternoon." The gate arm lifted, and I entered another world.

It was like driving into a beautiful oil painting. The whole place was like a movie set. Like something you might have seen in the opening of a southern gothic drama. A long lane stretching into what seemed like infinity, a glimpse of white columns in the far distance. Rows of giant oaks on either side, most likely planted over a hundred years ago, evenly spaced, their branches meeting above my head. Spanish moss, moving gently in the slightest of breezes, creating a dark canopy even though there wasn't a cloud in the sky.

The grounds were parklike, with topiary gardens and mazes and statues, flowers everywhere, mostly those camellias. The Lumets sure did like their camellias. I'd read that there were hundreds of species in existence and thousands of hybrids of the popular and beautiful flower, which was reminiscent of a rose, but much more impressive—the green shiny foliage providing perfect framing.

Everything about the estate was excessive and overdone but somehow tastefully overdone, if that was possible. It was formal, for show, not the kind of place anybody could possibly live comfortably. I knew the heir to the throne, Phaedra, and her husband, Sterling, had produced one child, sadly deceased. A boy named Oliver who'd been a couple of years older than me. I'd officially met him once when we were kids and had run into him a few times after that. He'd seemed a sweet person. I was sad when I heard of his death. I tried to recall what he looked like. Straight blond hair, blue eyes, light skin, pink lips. I'd had a bit of a crush even though he was just the kind of pretty boy my mother had warned me about.

Oliver and his early departure from this mortal coil were not the only unusual note in their family history. About a year after my mother's death, Atticus, Phaedra's twin and the family playboy, had gotten drunk and wrapped his sports car around a tree, killing himself and his date. It made national news, but things had been mostly quiet since then. A quick glance at the internet this morning, plus a few hours back in Minneapolis, had informed me that Phaedra's parents retired from the company several years ago. Her mother was dead, but her father, now in his late eighties, was still alive.

I gawked at the palatialness of the estate, as much as I could while keeping on the path, easing Maude into a lot with a sign that said, "Guest Parking." I grabbed my bag with my recorder and digital camera. With a start, I realized this would be my first gig since Sal's death.

Despite my calling the assignment a fluff piece, it certainly didn't feel like one right now. My mother had attended a party here the very night she died. Had Bennett known that when he suggested I write the piece? It seemed unlikely. He wasn't that thoughtless, and most of the things he'd learned about me he'd gotten from the press. Not from me.

"I don't need to be psychoanalyzed," I'd told him shortly before deciding I couldn't be married to him anymore. In retrospect, it was probably *why* I decided I couldn't be married to him anymore.

Before going inside, I took some shots. Phaedra and Sterling Lumet would get full approval before the article went to print, so there would be no going rogue for me, no subtle jabs or big revelations.

Tucking the camera away, I walked up a wide walk lined with red roses, took the shallow steps to a set of towering wooden double doors that were probably over a hundred years old too. They were at least ten feet tall, dark, maybe walnut. I was surprised to see that despite the formal impressiveness, someone had adhered to the southern practice of painting the porch ceiling haint blue, a blue that was a very specific and beautiful shade found in the South, a cross between baby blue and teal. I wondered if it had been painted out of tradition, or from an actual belief that the color would keep out evil spirits. For the most part, my mother had been fearless, but she'd bristled whenever anybody brought up the subject of ghosts, even in jest. And really, if any place was going to be haunted, it would be Camellia Manor.

The drive, the familiar lane, last ridden with my mother, had my heart beating hard, and my fight-or-flight hitting the red zone. But over the years I'd managed to perfect my projection of an outward sense of calm while my inner self collapsed. I think we all did the same thing to varying degrees, depending upon the situation. Unless you were like Ian Griffin, who just fainted. I suppose that could be a handy reset. Not that I didn't sympathize with him.

Recalling the Victoria Williams lyrics about fear meeting you half-way, I bolstered myself and rang the bell. I almost expected some austere butler dressed in black, a bow tie below a severe expression. Instead, the door opened, and the owner of the company, Phaedra Lumet, stood there, a smile on her beautiful face. She had to be around sixty-five but looked closer to fifty-five. She was a walking advertisement for their products. Not a line or blemish—her skin looked as if it had never seen the sun. She had platinum-blonde hair, the kind that, all by itself, exuded a sense of wealth. It was the kind of high-end hair I'd attempted to achieve with Salvador.

Phaedra was dressed in a white pantsuit with black buttons. She wore a statement necklace made of hammered silver and carved wood. A big watch with a white band. White high heels, pink toenails. Makeup that would leave me looking like a clown if I attempted it. Maybe some contouring going on, along with lipstick that matched her pink nail polish. She looked like she'd stepped off a magazine cover. Something like *Vogue*, if that was still a thing. She made me self-consciously aware of my own clothing, my own personal uniform.

It was weird how being around someone like her, someone who moved on an entirely different level of femininity, made me feel masculine in my jeans, boots, T-shirt, and arm tattoos. Like I'd suddenly dropped a few notches and was channeling my male ancestors, those people who worked on their own cars and didn't mind getting greasy. But even if I'd been dressed in my undercover clothes, I still think I would have felt awkward.

"Why, bless your heart," Phaedra said.

Her voice. Oh my God, her voice. Just what you'd think, but not what you'd expect. It had been taught, not born. Deeper than it should be, startlingly so, and an accent that had to have been designed just for her. Open vowels, a hint of England enveloped in the floral South.

"Don't you look just like your mother!"

I didn't look *just* like my mother, but we looked related in the same way Marie and Stella had. Though maybe my mother and I emitted some of the same things—one being an unfeminine bravado.

I wanted nothing more than to get in and out as fast as I could, but a good journalist took her time and absorbed her surroundings and let the interviewee roll. Because a story, a good story, was more than just what happened. It was putting readers in that spot so they could feel what Phaedra felt. It was finding something nobody had found before. It was exposing that an art forger really did love the art he copied, as well as the people he allowed in his circle.

I stepped inside, and she closed the door. "How about some sweet tea made with camellia leaves?" she asked.

That sounded horrid.

"We grow *Camellia sinensis* here on the property, just for tea. It's one of our most popular products." She smiled and shrugged. "I know. Not for the skin, but it does have antioxidant properties."

"That sounds great." I put my camera bag down on an end table. White walls, white marble floor. A mix of vintage and modern furniture. It had the spaciousness of a church or museum or capitol building. "This place is more breathtaking than I remember."

"Is it?" She looked around the vast foyer with disinterest, maybe as if she'd seen it a million times before. Or never. "Honestly, I can't tell," she said. "A prison is still a prison even if it's beautiful."

Wow. I'd been hoping for some honesty, but I'd really expected to dig for it. If this kept up, she was going to make my job easy.

"A business that has been in the family for generations can be a burden," she said with her curated accent. "We make beauty products for vain people. And I'm just as vain as everybody else." She gestured from her face to her shoes, shoes I would bet, if I knew about such things, were very expensive. "So my comment is hypocritical. I realize that. It's hard to live in that kind of dichotomy."

"But your products make people feel better about themselves, right? That's a good thing." I thought about how powerful and free I'd felt on Sal's arm, finally clearing the beauty bar.

"You are surprisingly kind. Your mother always had a little sour lemon to her. But let's face it. I live a shallow life."

She had so much sorrow swirling around her. I felt a growing kinship. We'd both suffered extreme loss. She'd lost a son and then a brother. I'd lost a mother and then a lover.

We sat down, and she poured tea from a pitcher into glasses that were as beautiful as everything else. Made of cut glass. She topped my drink with a mint leaf and handed it to me.

"What kind of life would you choose?" I asked, watching her as I took a sip. The tea was very cold, and, as I'd expected, it had a strong floral flavor. Not unpleasant, but way too sweet. I'd bet each swallow cost a small fortune. I imagined drinking liquid gold, picturing it going down my throat and moving through my digestive system, making the whole thing sparkle like the inside of this house.

"I don't know," she said with a reflective tone.

I didn't want to put words in her mouth, but I tried to help. "I guess everybody wants a choice. Or even just the illusion of a choice."

Her face brightened. "That's exactly it. But how can a person complain about something as lavish as this?"

"I appreciate your bold honesty. It's refreshing." I took another sip of the tea. I tried not to make a face, then thought I'd try some honesty for myself. "Not terribly excited about this drink, but I like you."

She laughed. "I can get you something else. Sterling tells me I make it with too much sugar."

I was surprised she'd made it herself. "I'm fine. It's a good way to tell if I have any cavities. Don't seem to."

"You didn't expect to like me, did you? That's okay. Most people, unless they're wealthy, don't."

"No, I didn't." Bald honestly was just flying around the room. "Sorry."

"We really are conditioned to distrust people who are different. I wish the world wasn't that way."

"Me too."

"To make myself feel useful, I have fundraisers, and we sponsor girls. Pay for their entire college." She shifted gears. "But I'm so glad you're here, because I'd like to tell you how incredibly sorry I was about your mother."

I usually hated it when people brought her up, but I could understand that Phaedra wanted some closure, especially since my mother had worked for her company. "Thank you."

"And I'm sorry I can't quit staring, but you look so much like her. You have that old Hollywood vibe she had. She was like Grace Kelly, only with dark hair and a vulgar mouth." Her face clouded a moment. "My mother was always trying to get her to control her cursing." The cloud passed, and she brightened again, laughing. "We aren't as concerned about things like that now, but we still have to be careful. But anyway, that face."

She tipped her head and held a finger to her chin as she considered what work I needed. A lot, I'd guess. "I have a stylist who could do wonders with you. Pull your hair back in a tight chignon. Some black, Audrey Hepburn eyes and red lipstick. Maybe pearls around your neck. I know pearls are dated, but you'd wear that look well. So classic."

"I prefer the destitute look, thank you."

She didn't even crack a smile. I found myself thinking that Bennett and my dad would have both laughed.

"We're having one of our affairs next week. It's black tie with the best chef in the Lowcountry. You should come."

It was odd and thoughtless that on the heels of apologizing for my loss Phaedra was inviting me to the very kind of party my mother had attended the night she died. But maybe I was being too sensitive. "I don't have a dress," I mumbled. Anybody could get a dress. I could order one from Amazon right now and have it in two days.

"We have lots of dresses. You can have your own room and stay the night. These parties go on and on, and you don't want to have to drive home. We're typically very strict about who attends, but we will make an exception in your case and even allow you to bring a plus-one of your choice. We don't even need to vet them."

I thought back to that day with my mother as we sped away from the mansion. She'd been so relieved to have the soft launch over.

"And here's another idea that's taking me by surprise," Phaedra said. "Would you ever consider being the face of Luminescent?"

Oh hell no.

"I even like your tattoos. Rather than cover them up, I think we could work with them. We haven't had one person, one face, representing our brand since your mother passed. I think it's time we did something about that. Marketing has been talking about pulling back on what we call our upscale branding, and trying to appeal to a broader audience." She leaned forward, put the back of her hand next to her mouth in a conspiratorial gesture, and said, "Our patrons are dying. I mean, really dying. They're old. We need some new blood."

"No, no, no . . ."

"Oh, come on. Would you at least think about it?"

"I appreciate the thought, but—"

I was saved by a commotion from another room. The clack of dog nails on tile and a flurry of movement announced Sterling Lumet's arrival. He was wearing long beige shorts and leather sandals. A white shirt with a straight hem, some sort of stitching along the buttons. The kind of shirt I might associate with the beach or a boat. His arms and face were deeply tanned. He had nice hair, thick for someone his age, light brown with gray at the temples, slicked back with some kind of product that looked like it would leave a mess on a pillow.

He would have turned heads in his day, and even now he probably got some attention in the right circles. Because of Luminescent, he'd chosen to take Phaedra's last name, abandoning his own, not even hyphenating it. I liked that. Just flip the American tradition. I'd always felt that if you're going to change your name at all, then the best name should win no matter who it belonged to.

He poured himself a glass of iced tea, walked across the room, and added a hefty splash of hard liquor from a decanter. An actual decanter.

Together, they gave off the aura of extreme wealth along with an unspoken dignity. I'd lived around extreme wealth for the past year, and I knew that aura of the unseen, worn like invisible clothing.

Sterling had three fluffy dogs in tow and joked that he was the dog walker. "You really need to stop hoarding pets," he told Phaedra.

He had an affable face, the kind that was most often smiling a bit rather than, like mine, frowning as I either concentrated on something or was just plain pissed. He turned his attention to me, his brows moving slightly, his mouth with a hint of a smile but no visible teeth. He had a twinkle in his eye that said we'd just shared a secret joke about the dog hoarding. Through no fault of their own, and by sheer proximity to their perfection, I continued to feel clumsy and unattractive. If my mother had been in the room, she would have eclipsed us all.

"You do look like your mother," he said. "Doesn't she?"

"That's what I've been telling her. I even asked if she wanted to be the face of our product. We haven't had one since . . . well, the unfortunate event."

"Oh, that's a marvelous idea."

"I'm not interested."

"She's not interested."

"Well, think about it."

"That's what I told her."

I really needed to stop this path of conversation, and since they were both in the room, I wanted to offer my own overdue condolences. "I was sorry to hear about your son," I told them. "He seemed like a kind person." He was the one I really remembered from that long-ago visit. We'd snatched a bunch of food off trays in the kitchen and taken it to the library, where we'd stuffed our faces and even drunk some champagne. After that, he'd taken me down some narrow back stairs, showing me secret tunnels. We'd gone all the way to the basement and the warehouse beneath the main house, where the products were stored.

The room went still. I swear even the dogs seemed uncomfortable.

"Thank you. It was a sad thing," Phaedra finally said. "Especially after your mother's and my brother's deaths."

I'd found that most people liked to talk about their loved one, so I related a little of that day, of how Oliver and I had taken food from the kitchen, my thought being that they might both enjoy the story. They didn't seem to.

"He could be a challenge," Phaedra said, her face and voice full of sorrow.

I wish I hadn't brought it up.

"Do you have children?"

"No."

"That might be for the best. They will break your heart."

I wanted to know more. How he'd broken their hearts. By dying? By doing something else? I was hoping she'd volunteer information, like how he died. She didn't. It would have been improper to ask. I knew how intrusive the questions of strangers could be.

The conversation drove Sterling away. He put his glass down and excused himself, calling the dogs to come with him, mumbling something about taking the helicopter to Hilton Head Island.

"I'm sorry," I told Phaedra once Sterling was gone. "I shouldn't have brought up your son."

"It's okay," she said. "I love hearing stories about Oliver. It keeps him alive. But Sterling has such a soft heart. He can't deal with it. Maybe someday . . ." She took a deep breath and looked back at me, leaning in. "Also, I keep telling him he should quit flying. These old guys don't like to admit they aren't as sharp as they once were. He's had a couple of close calls, and he really needs to get rid of the helicopter or hire a pilot. But boys have a hard time letting go of their toys."

She appeared to shake off her concern in order to return to today's popular topic. Maybe what seemed like an obsession was her way of coping with things she didn't really want to deal with.

"You really should think about doing some test headshots for us," she said. "That would do a lot toward freshening up our image. We're launching a new product, and we want a new face to go with it."

"Wouldn't that just be another gimmick?"

"I suppose so, but for me it's also a do-over. A chance to make things right. I don't feel we treated your mother the way she should have been treated." She took a long drink, rattled the ice in her glass. "Her contract was appalling."

"I was too young to get any details, but I've heard as much."

"It was worded in such a way that once she was dead, the company owed her nothing. It was really to protect Luminescent in case she bailed, but it was not in her favor. Her lawyer should have been fired."

I think her "lawyer" had been my father.

"But the truth is that my parents were not at all happy with your mother. Once she started the TV show, she was no longer the wholesome girl they'd hired. She was no longer a respectable and worthy reflection of the brand. They put up with it at first, but there were meetings. Lots of meetings. At first I think they just felt the show would bomb, and we could ride it out." She smiled. "Of course, that didn't happen. We also felt guilty for introducing her to her driver. That hung heavy over our heads. We vetted him, but you just never know."

She was talking about Luc Chesterfield, the man serving a life sentence for the murder.

"You and I should hang out," Phaedra said. "Even after we're done with the interview."

"I don't think I'm going to be in town much after that."

"You'll be in town a lot if you sign with us!"

I laughed at the way she wouldn't let it drop. It made her seem incredibly young and naive. But I suppose when a person grew up in

Found Object

such a protective bubble, it could stunt you. Or maybe it was that no one ever told her no.

"And now is the time to admit to having an ulterior motive in bringing you here. I wanted you to do the interview, but I also had something else in mind. A painting I wondered if you'd look at."

"Painting?"

"I was hoping you might be able to tell us if it's fake. We think we might own one of Salvador Cassavetes's forgeries."

10

I imagined a giant rock being dropped into a pool of water. It went straight down and hit bottom. That was what my stomach felt like. I wanted to run, make up some excuse so I wouldn't have to confront something Salvador had created, if the art was indeed his.

It took me right back to the island . . .

I watched as he walked toward the water, just a black silhouette, the half-moon's reflection off the waves crashing against the beach. He was up to his waist, then his shoulders. Then, like the sun, he vanished.

I shouted his name. I ran after him. Waves hit, washing the sand from under my feet, knocking me down. I choked. I swallowed salt water. I shouted again. I pulled out my phone. I aimed the flashlight at the place I'd last seen him. Nothing. I called his assistant back at the house where Sal and I had recently shared a bottle of wine.

At first, I think she thought I was kidding. Then suddenly people were swarming like ants, running to the beach. Salvador's driver dove into the water and swam toward the place where the sun had gone down and the place where I'd last seen Salvador.

Time was confusing.

More people showed up. Someone put a blanket around my shoulders and handed me a cup of coffee. Finally, and so oddly, it seemed, the sun rose behind us.

"It's because of your article!" his assistant said.

"What?"

"The article. The exposé, or whatever it was."

That made no sense. No one there knew I was a journalist.

At one point, at many points, I'd considered not turning it in, never turning it in. I think I was afraid if I didn't send it at the moment I'd sent it, I never would. And that might have been okay. What if I'd just embraced my pretend life and left my old one behind? Could I have done it? To protect him? To save him?

Yes.

"It's in all the papers," his assistant told me. "Every big paper in the nation and the world."

I'd been trapped at the little airport all day, with no internet, no television, no cell service. Bennett must have released the article even though he'd promised not to. And now Salvador's death, just like my mother's, would most likely haunt me for the rest of my life.

"I don't know why he even let you come here after doing such a horrible thing to him," she said. "You killed him!"

It made sense that he hadn't been able to face the public humiliation of the exposé. The admiration of strangers had always been so important to him, as it had been to my mother. And maybe he couldn't face the people he loved either, like his mother and sister. Was I one of the people he could no longer face? I touched my lips and thought about the parting kiss.

His assistant was right. I'd killed him.

He swam away from it all, into the ocean he loved, and just kept swimming until he could swim no more. Then he let the salt water take him. And he did it because of the words I'd written.

I imagined him sinking, surrounded by colorful fish and undulating seaweed, his arms above his head, his long fingers, the fingers he'd threaded through my hair, the fingers that could make any painting pass for the real thing, relaxed, waving goodbye. I could have stopped him. I should have stopped him. I should have called for help sooner.

Those were the big things. There were the silly things too, small, unimportant details buried in small and unimportant but quiet days. A look, a brush of the hand, a smile. The time he even tried to teach me how to paint a forgery, and we'd laughed at how awful I was. I couldn't even hold the brush right. He'd seemed delighted by that.

In my mind, I sometimes saw him staring at me with eyes that loved me. Love was a powerful drug. I'd never had much romance in my life, and he was good at that too.

You know how you can tell when something is exquisitely beautiful? he'd asked me one time.

How?

It hurts to look at it. It hurts your heart.

I kept saying I loved him and I missed him and that explained this hole in my stomach, but it might have been guilt just as much as love. I didn't know. I couldn't tell them apart.

"I'm no forgery expert." My voice wobbled, but probably not enough for Phaedra to notice. My heart was slamming. If I'd been in a cartoon, you'd have been able to see the whole outline pulsing under my T-shirt.

"But you lived with him and watched him work," she said, seemingly unaware of my distress. "I read your article."

I should have just left, but I didn't. Instead, I followed her up the sweeping staircase and down a long hallway with marble floors under our feet and cathedral lights above our heads. She used a plastic card to unlock a door.

"Only Sterling and I have the code," she explained, opening the door. "It's a controlled environment, with controlled temperature and humidity. But we also worry about theft." An alarm system was beeping. She walked to a keypad on the wall and poked in a selection, and the beeping stopped.

There were no windows in the room, and she explained about the special filtered LED lights that didn't shine directly on the paintings.

"Most people know sunlight is bad," she said, "but fluorescent is also very bad." There were mounted strings of bulbs, all the light bouncing off the ceiling.

I was no expert, and I wasn't even sure who'd created most of the art in the room, all oil paintings, some large, some small, in matching gold frames, maybe twenty pieces.

It had taken a while for Salvador to trust me enough to let me see his workspace. And then even longer before he allowed me to see him in action. But when he did, it was as if he'd been waiting for an audience. I was never even sure if his relatives knew about his forgeries until everything went down.

Once he let me in, like really let me in, I'd watch him paint. I had no video of it, because he was at least cautious enough to make me leave my phone in another room, but I would sit behind his shoulder on an art stool and watch him work.

If you were to study any of the masters, you'd quickly learn that the paint each one used came from very specific regions. Van Gogh's yellow, for instance, came from Julien Tanguy in Paris, France.

I leaned in, looking for that one fine brush mark, and couldn't find it. There was nothing about the painting that hinted it had been done by Salvador. "I'm pretty sure it's not his," I said with relief.

Salvador made sure his paint came from the right country and region. He bought old pieces from those locations, scraped off the images, and painted on top of the antique canvases, so even those were authentic. But his ego wouldn't allow him to finish a painting without leaving that little bit of himself somewhere on it. His "signature" was a tiny fine line that looked like a reflection, so tiny it was almost invisible to the naked eye. But I knew how and where to look. And once seen, it couldn't be unseen.

"I knew it! That's what I told Sterling," Phaedra said. "He read the article about you and began to obsess about this painting. I told him it was real, but he wouldn't stop."

"Like I said, I'm no authority by any means. I can only tell you that I'm fairly certain this is not a Salvador Cassavetes forgery. That doesn't mean it's not a forgery," I told her. "Hopefully it isn't, but if you're still worried, I'd advise you to get an expert to look at it."

"You mean one like Cassavetes?" There was an understandable sneer to her words.

I got it. Salvador's actions had undermined the whole world of forgery experts. Who could you really trust when the experts were lying? Because Salvador wasn't the only one who'd manipulated people. "I understand," I said. "The art world has some untrustworthy professionals, but there are very many ethical ones."

Phaedra moved toward the door. "The problem is sorting them out. This painting was certified, and I'm going to believe it's authentic. If Sterling has a mind to pursue something else, he can. I just want to enjoy it."

And that was the strange thing about art. If two paintings looked identical, had been painted with paint from the same town, such as a village in France, if the light fell the same way and it evoked the same response, did it matter that one was fake? Of course it would if you'd bought it only for an investment. But if you'd bought it to enjoy . . . ? That was probably some of the justification Salvador had used.

"Anyway, it's good to have you here," she said. "I feel a connection. You should stay with us, at least while you're working on the article. Really. We have plenty of room, obviously. It's a long drive for you. And you'll be pampered."

"Thanks for the offer, but I need my downtime."

"You can get plenty of that here. The whole west wing is empty. It's like your own world over there. Your mother used to stay with us sometimes. I'd offer you her room, but I can understand if you wouldn't want to stay there. We haven't done anything to it other than clean since she last stayed there. It felt wrong."

I didn't know what to think about the unchanged room. I was curious but also repelled.

"I won't push, but keep it in mind. If it gets too rowdy in Savannah. I know how loud it can be there on a weekend."

Phaedra fed me a light but delicious lunch while telling me more about the history of the business. Boring stuff I could have found online, but it sounded much more interesting coming from her. I took some photos, one of her with the dogs standing in front of a large portrait of her great-grandfather, the founder of Luminescent.

I was getting ready to leave—she was still begging me to stay—when she asked if I wanted to see the rooms where the old products were kept. I said yes but didn't admit I'd been down there before.

11

Phaedra and I took a sleek stainless-steel elevator down to the lower level. She suddenly seemed distracted and in a hurry, like a little kid who knew she was doing something she shouldn't. Once we were below-ground, we stepped out. With a flick of a switch, everything went bright with no shadows.

The tunnels weren't quite like I remembered, possibly because Oliver hadn't turned on all the lights that day, and we hadn't used an elevator to get there. It was almost like a giant bunker. At one end were massive doors big enough for trucks to drive through. The vastness of the space, the rows of lights leading to the exterior doors, would make a nice image for the article. I started to pull out my camera, and she put a hand on my arm.

"No photos down here, please."

"Of course."

I found it especially interesting how everything had been modernized. She waved a keycard over a sensor and opened a heavy door. There hadn't been any card-reading sensors before. Oliver and I had run unchecked through the tunnels, ducking in and out of doorways. We'd settled in one room where he'd opened a jar, scooped out a fingerful of lotion, and drawn on his face with it. Then he turned off the lights. The lines on his face glowed green. He offered the container to me.

"Try it."

I stuck my finger in the jar. Using a glob of lotion, I gave myself glasses around my eyes. "Am I shiny?"

"Yes." He giggled hysterically.

This ended up being more fun than I'd expected.

We talked about school. He went to a private one in Savannah where they had to wear uniforms. He was two years ahead of me. We talked about chess. He was on the chess team.

"Your mother seems pretty cool," he said at one point.

"She is." But why was he talking about her now? Everything always wound up being about her.

"I like her show."

Even though my parents were chill, I'd seen only a few, kid-friendly clips. "Are you allowed to watch it?" I asked, half-jealous and half-shocked.

"No, but I do anyway."

We both laughed.

I didn't want to leave our little hideaway, but at some point I realized quite a lot of time had passed. "We should go," I said.

He returned the jar to the shelf, and we went back upstairs. Later, when I left the mansion with my mother, I'd wondered if my invisible glasses would appear once I was in bed and the lights were off.

"We store a lot of the old products here," Phaedra said to me now. "Collectible goods dating back to the beginning. Here, follow me."

She took me deep into an area of shelves stacked floor to ceiling with carefully organized merchandise, the vintage packaging faded, edges brown with age.

"These are some of the very first Luminescent offerings."

"Amazing."

We moved to another section, and it was suddenly like a wall of Andy Warhol art, my mother's face neatly and precisely repeated hundreds of times on rows of products.

"See what I mean?" Phaedra said. "Couldn't you imagine being on something like this? I can totally see it."

As disturbing as it was to see so many images of my mother, I still laughed at Phaedra's stubbornness. "I can't."

"Don't give up on my idea. Don't forget about it."

"Not sure how I possibly could," I said dryly. "Are you certain about no photos?"

"Sorry."

We left, and the door locked solidly behind us.

We peeked in a few more rooms, all with shelves of products, some newer, without my mother's face. When I realized we were heading back toward the elevator, I asked, "What about that door?" I pointed to one we'd missed. I might have been mistaken because it had been years ago, but it seemed like it could have been the room I'd gone inside with Oliver.

"We never open that."

I spotted a Geiger counter on a metal table and understood her unease and need to hurry. I'd heard radiation detectors would still react if you walked over the graves of women who'd used the older products. Could be rumor, but the way Phaedra was acting, I was beginning to think it was true.

"They're still hot," she said. "Even after all these years. But the room is lined in lead, so we're safe. Or safe enough. It was built to withstand an earthquake or fire. Once a year we have the vault inspected to make sure there's no leaking radiation." At my expression of horror, she said, "I know it seems frightening, but we've been told this is the safest way to deal with it. Just lock it up."

Like Chernobyl. But last I heard that wasn't going so well.

Upstairs, Phaedra and I hugged.

"We should be gal pals," she said with a laugh, maybe about the corniness of *gal pals*. "I won't make a nuisance of myself. I know you're here to work, but I'd love to go for coffee sometime, or just have someone to text with. Let me give you my mobile."

I couldn't help but smile at how nervous and shy she seemed about the whole exchange. I intended to add her number myself, while feeling intrigued yet cautious about the gal pal thing. Once again reminding me of a naive teen, she grabbed my phone from me, rapidly double-thumbed the keypad, sent a message to herself, and handed the phone back. "I'll warn you. I'm a chronic texter. I hope you are too."

Guess I'd find out. I told her I'd come back for another interview once I had the article underway and knew what I might need to flesh it out. Then I drove back to the Airbnb and did an online search for Oliver.

It was hard to find much on him beyond what I already knew. It took a deep dive into some private and possibly unreliable sites to find the reason for his death. Cancer. Tragic, but no surprise. I wondered how often he'd played down in the radium room. Was his death a direct result of putting those old products on his face? No wonder the family had tried to keep the cause quiet. I also suspected they'd paid big bucks to scrub the internet of the information.

Next on my to-do list was talking to Ian Griffin. It might seem a stretch to ask someone about a dream, but I didn't like to ignore even the faintest of leads. I called the police department and asked to speak to him.

"He's not here today."

No surprise. He was probably on patrol. "What's a good time to catch him in the precinct?"

"He's actually not going to be here for a while. He's taking some personal days."

Because of what happened in the woods? If so, I felt weirdly responsible. After disconnecting, I remembered the home address I'd put in my phone. I pulled it up, mapped it, and headed back out.

12

I didn't know what I expected, but it wasn't a cute cottage on the edge of a marsh. The home, which was small despite being two stories, had a screened front porch. The wood siding was painted a happy shade of pink, the trim a bright teal with lime-green accents around the windows. I got out my camera and snapped a few shots.

As I stood there eyeballing the house, the sun felt wonderful on my back, through my T-shirt, especially after the gray skies of Minnesota. I could almost forget my mission. I could almost stay awhile.

Along with the view, the smell of a marsh was distinctive, and I even recognized plants I thought I'd forgotten the names of, like saw palmetto. But I could never forget the infamous kudzu vine. Pronounced like *could-zoo*, emphasis on *could*. Kudzu not only *could*, it did. It was often known as the vine that ate the South and was ranked as one of the top six invasive plant species. Kudzu had been introduced to the US at a plant exposition in the mid-1800s. After that, one million acres were planted to reduce soil erosion. I'd heard it could grow up to a foot a day, which meant chopping it back only delayed the inevitable unless you trimmed it daily. It smothered everything in its path, from plants to giant trees. Some described it as having a grape scent. I thought it smelled like bubble gum and death.

I'd always had a strange and secret fascination with the plant, even an admiration, and I doubted anything could really compete with it. A plant of lore and myth, said to crawl under the door or through open windows to strangle you while you slept. It was known for swallowing houses whole, darkening the windows, rotting the wood, spreading mold through the walls until there was nothing a person could do but run away.

A pair of men's leather flip-flops had been kicked off next to a doormat that said *meh*. There was a paper sign instructing visitors to just step onto the porch. I did so, noting the knocker on the interior door was shaped like a mermaid. I liked that. Nobody answered, but I heard sounds coming from inside. Ian could be home, but some people left their televisions on to keep pets company or deter burglars.

I used the knocker again, louder this time.

Looking through the porch screen, I noted a garage to the right of the main structure. It was also painted brightly. I thought about Ian and his dark history. His living there seemed an attempt to create something happy outside his own skin.

Close to giving up, I tried the door once again, this time rapping with my knuckles rather than the gentle treatment of the mermaid. I heard a crash, possibly a startled movement. That was followed by a shudder of footsteps, then the door was jerked wide.

The interior of the cottage was dark, the ceiling low. Wooden beams, painted white, above my head. Ian stood in the opening, blinking against the bright sun. No shirt, just a pair of baggy shorts and an unshaven face. In the darkness behind him were a couch and a coffee table with a laptop surrounded by fast-food wrappers, chip bags, and clear plastic cookie inserts with no cookies.

His hair was curlier than I remembered. Maybe because he didn't have hat hair today, and he wasn't sweating. It was longer than anything he'd be able to get away with in Minneapolis. It didn't seem to be a style, but more a lack of self-awareness and a sign of preoccupation with other things.

When he recognized me, he scurried back to the couch, grabbed a wrinkled orange T-shirt, turned it right side out, and pulled it over his head. It advertised a café famous for crab legs and locally brewed beer. After his initial flare of panicked recognition, he looked away, as if afraid that too much eye contact would make him faint again. I felt like Medusa, the mythological Greek figure who turned people to stone when they looked into her eyes.

He tugged at the hem of the shirt and gestured behind him. "I'm working from home."

"I see that."

He dropped back down on the couch and resumed watching the cat video playing on his laptop. A couple of times he laughed out loud.

"Do you mind if I come in?"

"Oh. Yeah." He was acting as if he didn't get company very often. I closed the door behind me, saying, "I called the police station, and they said you were taking some personal days."

"I needed a little time off."

I guessed it was because of me, but maybe not. Yet his fainting seemed to indicate that seeing me might have sent him into a downward spiral.

"I looked up your name when I got to Savannah, and I remembered who you were. Why didn't you say something?"

He let out a sigh. "I should have. I don't know why I didn't."

It was questionable behavior, but maybe, like me, he'd just wanted to pretend that day had never happened. I understood that. Or it could be he'd recollected the blood on his hands.

Using a plastic shopping bag retrieved from a chair, I picked up trash as I walked around the room. I filled the bag, found another with the logo from a nearby store. I filled it too. "I see you're doing your part to reduce waste."

"I don't normally buy fast food."

"Only when you're upset?"

He glanced my direction, seemed to remember the Medusa thing, then quickly averted his eyes and looked back at the screen. "You should watch this video. It's pretty funny. The cat plays a piano."

"I think I've seen it, thanks." I carried a stack of dirty dishes to the sink, turned on the water, and squirted in some dish soap.

"You don't need to do that," he said. "I'm not into outdated gender roles."

"That's okay. It's not about gender. People need to take care of one another. Not you and me, specifically, but in general." I might have been fooling myself, but my career had been about righting wrongs, exposing evil, helping people in need. Which could be one of the reasons why what had happened with Salvador had hit me so hard. I wasn't the kind of person who inflicted pain. Or at least I tried not to. And I certainly hadn't wanted anybody to die.

My cleaning Ian's mess was reminiscent of how Bennett had straightened up at my condo. Or how I had watched after my father in those early days after my mother's murder.

When I finished the dishes, I looked in the refrigerator and found a carton of eggs. Noticed a child's colorful artwork on the door and spotted some dishes more suitable for children. Did he have kids? He seemed too fragile to be a parent. A ridiculous thought, considering the fragility of my own father.

I turned on a stove burner and placed a just-washed skillet on it. As the pan heated, I cracked several eggs into a bowl, beat them with a fork, then poured the mix in the pan. It sizzled, getting Ian's attention. I found some bread and popped slices into a toaster.

"I said you don't need to do that."

"I'm hungry." I kind of was, but the array of junk food wrappers told me he probably needed some real food.

A few minutes later, I placed two plates with scrambled eggs and toast on the table.

He glanced at me, closed his laptop, and got up from the couch. Without conversation, he dug a bottle of salsa and a jar of apricot jam out of the refrigerator. From a drawer, he produced forks and knives and placed them near the plates. We sat down across from each other, and he finally looked at me longer than a millisecond.

And didn't faint.

He ate a few bites of food, then blurted out a confession. "That whole ridiculous episode in the woods was on my body cam. And the next day, when I got back to work, people were watching it and laughing. So I took some personal days."

Cop culture. It was a real thing.

It was my opinion that there were a few basic kinds of cops. You had the ones who'd been bullied as kids, and they became cops so they could bully other people, thereby, in their own minds, rectifying their shitty and unbearable childhoods. Then you had the ones who just needed a job and had no idea what kind of darkness they were getting into. Those cops could, at the tutoring of the bullies, become bullies themselves. Or they learned and became better cops. Some of them just quit. Then there were the cops who became cops because they thought it was a worthy profession, and they wanted to help people. Those cops fell the hardest. I suspected Ian was a hard faller. Someone with a good heart, someone easily hurt, who probably gave good hugs when someone needed one.

But I couldn't get the image of the blood out of my mind. He'd been so kind to me the day of my mother's murder, but I was a kid. I didn't know what I now knew about the evil in the world, about the kind of lies people told and how they disguised their crimes.

I planned to ease into the bloody-hands question with some honest sharing about myself. Personal things could break the ice, making him feel more comfortable before I hit him with the big stuff. "I'm not just here to do the Luminescent story," I said.

Panic flared in his eyes. "I was afraid of that."

13

When Ian had seen Jupiter standing on the stoop, he'd been shaken all over again. But he swore not to faint twice in a week, and certainly not over the same event, an event that had consciously and subconsciously shaped and impacted the rest of his life.

It had been twenty years since he and Jupiter first met . . .

"Go inside. Try to talk to the girl," his partner had told him. "You're closer to her age. Take her out the front door." She dug out her keys and handed them to him. "Give her a ride home if she needs it. I'm going to question the father, who's having a meltdown."

Ian found Jupiter in the house.

She was standing in the middle of the living room, screaming, going from one person to another, telling them her mother wasn't dead. "I can't believe any of you fell for it!"

She was young, high school. He might have seen photos of her next to her mother at some awards event, the kind where the stars stopped and posed for the photographers. She was wearing a dark dress, dark tights, and black boots. Her brown hair was braided, and her wrists were full of leather bracelets and beads. A girl whose mother had been alive hours earlier but was now dead.

Moving sideways, excusing himself, he cut through the throng of people who were trying to calm her down. He reached the girl's side, spoke her name, took her arm.

She was panting. No other way to put it. Eyeliner and mascara melted down her cheeks. It didn't seem like she heard him at first, but then her eyes locked on his, and she whispered, "Get me out of here."

He glanced at the blood on his hands and hoped she didn't notice. Then he took her by the arm and guided her through the crime-scene personnel to the front door.

The street was lined with squad cars. The Georgia Bureau of Investigation was already on site, along with a white van with *Coroner* written down the side in large black letters. Nothing subtle about that. Just its presence alone was increasing the crowd by the second.

Two officers were stringing more yellow tape around tree trunks. Others were erecting barricades. A pair of detectives, a man and a woman, milled around, hoping to find something nobody else had noticed. Officers were being dispersed to take information from the gathering crowd and knock on doors. Neighbors would be asked if they'd seen or heard anything. Security camera footage would be requested from those homes that had it.

Reporters were arriving. Some he recognized; others he didn't.

The girl swayed. He grabbed her arm and steadied her, then led her to a somewhat secluded area of the yard, a place tucked away in a corner. Her face was ashen, and her lips were blue. The arm under his hand felt cold and clammy.

"Sit down." Ian helped ease her to the ground. When she was close enough, she dropped the rest of the way. He crouched beside her.

One of the detectives, the guy, spotted them. Came over. He stood too close and towered over both Ian and the girl.

"Why'd you come here today?" he asked Jupiter.

She was too upset to be questioned right now. Ian wasn't even sure she'd heard. The detective asked her again.

She stammered, confused, obviously wondering who he was and why he was even talking to her. "To see my mom. To surprise her."

Ian straightened. "Back off," he told the detective.

"Who the hell are you?"

"It doesn't matter."

The detective looked at Ian's badge. "Maybe you don't have any business being a cop."

"Maybe I don't."

He might have walked away if not for being the only one who seemed to be watching out for Jupiter at the moment. He didn't feel comfortable abandoning her to the detective. Her dad was obviously in no shape to stand up for her.

"Since when is babysitting part of your job description?" the detective asked.

Ian wasn't a fighter. He'd never been in a fistfight in his life, but he boxed, and he imagined hitting the guy in the face. Ian stood up for people. Not anything to brag about. Just something everybody should do.

A man came running toward them. He'd ignored the yellow tape or maybe convinced someone to allow him to pass. Or maybe his good looks just left everybody helpless and starstruck.

Christopher Crane.

He looked just like he did on the show—a cross between Brad Pitt and Heath Ledger. Ian had even seen that smooth, athletic run, seen the blue sky behind him, seen his blond hair moving in the wind. He played the male lead, Nova's off-and-on love interest. If the tabloids were right, they'd had a hot affair in real life too.

And then Crane was there. He grabbed Jupiter and pulled her to her feet. The girl let out a sob and flung her arms around him, burying her face in his neck.

Crane asked Jupiter if she was okay.

What a question. Of course she wasn't okay.

She nodded, just a conditioned, habitual response to a common question.

"Is it true?" Crane asked. "Is Marie dead?"

The girl began crying again. In the middle of a series of sobs, she stopped, looked around, and said, "Where's Blanche DuBois?"

"Blanche DuBois?" Ian asked. "Does someone else live in the house?"

"It's her mother's cat," the actor said.

Ah. Nova had starred in the movie remake of *A Streetcar Named Desire*. If he remembered right, that was where she and her husband met. Ian had spent a little too much time reading about her career while standing in grocery store checkout lines. As a teen, he'd been a fan and even attended one of her movie premieres.

"I'll find her. Wait here." Ian left them there and strode toward the house, resisting the urge to run, just run and keep running while he ripped off his uniform and threw down his name tag.

There were clusters of people inside, all working on the crime scene. Through windows, he could see more crew outside.

"Anybody seen a cat?" Ian asked.

Negative.

"Mind if I look around?"

"Grab a pair of gloves and slippers." A guy motioned to a supply area. "And don't touch anything."

Funny, not funny.

Ian snapped on the shoe covers and gloves.

"We've pretty much combed the first floor," a woman said. "And the house was secured before we entered."

Ian headed upstairs, thinking about how his sister's cat liked to lurk under the bed and had even chewed a hole in the box spring to create a private little nest inside to hide. He didn't see any blood on the way, but luminol would reveal stains if someone had done a sloppy job cleaning up.

He found what looked like the main bedroom. The bed was unmade, but there were no obvious signs of a struggle and no blood on the sheets. It was possible they'd been washed. Killers often took the time to do laundry. He got down on his knees and peered under the bed. No cat.

"Here, kitty kitty," he said softly.

There was a painting on the wall of a black cat. Was that Blanche? "Here, kitty kitty."

He paused, thinking he'd heard a meow. Not nearby, but faint and distant.

He shoved himself to his feet, not that easy because of the belt he was wearing, which held forty pounds of equipment, including a handgun and Taser. He checked the bathroom and checked the closet, but he felt sure the sound had come from farther away.

He searched and found another flight of stairs leading to the third-floor office and TV room. A shelf with awards.

He heard it again. A meow, a little louder now.

Definitely a cat, and he was definitely closer.

There were other rooms on the floor, but they were unfinished, dusty, obviously unused. Back to the office. He opened and closed closet doors. Called the cat again. Heard another meow.

Above him.

Was it in the wall?

Another circle of the rooms, then back to the closets, going deep this time, finding a narrow door he hadn't seen before because it blended with the shiplap walls that had been painted white. Then he remembered the turret.

He wasn't tall, just an average-sized guy, but he had to keep his head down, the stairwell so narrow his shoulders brushed the sides. Cobwebs hit him in the face, and he wiped them off and shook the stickiness of them from his hand.

He called the cat again.

It answered.

He pulled out his flashlight and clicked it on. The walls in the curved and narrow stairwell had long streaks of blood on them. His heart pounding, he held fast while passing the flashlight beam around the curved space, stopping when the beam landed on a man sitting against the wall, knees to his chest, hand up, trying to block the light.

It wasn't just the guy's hands that were covered in blood. His face and clothes were covered too. Without taking his eyes off him, Ian reached for his gun, unsnapping the holster.

A cat burst out of nowhere, shrieked, and tore off. Ian stumbled, reached out, caught himself. At the same time, the suspect launched to his feet, shoved past Ian, and almost flew down the stairs, landing hard at the bottom.

Ian ran after him, back through the closet and into the office, where he tackled him, brought him to the floor. The guy screamed. Ian yelled for backup.

Breathing hard, he cuffed the man, then pulled him to his feet.

It looked like he'd caught the killer. At least that was what everybody thought that day.

14

"Are you back here looking for closure?" Ian asked me.

"I don't know about that. My boss sent me to take a break and write something he thought would be fun and easy." I laughed a little scornfully. "Sometimes I think closure is a myth, or something only other people can achieve. But being here, talking to the Lumets, there's so much about my mother and her murder I don't know. I've thought about it, and I'm going to try to get an interview with Luc Chesterfield."

He kind of recoiled. "Is that a good idea? That's not really the kind of closure I was thinking about."

I'd also decided to interview Christopher Crane, my mother's costar on the show. He'd reached out to me a few times over the years, but I'd never responded. I felt bad for him for a couple of reasons. After the murder, the production company tried to replace my mother with another actress. It was a disaster, and the show was cancelled. I don't even think they aired the last episodes. Crane, who'd been rising fast on my mother's stardom, crashed and never regained momentum. I'd seen him in a few things, usually bit parts. Like the kudzu vine, death had a way of digging into cracks and crevices, destroying and consuming.

"I've never felt completely convinced that Chesterfield was the killer," I said, testing him.

He stared at me. "Really?"

I was looking for any sign of unease or guilt, but I was having trouble reading his expression. Was he a little nervous?

"If it's not Chesterfield . . . do you have any suspects?"

"No solid ones." I put apricot jam on a piece of toast as I contemplated how much information I wanted to share. "Now that I'm older and more experienced, I question some things that happened, and I question how the case was handled. It was all too easy, in my opinion."

A lot of police work was about observing people. Everybody was a suspect, especially family members. And even teens with raging hormones and hot tempers were known to kill. I'd never had that much of a temper, but I was sure I'd thrown a few beautiful tantrums in my life. Nobody had even questioned me. Max had been interrogated, but, looking back on it now, I could see the holes. I would have asked about their fights, about their evenings, about everything.

I took a bite of toast. The jam was good. I wouldn't mention my father, who was at the top of my list. Or Ian himself. Not yet. "Chesterfield? My mother's driver? That's like saying the butler did it. Maybe someone in the Lumet family. Maybe Christopher Crane."

"Often the simplest answer, especially when it comes to crime, really is the correct one."

True. I was about to question him about the blood when I heard a car pull up, heard slamming, then the front door opened, and a young girl stepped inside. She was wearing a backpack and pulling a bright pink overnight case on wheels.

"Honey, I'm home!" she shouted with ridiculous flamboyance, obviously imitating Ricky Ricardo on *I Love Lucy*.

She must have been eight or nine, and she had a light about her that chased the shadows from the little cottage. Dark curly hair, thin and tan arms and legs, wearing denim shorts and a purple T-shirt with a character I didn't recognize because I had no idea what kids watched nowadays. Behind her was a woman who stepped inside as if she belonged there.

"I think she had a great time at marine-life camp." The woman wore beige shorts and white flip-flops. A blue T-shirt with a dolphin on it. "Poppy can tell you all about it. I've got more kids to drop off. Call me if you have any questions." She told the child goodbye. Then she left, closing the door after her.

"You're a dad?" My question was a whisper, but the girl heard it and looked up at Ian.

"You're a dad?" she asked.

"She's my niece," Ian said.

"Ah."

The niece—Poppy seemed to be her name—let go of her suitcase, and it tipped over. I hated when that happened, and I felt annoyed for her. Then she shrugged out of her backpack, put it on the floor, and crouched and unzipped it, the contents spilling out. It seemed to contain things she'd made at camp. "On the way here, Bianca asked me if you were married or in a relationship." She glanced at me, obviously wondering.

I quickly shook my head in horror.

She pulled out some artwork, walked over to the refrigerator, and used magnets to hang her creations on the door. *Ah, the artist.* Most of the colored-pencil drawings were jellyfish, but there were some sharks with open mouths swimming below the surface of the water, an unsuspecting swimmer above. The universe must have been laughing at me, because even her artwork reminded me of Sal.

"I told her you were divorced," Poppy said. "Was that okay?"

"Fine," Ian said.

She opened the fridge door and pulled out a carton of milk. Ian got a blue bowl and spoon and placed them on the counter as she climbed up on a wicker stool. The girl poured cereal into the bowl, then with two hands, added milk from the carton. "He's divorced because of the fainting," she said, with further acknowledgment of me, keeping her eyes on the milk coming from the carton.

"Not true," Ian said.

101

"That's what grandma says."

He mouthed something to me that might have been the word *precocious*. Then he said to Poppy, "Grandma told you that because she didn't think you were old enough to hear the truth. Grandma doesn't know everything."

"She says she does."

"There you go."

"Are we riffing?" the child asked.

He placed a red apple on the cutting board and began slicing it. "We are."

The girl looked at me. "Ian says riffing is the secret to life."

He placed the plate of sliced apples in front of her and glanced at me, a look of embarrassment on his face. "Poppy's mother is out of the country for a few months, so I'm holding down the fort while she's gone. This is her house."

That explained the mermaid stuff.

"I riffed a lot at camp, and they told me to stop."

"You can't do it all the time," Ian said. "That can be annoying. And potentially inappropriate."

She began eating the cereal. I took a slice of apple Ian offered me. The white was already turning yellow.

"I didn't scream when I played," Poppy said around a mouthful of food. "I told the kids at camp they needed to stop screaming. They were scaring the wildlife. And they got mad at me."

Ian brushed a strand of hair from her face. "I'm sorry about that."

I had to agree with her. Kids made too much noise. When they were playing, it sounded like someone was being murdered. Like they needed to be rescued.

"The camp counselor got mad at me and said the kids were just having fun."

"Screams are for alerts, not happiness," I said.

"Ian tells me to only scream when I'm in danger."

"I totally agree."

I wasn't a big fan of anybody between the ages of one and fifteen, but she might have been a kid who could change my mind.

"Like if you were just sitting there coloring and you suddenly started screaming." I shrugged. "Not a good vibe."

"Right!" she said.

"Her mother was going to turn down the job, but we talked it over," Ian told me. "It seemed like something she shouldn't miss. Six months, though, but they FaceTime almost every evening."

"Mom says if Ian hadn't become a cop, he'd be a hipster. And that he had a horrifying first day on the job."

"That's enough," Ian said.

"But I'm not supposed to hold my thoughts in."

"Remember what I said the other day? About being sensitive?"

"You mean about reading the room?"

"Yes."

"Well, this is Jupiter Bellarose. Her mother was murdered that first day of my job."

Even I knew that was too much information to dump on a child so quickly.

The corners of her mouth turned down, and her mood shifted rapidly. She suddenly looked like she might cry. She grabbed a stuffed animal and hugged it to her, burying her face in the fur. I felt bad for her and battled between finding words of comfort and not wanting to contribute to her anxiety. When it seemed like she might be over it, she suddenly burst out with a question.

"Where do people go when they die?" Her bottom lip trembled.

"I don't know," Ian said.

"Google it," she said in obvious panic. "Can't you Google it?"

"I don't think Google will have the answer."

"So they just go away?"

"I don't know, honey."

She jumped off the stool, ran to her backpack, pulled out a pad of paper and crayons, and began drawing and coloring furiously.

"Her mother is a journalist in Yemen," Ian said.

"What's her name?" I asked.

"Liz Griffin."

"Oh, wow. She reached out to me to see if I'd be willing to be interviewed for a piece she did on my mother's murder. I hate to say it, but I didn't respond to her email." Typical behavior for me, I guess.

"She asked me too, and I said no. I couldn't do it either."

"Mom said you were afraid you might faint in front of the camera," Poppy said from the floor.

"If I had, your mother wouldn't have run the footage. But yeah, it was a concern." He looked back at me. "She never found anything to support the idea that someone else committed the crime."

"What about the man in the mask?" Poppy asked.

"Well, honey, it was a few days before Halloween, so if someone really saw a person in a mask, it wouldn't have been that unusual."

Sometimes it could be annoying when adults talked to kids as if they were adults, but this relationship seemed to work. It stood in contrast to my own. While I'd been raised by a mother who'd never seemed to consider me anything but a small adult, it hadn't been casual or comfortable. At the time, I'd found it euphoric to be included in grown-up conversation, but there wasn't a lot of space for me to just be a goofy kid with her.

To me, Ian said, "We could never find anybody else to substantiate that report. And my sister is a good investigative journalist but was unable to uncover any new information."

"She's an excellent reporter."

"I'm proud of her. What you're doing is important too. Just a different kind of important and more of a slow burn. I read your piece about those kids. And the most recent one about the forger. Liz's reports are mainly live and on location now."

The girl handed me the drawing she'd been working on. "To make you feel better."

I looked at it. I think it was supposed to be me. Same clothes, same hair, arm tattoos, but the person was crying. Needless to say, it did not make me feel better. She turned quickly away and plopped down on the floor in front of the TV.

"Is there somewhere we can talk?" I whispered to Ian.

"Out back on the deck."

At the sink faucet, he filled two glasses with water and handed one to me.

"She needs ten jokes, Uncle Ian!" Poppy said from the floor, suddenly much brighter. The drawing seemed to have given her some release and brought her light back. With no explanation of that outburst, she pulled a spiral notebook closer and announced, "I have to work on my novel. At camp we never had any downtime, and I wasn't able to get anything done."

"Everybody needs downtime," Ian said. "It can recharge the brain."

"Novel?" I asked once we were sitting on the back deck overlooking a marsh.

"She wants to be a writer, but not a journalist."

"Have you read it?"

"Nope. Big secret. But I'm sure it's destined to be a bestseller." He smiled at his own joke, but it was easy to see he adored the child.

I placed her drawing on the little glass-topped bistro table between us. Ian turned it around so he could see it. "Poppy is kind of an old soul." He leaned back. "I worry about her because this world is tough, as you know, and she feels the pain of strangers. She shouldn't feel the burden of someone else's sorrow at such a young age."

"And how about yours?" I asked. "Does she feel it?"

"I swear that kid can walk into a grocery store and see somebody and start worrying about her. And yeah, me too. And you. She's worried about you. She should not have to feel our heartache. She has enough with her mother being gone. And Liz is in a dangerous place. I realize there's a chance she might not come back. But I can't think about that. You know what she said about you? That you needed to hear ten jokes? It's her measurement of sorrow. How many jokes it will take to make a person happy. I'm probably a one-to-five-joke guy most of the time."

"So ten is bad."

"Yeah."

I could see he was waiting for me to explain why I was here. "I remembered something from the day my mother died." I decided not to mention that it was a dream.

"Ah."

"And I wanted to ask you about the accuracy of my memory. I know how false memories can affect stories, and this one seems like it could fall into that category. This isn't going to make you faint, is it?"

"Like I said, I hadn't fainted in years. I have to be taken by surprise. That's why it happened the other day."

"Her death impacted so many people. I've had a hard time wrapping my mind around that."

"I know you lost your mother, so we didn't have the same experience, but I feel a connection to you because of what happened. But tell me what you remembered." He suddenly seemed nervous, almost as if he knew what I was going to say.

"You led me out of the house."

He nodded. "That's right."

"And you handed me something. It might have been water. Yeah, I think it was. But I noticed something. Your hand was bloody. Both of your hands were bloody."

Sweat popped out on his forehead, and his mouth went slack.

Here we go.

Before I had time to consider what I was doing, I jumped to my feet and tossed my full glass of water in his face. "Oh my God." I put a hand to my mouth. "I'm sorry."

He blinked hard and wiped water from his face, then laughed a little. "That's okay. I'll have to remember that trick." He gave his head a shake, spraying water, collecting himself. "Your memory is correct. I'm not going to go into detail about the how and why I had blood on my hands. I don't think it's of any benefit for you to hear about it in vivid detail, but I was first on the scene, and I made an error in judgment that day."

And then, when I once again thought he was going to faint, he covered his face with his hands, and his shoulders began to shudder. And damn if he wasn't crying.

15

It was his first day with the Savannah Police Department, just hours on the clock, when Ian and his partner were dispatched to a home with a possible dead person, called in by an anonymous 911 tip. No other details.

"It's Marie Nova's house," his partner, Belinda Harper, a blonde woman in her fifties with a southern accent that was more Texas than Georgia, said as the siren screamed above them and she blasted through intersections.

Ian, like everybody else in the country, watched *Divination*. Campy and sexy, it had mermaids and vampires, and Nova played a psychic who not only saw the future but could control it. But the real reason it was a hit was because of the star. Everybody, male and female, young and not young, was in love with Marie Nova, Ian included. He was too old for a poster on his wall, but in high school the story had been different. So to be called to her home just hours into his first day of work was surreal.

Fifteen minutes later, siren now off, no lights flashing, they pulled to a stop in front of a narrow three-story Victorian home painted various shades of purple. He would have expected nothing less.

It should have looked garish or even cheap, but it was regal, the colors giving it an air of mystery that fit her show's character. Along with the three stories, it also had a turret. He imagined the turret with a table and crystal ball. More likely it was just a room, maybe a bedroom, maybe an office, maybe storage. To the left and attached to the house was a garage that didn't fit the style but was understandably practical.

They were the only squad car there. No one else would be dispatched until they had confirmation and reported back.

He and Officer Harper walked to the front door. Harper knocked, spotted the doorbell, rang it. They waited, feet planted, hands on hips, looking around. All seemed quiet. Nothing that spoke of anything out of the ordinary.

When no one answered, she said, "Go around back while I check for anything suspicious in front."

A curved walk led to the right side of the house and a solid wooden gate that was at least seven feet tall. An actress like Nova would need her privacy. Ian pushed down on the metal latch, surprised to find that the gate swung open. He stepped through and continued to the backyard.

Fall sasanqua camellias were blooming. The entire space was filled with their bright pink blooms and sweet scent. In the center of the yard, near the base of a massive tree that shaded much of the area, was a scattering of objects that at first his mind recognized as a broken mannequin. An arm flung there, a leg several feet away, a torso near the birdbath.

He stepped closer, leaning in.

Were they show props? That was what they looked like. *Divination* was known for its graphic violence and sex. This had to be his initiation, he decided. It probably wasn't even Nova's house. He'd heard about some of the immature things done to rookie cops. He hated that kind of cruel humor. He'd never pull that kind of shit on anybody.

He was about to shout to Harper, tell her *good job* and *ho-ho-ho*, when he spotted a head propped up in the birdbath. A human head with long, shiny red hair. Still feeling angry at being the butt of such an elaborate joke, he strode swiftly across the yard and picked up the head with both hands. It was heavier than he'd expected, and he lifted it high, so he and the head were face-to-face.

His heart began to slam, and his ears roared. It was a woman, eyes open just slightly, mouth, with Nova's signature bright red lipstick, wide, as if caught in a silent scream.

Plop, plop, plop.

He looked down.

Thick, congealed blood, darker than the lipstick, was dripping on his black shoe. He let out a muffled sound, something between a whimper and a scream. He backed up. He threw the head. Not far, just far enough to get it away from him, get it away from his shoes.

It rolled across the grass, stopping a few feet from the birdbath.

Brown leaves from the live oak fell into the water and floated there, etching a design on the surface that also reflected the blue sky and puffy white clouds. Behind him, he could hear the leaves falling on the sidewalk. They made a clicking sound followed by a soft *shush* the way live-oak leaves did. They never stopped falling, day and night, every season.

Shouldn't have thrown the head. *Thrown the head.* Shouldn't have even touched it. He'd thought he'd stepped into a joke, but this was a crime scene. Tumbling deep into mental panic and disbelief, he lost time. At some point, he heard the gate creak, heard footsteps on the sidewalk, footsteps stirring the leaves. Then weighted silence followed by a gasp.

Ian turned to see his partner standing a few feet behind him, a look of horror on her face. She fumbled for her shoulder radio, got dispatch, said something. Ian was only partially hearing anything above the roar in his head. Then he buckled and hit the ground like someone who'd been shot.

When he finally came back around, Harper was leaning over him. "You okay?" she asked.

He couldn't make sense of anything. He was starting to think nothing was real.

Cops began appearing behind her.

"Are you diabetic?" she asked. "Do you need sugar?"

He expected the other officers to laugh and make fun of him. Nobody made a sound. Someone extended a hand and pulled him to his feet, patted him on the shoulder while not making eye contact. He went to the squad car and sat there awhile, heart pounding. Beyond the vehicle, others were arriving, along with the coroner and medical examiner. People were gathering on the street. He didn't want to, but he finally forced himself to leave the car, went back, and found his partner.

"Somehow, in all the chaos, Nova's husband and daughter arrived on site before we got the area contained," Harper told him. "The girl saw the body." Harper squeezed his shoulder. "I'm really sorry. This is a tough first day, a day that would be hard for a seasoned cop." She paused, looked down. "Your hands."

He turned them over. Both palms had blood on them. He wiped them off on his dark pants.

"Did you touch something?"

"I thought it was a joke."

She pulled a tissue from her pocket and handed it to him, glancing over her shoulder, then back. "Clean yourself up," she whispered.

He made a feeble attempt, but the blood was already dry. He stuck the tissue in his pocket, and they both looked over to where people wearing black jackets with *Crime Scene Investigator* across the backs were crouched over the head he'd tossed. One of them was taking photos, and another was measuring the distance between the head and the torso.

Ian wiped the back of a hand across one cheek and realized his face was wet. He was crying and hadn't even noticed.

16

I didn't know what to do with the crying people I knew, let alone someone who was almost a stranger. I patted Ian's shoulder awkwardly but managed to restrain myself from saying, *There, there.* When he finally seemed to get himself a little under control, I said, "Tell me what happened."

He pulled in a shaky breath, looked up at me, and said, "I don't think I can. Not you. Not her daughter."

"You asked me about suspects. I didn't give you my complete list. I left off your name."

He made a little sound of despair.

"Did you do it? Did you kill her?" I knew I sounded ridiculous. Looking at him, I didn't believe it was possible. But I had to know.

"Me?" He appeared convincingly horrified. "I hate to tell you, because you'll use this information to support your weak theory about Chesterfield. I didn't commit the crime, but I'm guilty."

I must have let out a gasp.

"It's not what you think. I compromised the crime scene."

He explained it all in short, broken sentences. He told me how he'd found Marie's head in the birdbath and picked it up. "When I realized it wasn't fake, I yelled and threw it." He buried his face. "Oh my God. I'm so sorry."

Sometimes things could be so horrific you wanted to laugh. Not a real laugh, but a release that wasn't crying or screaming. I felt that way now. It was all so horrible and all so stupid. People did not get their heads cut off, and cops didn't scream and throw severed heads across the yard. And yet I myself had insisted the body parts had been props.

"I'd like to see the files," I told him.

"I can do better than that. Since the case is closed, I can get you a copy. I'll stop by the archive department tomorrow and have them to you by tomorrow night."

Maybe he felt it was the least he could do. We shared phone numbers and I left, but not before telling Poppy goodbye.

Once I got back to the Airbnb, I used a *Bird Girl* magnet to stick her drawing to the refrigerator door. Despite my initial reaction, Poppy's art suddenly made me feel better. I don't know why. Maybe because it was an innocent and heartfelt display of human connection.

17

The following day I hunkered down to work on the Luminescent article, only taking a break long enough to grab a bite to eat and buy clementines from a nearby fruit stand within walking distance of my Airbnb. When evening rolled around, I got a text from Ian letting me know he was outside with my mother's case files.

The street-level door was locked, so I went downstairs, expecting him to just give me the goods. Instead, he stood there holding a large white cardboard box, punch-outs for handles, seemingly waiting for an invitation to come inside. I wasn't in the mental state for company, but then I rarely was. I stepped back and mumbled something halfway friendly. He followed me up the stairs to the third floor. Inside the apartment, while I cleared my work area and moved my laptop and notebooks aside, he set the box down on the table.

"Nice place," he said, looking around. "Love the plank flooring."

I saw the space with fresh eyes and without the panic of just arriving in Savannah.

"The requisite *Bird Girl* decor, I see."

"It's wild that after all these years, tourism is still being driven by the book and movie," I said.

"Also by *Divination* and *Forrest Gump*. But I think *Midnight in the Garden of Good and Evil* really took hold because it's based on a true story. People find that aspect fascinating."

"My mother auditioned for *Midnight*," I told him. People from the area often just called it *Midnight* or even *MGGE*. "She was devastated when she didn't get it." I hadn't thought about how badly she'd wanted that part in a long time. "A year later she tried out for *Divination*, and the rest is history."

I'd often wondered how different things might have been if she'd gotten the movie role. She wouldn't have been cast in the TV show, and she would not have become a global phenomenon. She might very well have still been alive. She and I might have been sharing an Airbnb right now, just hanging out.

Ian and I sat down across from each other at the table. It was a farmhouse design, long and narrow. Old, sturdy. Behind us was the small kitchen with its granite countertop. The bedroom was down the hall. I had the view. I could see through the French doors to the balcony and wrought-iron railing. From somewhere came a whisper of music, maybe someone busking on the square.

"Poppy says hi." Ian lifted the lid from the box and set it aside. The first item he pulled out was colored-pencil artwork with Poppy's signature in the corner. He handed it to me. "For you."

The drawing was a mermaid. They sure liked mermaids.

I'd never been around kids much. I'd always gotten the idea most of them were selfish brats until they learned that wasn't cool, but I was impressed by Poppy's thoughtfulness.

"These aren't the originals," Ian said, unpacking the box. "So I don't need them back, but there wasn't a lot. Most of the crime-scene photos were gone. No surprise. We tend to keep and store things longer now since we have dedicated space, but twenty years ago we just didn't keep files on closed cases. To have anything left from your mother's time period is unusual."

I was familiar with those deep purges. Minneapolis rotated out records and evidence after five years unless it was a cold case. More than once I'd run into a lack of evidence while working a story.

"Why do you think any of this still exists?" I asked.

"Probably because it was Marie Nova. People couldn't make themselves shred it. I'm guessing it feels like a piece of history."

He pulled out four manila folders, plus a stack of unbound sheets of paper he held with two hands and tapped against the tabletop. "Fresh from the copy machine," he said. "I haven't gone through it, so I wouldn't mind giving it a look myself to see if anything jumps out."

And he wanted to gauge my reaction. I was familiar with that tactic.

Most of my note-taking was electronic files, but I still liked to jot down information on a pad. I grabbed my favorite—a little narrow reporter tablet—and a gel pen, black ink.

Among the paperwork there was the expected pile of phone records, a year's worth. There were interviews with some of Marie's friends, fellow actors, and associates, but given the confession, investigators hadn't spent much time on them. One person said Marie hadn't seemed herself lately, and had appeared preoccupied at times. Someone else said she'd confided that she hadn't been feeling well.

The murder weapon, a butcher knife, had been found in the dishwasher. Blood on the washing machine. Trace amounts had also been found in the shower. The next morning, after Luc Chesterfield was caught, his blood alcohol level was still high, 0.20, and a tox report had come back showing methamphetamine in his system.

"That's an impressive amount of impairment," Ian said, passing the report back to me.

"Surprising he could even walk that night, let alone kill someone. Or try to clean up after."

"But then again, meth can give a person superstrength."

"Yep."

There were copies of angry emails from Max, dated the days leading up to her death. The emails didn't surprise me, because I knew they'd been fighting. There was bank account information that would take time to decipher, if it could ever be deciphered. And something else: a fairly large insurance policy of which my father was the beneficiary.

Seeing my surprised reaction, Ian said, "You didn't know about that."

"I didn't. He's never mentioned it."

Next were notes from the detectives who'd arrived on the scene that morning. I vaguely remembered a guy in a dark suit. There were pages of observations and remarks, yet it appeared he'd ignored the insurance policy, a strange oversight.

Ian produced something else, a book, and placed it on the table. *The Black Dahlia* by James Ellroy, fiction based on the gruesome and unsolved Elizabeth Short murder. I tried not to flinch, thinking about how Short had been dismembered, thinking how my mother had been dismembered. Both of them actresses. The book was one of the early editions of the paperback, published in the late eighties.

I forced myself to pick it up and look inside, saw a familiar used-bookstore stamp on the inner cover. Everything about it felt tactile and familiar, even the smell.

"That should have gone back to your father once the file was disbursed," Ian said.

I kept my face down so he couldn't see my expression. "Maybe he didn't want it."

I had no memory of leaving the book at her house, but it would have made sense for me to have been reading it there. I'd been obsessed with the story, worried about the life of an actress and trying to figure out just why the case couldn't be solved. I'd carried the book around a lot and read it several times. But then many people had been obsessed with it, including my father. I said nothing and moved on, blocking the memories and lack of memories for now and maybe forever.

I pulled out a small, folded card, the kind that came with flowers. I was still shaking inside, but my hand was steady. It was a note to my mother from Atticus, Phaedra's dead brother.

Please accept my sincere apologies. I know being drunk is never an excuse, but I was drunk in more ways than one. One from the alcohol, and two from your presence. Please accept this small gift.

There had been rumors that they'd been an item. And what was the gift? Flowers, or something else?

There were a few photocopy images of my mother's bedroom, the hallway, the stairs, and the kitchen. No surprise that blood was everywhere. I remember taking off my black boots that night after my father and I returned home and finding blood on them. I'd tried to clean them, but there was so much I ended up throwing them away.

Every room was in disarray, but it was impossible to know how much of the mess was just my mother's normal slovenliness. And yet, looking at the pictures, it wasn't hard to imagine signs of a struggle in both the bedroom and kitchen.

The whole thing seemed to make Ian uncomfortable, and at one point he stood up abruptly. "I've got to pick up Poppy."

"Tell her thanks for the drawing."

I walked him toward the door, stopping to put the colorful mermaid on the refrigerator next to the sad picture she'd created yesterday. I wished I had something to send back to give her in return. I looked at the framed prints on the walls and the decorative dish on the table, none of them mine to give, and none of them anything a kid would want anyway. I plucked a clementine from the bowl and handed it to him. "For Poppy."

He tossed it in the air and caught it. My host skills were nonexistent. I should have offered him something upon arrival. He looked hungry as he considered the clementine. I gave him a second one before he left.

Once he was gone, I returned to the box and quickly came to the realization that I was glad Ian wasn't there. Because at the bottom I found my mother's autopsy report.

In my job as an investigative journalist, I'd read my share of them. Until now, I'd always avoided hers. Had his quick exit been intentional? Before opening the manila file, I sat down, this time on the couch, my bare feet tucked under me.

Autopsy reports all looked similar. They used the same human figure, just an outline. I guess they didn't have one for decapitations, because there were actual drawings of that, along with notes.

I was doing okay, considering, then my heart suddenly lurched. Included in the packet were photos of her bloody hands. They were curved, palms up, as if gently holding a bird. Close-ups revealed nails packed with flesh, much more than I'd ever seen mentioned in any report. She'd fought hard and done some serious damage in the process.

My phone alerted me to a text message. It was from Phaedra.

Just saying hello and hope your day is going well!

I closed the file and found myself welcoming a light conversation. I didn't tell her my day was not going well. Instead, I pretended I hadn't just been looking at my mother's autopsy report. We talked about the upcoming party and the weather. I felt myself relax and thought it might be nice to have a female friend.

18

I got up early the next morning, swung by the nearby downtown Parker's Market on Drayton Street, grabbed some deli food, along with ice for my cooler, then headed out of town, toward Atlanta.

It would have been a pleasant drive if not for the destination.

After going over the autopsy report last night, I'd looked up Chesterfield on the Bureau of Federal Prisons website. Prisoners got shuffled around all the time. Right now, he was being held less than three hours away, in a maximum-security facility in South Carolina. The real challenge was going to be getting in to see him. It could be tough to snag an interview with a prisoner. There were a few ways to go about it. One, which I didn't have time for, was to send a letter and wait for a reply. Another was to contact one of the prisoner's friends or relatives to see if they could put in a good word. The third, and least likely to produce results, was to just go to the prison and request a visit from the warden and Chesterfield. I chose three.

A few hours later I was inside the building, putting in my request with the woman in the bulletproof vestibule. I filled out paperwork, showed my press credentials and driver's license, and then sat down to wait to see if Chesterfield would see me. Thirty minutes later he'd okayed the visit.

I think part of me had hoped he'd say no.

I had to leave everything in a locker, then I went through a metal detector and was met on the other side by a guard.

The light was always strange inside a prison. No windows, a lot of bright bulbs that made everything kind of gray and harsh, but also, oddly, dark and blindingly bright at the same time.

I knew this beat. I covered murderers in my work. I'd once accompanied a family on a visit to meet the man who'd killed their daughter. It might seem strange looking in from the outside, but many people wanted to talk to the person who'd ended their loved one's life.

I wasn't sure where I fell.

There were many roads to closure, or many roads to an attempt at closure. Some felt the need to tell the monster how horrible he was, how they hoped he died a long and painful death. Others secretly plotted to end the killer's life, a foolish thing to attempt in a prison. That effort might be planned with a tool they tried to sneak in. Some thought they could accomplish it with their bare hands. Others just felt the overwhelming need to be near the human who was there when their loved one died. Behavior in such a situation very often didn't make sense.

I'd like to think I'd prefer to be the family member who wanted to jab a pen in an artery, but I suspected I might have been someone who craved that tangible connection to the person who'd ended my mother's life, the person who'd breathed the same air she was breathing when she died. The person who'd witnessed the life leave her body.

I was led to a room where a man sat at a table, shackles around his waist, chains attached to the floor. I pulled out a chair. The legs scraped the concrete, and the sound bounced around a space equivalent to an echo chamber as I sat down across from him. I could see no recognition in his eyes and no fear or remorse or shame, things that often came with a killer confronting the relative of the person he'd killed, especially in prison, because here there was no way to pretend it had never happened. There were no big diversions, no new landscapes or obsessions or jobs or interests or plans for the next hour or day or week or year. You were just in this place, with your old memories and few new ones.

He had the look I called prison ick.

Almost everybody you saw, if they'd been inside long enough, had a certain doughy, translucent quality to their skin, a little reminiscent of a dead and bloated fish that had washed up on the beach. I noted that he had no scars on his face, which could have been evidence of Marie having defended herself, but everybody healed differently.

His cuffed hands resting on the table between us had long, bony fingers, the kind that would do well with a keyboard—when not killing someone. He had no scars on his arms either. If he'd done it, her nails could have dug his flesh elsewhere on his body, but such wounds were typically found on the face or arms or both.

I swallowed before inhaling the stale aroma of stagnant air. I stared at him. Had he always looked so fragile? It would have taken a lot of strength to cut the head off someone. Or a lot of hatred. He didn't seem like someone who would hate easily.

I was suddenly hit by an old childhood memory.

"I once went to a Christmas play at a minimum-security prison when I was a kid," I told him. "The play was put on by the prisoners." At his look of surprise, I continued, "I know it's hard to imagine that today. All the actors were inmates." Chesterfield seemed to appreciate my little story. There was a spark of interest in his eyes.

"No way would that happen now," he said.

His voice was higher than I'd expected and more youthful. I'd always imagined someone my father's age, but he was only forty-eight. He'd been in prison twenty years.

I didn't remember much about the play, but the part that stuck in my mind was how the adults had been stamped with ultraviolet ink that showed up only under a black light. But they didn't stamp the kids, because it was an adult prison. Adults were screened coming and going.

When we went in, I held up my hand to get a stamp, but everybody just laughed. So I sat through the whole play worried that I wouldn't be able to leave because I didn't have a stamp on my hand. How would they know I didn't belong there?

The things we think of and fear as kids. They were so irrational, and yet the *fear* was real. I still felt a little that way when I stepped into a prison. Like I might not be leaving. Like somehow there would be some mix-up and they'd think I was someone else, and nobody would believe me when I tried to say I didn't belong there. Because what prison guard hadn't heard that line before? And the thing I hadn't wanted to face until now, until Sal's death, which I was responsible for, was that maybe I *should* be locked up.

"Do you know who I am?" I asked.

"At first I wasn't sure."

I remembered him from that earlier life when he worked for my mother, but had I ever heard him speak? I couldn't recall, but then teens had a selective memory, even when it came to the mundane. Yet I could certainly forgive myself for erasing all recollection from my mind if he'd ever been there. It seemed a smart and protective thing to do.

"When I saw your name on the request, I thought you might be an impostor. People do that." He shrugged, sharp shoulders moving under the orange jumpsuit. "Journalists who want a scoop. But a lot of times it's just nutcases who are trying to meet me."

He smiled, and I could see he was missing an upper tooth. Prisoners got medical and dental care. I wanted to ask how he'd lost it, but I didn't. I was going to guess it was his choice to have a bad tooth pulled rather than repaired. Looks weren't a priority in prison.

"I've had a lot of marriage offers." His words explained the smile. "And offers of conjugal visits. I thought it might be someone pretending to be her kid, but as soon as I saw you, I knew you weren't lying. You look a lot like your mom. She was a beautiful woman."

I tried not to wince at his words. I hated that he was speaking of her in the way a person might mention someone who'd died of a disease. "Was," I said, driving home that she was dead because of him.

He stopped smiling and seemed to fade away.

As years passed, prisoners lost their ability to interact with others, especially people from the outside. You could see when things went dead in their minds as they inwardly struggled to restructure and rearrange and find the beat of the conversation. But then he looked at me, right into my eyes. I didn't even blink.

Good job, Jupiter.

"Did you come here to forgive me?" he asked.

I hadn't expected that. My throat went tight, like a band had wrapped around it.

It was hard for anything to surprise me anymore. I should have been prepared for the question because it often came up with killers and survivors, but I'd probably blocked out that possibility like everything else. And now I wondered if I should run with it. I would never ever forgive him, but I could lie. I was good at that. I'd lied to my parents. I'd lied to child traffickers. I'd lied to Salvador. There was no honor among thieves or killers, and Chesterfield and I were both killers.

"Yes," I croaked, then immediately regretted my answer. I knew the best way to the truth was with the truth. I quickly corrected. "No."

Unable to maintain eye contact any longer, I looked up at the clock on the wall and was surprised to see that only a couple of minutes had passed. It felt like forever. I stared at it for a few ticks, then forced myself to look back at him. "I can't do that." My voice sounded weird to me, but probably not weird enough for him to notice. He might have killed her. He might be the one, the right guy sitting here right now, locked up, unable to hurt anyone else. I wanted him to have killed her, because the alternative might break me one final time. "I can't forgive you. I won't forgive you. You don't deserve forgiveness."

He bit his lip and nodded. "I understand."

We've been conditioned to think we should always forgive, that forgiveness will heal us. But with my decision to never forgive him, I felt some of the burden lift from my soul. The constriction around my throat loosened.

"What do you miss?" I managed to ask casually. "From the outside." It was a favorite question of mine.

He thought a moment.

"Trees," he said after consideration.

I'd expected him to name some kind of food.

"I really miss trees. The shade, the way they sound. Weird things about them. The way the sun falls through the leaves, especially when the wind is blowing. And you know how the leaves can kind of make a strobe sensation when they move? I miss that. There aren't any trees here. It would be nice if there were."

Trees were always good. "I heard you're going to be up for parole soon." No chance in hell he'd get out. Would he? "What do you think about that? Would you want to leave here? Some inmates don't," I said. "Some people never want out. And some get out and commit another crime just to get back in. The prison becomes a womb. What about you? Where do you fall?"

"I worry about supporting myself, but the big thing is that I feel safe here. It's about growing so used to it that I can't imagine living anywhere else."

"I understand. As much as I can anyway." And other places could feel like prisons too. Phaedra had even mentioned the vast Lumet mansion feeling like one to her. My life with Bennett had felt smothering at times. Maybe I couldn't be in a real relationship. Maybe that was also the reason I'd been so attracted to Sal. I'd kept things from Bennett, but with Sal I'd left myself behind completely.

"I also don't want to hurt anybody," Chesterfield added. "So being here . . . It's probably for the best." After that blunt admission, he drifted again, saying, "You know, your mother used to call me to do things for her. Didn't matter what time it was."

Had she called him that night? "Where did you first meet?" I asked.

"I was working for the Lumet family as a driver and kind of gopher, I guess. Any odd job or errand was given to me. One time when she'd had too much to drink, I gave her a ride home. Then she hired me."

"I've heard those parties were wild."

"That first one was just a small dinner, but yeah. Their yearly event was like something you'd never seen before and never would again. Each was spectacular in a different way, nothing repeated. I was actually a guest once. Your mother's plus-one."

"I didn't know that." She might have hated the parties, but she'd also hated being alone. But taking a driver was weird even for her. It certainly would have caused even more friction with the Lumets. But then again, she'd loved to wind people up, and I could imagine her doing it for just that reason. To piss them off and enjoy the ensuing pearl-clutching. "Did you ever have a sexual relationship with her?"

"Marie? No! God no." He looked genuinely shocked and horrified by my question. "She was unattainable. I would never even have tried."

"But you wanted to." That could have been a volatile situation. It was the motive behind a lot of celebrity deaths. It was why people had bodyguards. The only way to satisfy that desire was by killing the person they could never attain.

"I don't want to talk about this." He was getting agitated. I'd obviously hit a nerve. "I don't even know if I thought about her that way. She was so . . . above me."

"So maybe finding out she had many men in her life . . . Maybe that bothered you."

"That's what some people thought. I don't know. I don't think so. I mean, I might have felt like her lifestyle could have been a little more traditional, but it wasn't my business."

I'd seen her decapitated body, but that memory was a blur, something embedded in my brain by reruns. I once again recalled the photos I'd caught my dad with. Where had he gotten them? Had he taken them himself? Printed them out at home? Or had someone else given them to him? If so, who? Why?

I had to focus. In order to do that, I couldn't be me right now. I needed to adopt an undercover persona, not be Marie's daughter but a reporter. This was a case I was working, nothing more. I was good at pretending, as Salvador had pointed out before he swam to the sun.

My strategy helped. "I'm here because I want to give you a chance to tell your side of the story," I said pointedly. "Would you like to do that?"

"I don't know. I guess."

"Let's start with the why."

"Honestly, I've asked myself that a lot. I don't understand it." His voice got tight. "I was drunk and high. I don't know why I did it." He let out a little sob, then collected himself. "I adored her. Adored her!"

"Okay, then when did you decide to kill her? Was it a conscious decision?"

"I don't think it was."

"Would you say it was impulsive?"

"Maybe. Like I said, I was high."

"On what?"

"Meth and alcohol."

It tracked. "I saw your tox report. Those were some high numbers." But he might have gotten extremely high *after the fact*.

"It's always been hard for me to say." He started crying. He put his head in his hands, as much as he could with the chains around his waist and attached to his wrists. "I loved her. I don't know why I did it."

I didn't cut him any slack. I knew he could end this whenever he wanted, any second, so I pressed harder. "Let's go over the details."

"I've related what I know a million times. You could just read the transcripts. I thought I wanted to talk about it, but this makes me feel terrible. It makes me uncomfortable. You here. Looking like her."

"I want to hear it from you."

He let out another choked sob. "Okay, okay. I'll do it. I'll try. We were in the kitchen, and she was talking about the party she'd just been to and how she'd hated it. And there was one of those butcher block things with knives in it. And she was always talking about how she hated doing a lot of the stuff she had to do. She looked at the knives and said she'd just kill herself if she had the guts. And I think I thought I was going to help her. That I could stop her pain, do something for her nobody else could do. I grabbed the biggest knife, and I stabbed her. Over and over."

I'd never heard her speak of killing herself, but I would file that for later contemplation. Now we'd reached the part I really wanted to hear about, the question that had never been asked as far as I knew, one that had haunted me since the day I found her body. "I understand now. You wanted to stop her pain and misery. I get that, and I appreciate hearing that you did it out of kindness." I was serving up some real bullshit as I tried to keep my voice level. The whole thing was surreal, and I was aware that I should have been more freaked out than I was. But I was oddly composed, my voice level and tranquil, maybe even hypnotic. "I don't understand why you cut her up. Why you cut off her head."

Cut off her head.

"I guess I was trying to copy murders I'd read about."

"Like the Black Dahlia?"

"Yeah."

I wasn't the only person obsessed. "Did detectives suggest that to you? That it was maybe why you did it?"

He thought a moment, then nodded. "I think so."

"They shouldn't have done that," I said. "Why do *you* think you cut her up?"

"I think I wanted to make it more confusing. I don't know."

"Was it hard to do?"

"Not as hard as you might think. And I was on meth. That shit makes people strong. I just cut off her head right there on the kitchen floor. And then I remembered that she loved her backyard, so I wanted to take her out there. I dragged her body outside, then returned for the head and put it on the ground, near the birdbath."

I was on autopilot now. Thank God for autopilot. "On the ground?"

"Yes."

It didn't fit with what Ian had recently told me.

"Then I heard something, maybe the street sweeper, and I panicked and ran back into the house. I started cleaning things up, and at some point I maybe blacked out. Later, I ran through the house, calling her name. I couldn't find her. Then I walked outside." His hands were shaking. The violent tremors moved up his arms until his whole body was vibrating and the chains around his waist rattled.

I know it was weird, but without thought, simply reacting to another human in pain, I reached across the table and touched the back of his hand, even patted it, to my own secret horror. "It's okay. That's enough. Let's don't talk about this anymore."

He kind of pulled himself together and looked at me, his eyes swimming with tears. "I can do it. I can keep going."

I moved my hand away, and he wiped at his nose with a bare arm. "I was afraid to leave, so I hid upstairs, and I think I did some more drugs. The next thing I knew, I heard a lot of people, and I just kept hiding. Until that young cop found me."

"Ian Griffin."

"Yeah. He was looking for the cat, Blanche. He found me instead."

"You ran."

"I did."

"And you had blood on you."

"I did."

"And you confessed to killing her."

"I did."

I couldn't pretend to be someone else any longer. My heart was pounding, and I felt like I might pass out. I had to leave.

"I'm going to go now." I looked over my shoulder and motioned to the guard at the door, letting him know I was ready. I had to get out of there, had to get away from Chesterfield. And then I was suddenly standing up, walking away, my head feeling floaty as the guard unlocked the door.

"Will you come back?" Chesterfield asked.

I paused and turned. He seemed to have grown lighter after passing his burden to me.

"Maybe," I said. *Hell no.*

"What happened to the cat?" he asked. "Did he ever find the cat?"

"Someone found her and we took her home."

"Good. That's good. I'm sorry, Ms. Bellarose. I'm so sorry I killed your mother."

I somehow managed to walk down the cinder block hallway to the checkout point. I'd hoped to leave feeling confident that the right man was in prison. Instead, my doubt had increased. I didn't like the holes in Chesterfield's memory. I didn't like the slight discrepancies between his story and Ian's, but I knew memory was unreliable. I was the queen of unreliable memory. I also didn't like that detectives had fed him information he'd simply agreed with. To date, sixty people had confessed to the Elizabeth Short "Black Dahlia" murder. Sixty. Still, not one of them had actually been found guilty.

19

The night after visiting Jupiter, Ian called his sister for their FaceTime chat and the evening ritual of tucking Poppy in. They talked about their day, then mother and daughter kissed the screens and said good night. Once Poppy was under the covers and cuddling her stuffed black cat, Mr. Darcy, Ian carried the iPad into the living room for a private conversation with Liz.

"I want to talk to you about something before we sign off." He asked her about the piece she'd done on Marie Nova. "I know you worked on it a long time, and I wonder if anything interesting ended up on the cutting room floor."

"The segment was under fifteen minutes, so it's not as focused as I would have liked," she said. She looked tired, and he was worried about her. "I've got tons of footage and notes I didn't use. It would take you weeks to go through it all, but I can send you a link and password to the files I saved."

"That would be fantastic."

"And I'll bet the aired piece can be found on YouTube."

He'd never watched it, but it was probably time.

"One more thing." She lowered her voice. "I didn't want to say anything in front of Poppy in case it doesn't happen, but it looks like I might be coming home soon."

His shoulders sagged in relief. He'd seen the news about an increase in danger in Yemen. Some were even worried about another coup. He wanted her safe. "We'll be here," he said before they signed off.

Liz had been right about finding the documentary on YouTube. Watching it, he felt a familiar sense of pride in the job his sister had done. It wasn't sensationalized or intrusive. The piece began with old footage of Marie Nova, most of it shot before she became famous. He'd been a fan, but just minutes in he could see why the whole world had been infatuated with her. She exuded life, and while Jupiter was quiet and pragmatic, he spotted similarities between mother and daughter, although it almost seemed Jupiter was going out of her way to avoid looking like Marie. He could understand that.

In some of the later footage, there were noticeable bruises on Nova's arms. Some people bruised easily, and actors often got knocked around on set. If he recalled correctly, the show had involved the weekly requisite fight scene. It was impossible to know the cause of her injuries, but he'd mention it to Jupiter.

There was also news footage of the day the body had been found. It took him a moment to recognize himself and Jupiter framed in a scene, standing in the front yard. *So young.* Both of them had been just kids, really. Shortly after that clip, he'd left to search for the cat while she stayed with Christopher Crane.

He reached the credits and realized he'd managed to get through all fifteen minutes without passing out. He'd watch it again later, when he wasn't feeling as much anxiety.

Even though it was getting late, he followed the link his sister had sent while he'd been viewing the documentary. There were tons of files, some small, but a lot of them larger. Among them, he found one labeled *Family Videos.* It contained old footage, maybe mined from other pieces on Nova. Was that a very young Jupiter in the background having a tantrum as her mother languidly smoked a cigarette while having her hair done? He laughed. Turned out Jupiter hadn't always been the cool cucumber she was today. In a later clip, he again noticed bruises on Marie's arms, and this time her face was flushed.

He logged off and called Jupiter. "Sorry. Didn't realize it was so late," he said when she picked up. "I wanted to ask you something. Something about your childhood. Did your father ever hit your mother?"

"They fought all the time."

He was surprised by the speed of her admission.

"I actually think my mother was the instigator, but it definitely happened, and it was often very dramatic."

He felt bad for her—and suddenly appreciative of his boring childhood.

"And I'm sure I only saw a fraction of it." With seeming reluctance, she added, "I've wondered about my father for years. The fights, now the insurance policy. Her public affairs that broke his heart. Other things, like the smell of her perfume in his car. The way he not only kept the house, he moved into it."

"The book."

"Maybe," she mumbled.

"I wish I could get a search warrant."

"Please, no."

"Don't worry. No judge is going to issue one without more circumstantial evidence than this, anyway." He had an idea. "I know you have a nice Airbnb, and I'm guessing you aren't staying with your father because that would be hard for you, but would you consider it? Staying at his place? Having a look around?"

That suggestion was greeted by so much silence he thought they might have lost the connection. "You still there?" he asked.

"Yeah." Her voice was tight and low.

"Forget I said that. It's too much to ask. And it could put you in danger."

"He would never hurt me," she said with conviction, sounding a little stronger. "And staying there is something I should have done long ago. I just couldn't face it, but I'm ready now. It's time. Past time."

20

The next morning while parked in my van, waiting for someone to emerge from a house I was staking out, I texted Bennett to let him know I'd be moving to my dad's. I didn't say why. He immediately called me, something I found annoying, and he knew it. If I'm texting, it's because I don't want to talk on the phone.

"When I said hang out with your dad, I didn't mean stay with him," Bennett said.

I was losing interest in the Luminescent story. I was too distracted by my mother's case, but at least today I was pursuing something that might be connected to both my mother and the story I was doing on the Lumets. I'd managed to track down a few people who'd worked at the estate back in the heyday of the company, and I'd found at least one person who still lived in the Savannah area, a woman named Anyika Freeman.

She'd answered my initial call, but after finding out I was a reporter and before I could fully introduce myself, she hung up on me. So now I was watching her house. I rarely resorted to such undignified and invasive measures. I preferred to insinuate myself into people's lives before destroying them.

"What's the weather like there?" I asked.

"Warm."

"I'm going to need more information."

"Sunny and ten degrees."

"That's what I figured. It's sunny and sixty-five here."

I was parked just a few blocks from Bonaventure Cemetery. A lot of people, especially tourists, thought of Bonaventure as being part of Savannah. It was actually in Thunderbolt, a town a few miles south of my Airbnb.

"That's why I wanted you to go there," Bennett said. "Warm weather. But not stay at your dad's."

I spotted movement. Anyika was coming around the house, moving toward the street.

"I gotta go," I said. "I'm on a stakeout. Tell you about it later." I ended the call, jumped from my van, and caught up with the woman I hoped to talk to.

"I won't take much of your time," I promised as I dropped into step next to her.

She was making a beeline for a sedan parked at the curb. "I have no interest in talking to a white girl who's trying to sell me a new roof."

She'd be driving off in a moment, so I got to the point. "Just a few questions about the party that took place at Camellia Manor the night Marie Nova died."

She froze, her hand inches from the car's door handle. She turned and looked at me. Her mouth dropped open, then she whispered, "Oh Lord. I feel like I'm seeing a ghost. You're her *titi*, right?"

Titi meant *girl* in Gullah. "I am. And I was hoping to ask you a few questions."

She put a hand in the air, palm out. "I cannot talk about anything. I signed an NDA."

"I'll protect my source."

She glanced around. There was nobody nearby. "I'm sorry about your mother," she said in a low voice. "I really am." She let out a sigh and stared at me.

She was probably fifty, wearing a colorful sleeveless dress and gold flip-flops, her gray-and-black hair in dreads that fell past her waist. After some consideration, she nodded toward the house. "Come on. Let's go sit on the porch."

We settled into matching rocking chairs. Haint-blue ceiling above our heads, hanging ferns, and a mild breeze speaking of a hot day to come, but enjoyable now.

"I suppose the wild parties are no secret," she said. "And the money they spent. I think most of it went to drugs. Your mother was there a lot of the time. And of course I saw things. I can't talk about any of that. I'm just gonna say those people were weird, even for rich folk."

"What about Phaedra?"

"Her?" She seemed disinterested and shrugged. "I kinda liked her. She was snooty, but never mean to me like some of the others. Sad, a lot of the time. Her son died, you know. So I guess I did feel sorry for her. But none of 'em really had any common sense, or understood the value of money. They just burned through it. I don't think they knew if $10,000 was a lot or nothing."

Yeah, no surprise there. "And what about my mother?" I really wanted to know what Anyika thought of her.

"Oh, everybody loved your momma. Sometimes, when the party was going on in the dining room, she'd get bored with all those rich people and come in the kitchen and just hang out. I can even remember sitting with her in her room and just talking." A sudden memory lit up her face. "You've heard about the ghost, right? It was foolishness, but some people who stayed overnight said a ghost visited them in their room. Your mother told me that too. Said she woke up and saw a creature standin' over her bed, breathing hard. But you know they were all high, doing cocaine and who knows what else."

"You never saw anything?"

She let out a snort and pulled her head back into her neck. "No! And I worked there for years. And my mother before me. I think I made some joke about a boo hag or slip-skin hag. Everybody from around here knows that story. They come into your room when you're sleepin' an' try to smother you or steal your skin to wear during the day until it rots and then they have to find another victim. But that's just a Gullah folktale all our mommas told us growing up. I was just kidding around because it's all so foolish, but your mother didn't appreciate it."

Marie hadn't been a fan of ghost stories, something I'd always found odd since she was so brave most of the time.

"My favorite memory of your mother was the time they brought in wild animals. They had them shipped in for one of their parties, and they set up the cages for attendees to admire. Your mother was furious."

The Lumets would have known how she felt about such things, because she'd refused to wear fur for their ads. Made me wonder if they'd done it deliberately.

"Your mother got drunk and released a tiger. Oh my Lord." She pressed a hand to her mouth and laughed so hard tears rolled down her face. "Nobody got hurt, but seeing those people screaming and scrambling in their fancy gowns . . ."

"I heard about that but honestly never knew if it was true." It was particularly satisfying to get a firsthand account from someone other than my mother, since it had always been impossible to separate her truth from her fiction.

"I want to tell you something about your mother. She knew all our names and even the meaning of names. Mine is Gullah for *She is beautiful*. And it wasn't that phony kind of thing. She really seemed to care, and she'd ask me how my kids were, and how they were doing in school, and did they need anything."

"My great-grandmother was Gullah and grew up on Sapelo Island. She died before I was born."

"I knew your momma must have had some Gullah in her! But here's what I really want you to know. She'd come into the kitchen and open her fancy little purse. Instead of digging out a compact mirror or lipstick, she'd pull out these little envelopes and start passing them around. If it was a holiday, she'd say happy whatever day. And if it wasn't, she'd just say thank you. For just being alive, I guess.

"She knew how hard our lives were, and she understood the financial struggle we had. Each envelope contained a hundred-dollar bill. I know that doesn't seem like a lot, but it seemed like more then, and there were at least twenty people on staff. And I got the feeling she suspected we weren't paid enough. She wanted to do more, but it wasn't her place. I mean, this was a gift."

My eyes stung and my throat burned. It was hard to remember or think of Marie as anything but the sensationalized victim that had been burned into all our memories, the person who'd been murdered, the headless torso. But Anyika's story brought back the humanity that had been my mother's.

When I'd pulled myself together enough, I asked, "What about the night she died? Did you work that night?"

"I did. And things felt off. I can't explain it. I went to your mother's room just to say hi and see if she needed anything. Maybe talk a little like we did sometimes. She seemed distracted and upset. I could see she'd been crying. I didn't think she looked good either. Her hair seemed thin, and she had dark circles under her eyes. She'd removed her makeup so the Lumet person could do her up right. Without concealer, she seemed sickly, but then I wasn't used to seeing her naked face, so it might have just been that. Anyway, I left her alone, and I wish I hadn't. But I got the idea she wanted to be by herself. I spotted her a few times that night, radiant, makeup perfect, wearing a red dress."

"But you got the sense something wasn't right?"

"Yes. And then the next morning we got the horrible news. And really, doesn't it seem like the whole world changed that day? Nothing has been as bright or as promising since." She shook her head. "That family. I think they're cursed. First the baby, then Phaedra's brother, then the boy."

"Baby?"

"They used to call it crib death. Now it's sudden infant death syndrome."

"I didn't hear about that."

"She was only a couple of days old. Phaedra had mostly kept the pregnancy a secret. This was before social media. I felt so bad for Oliver. He seemed to adore the baby. He was only about five, so I think it really hit him hard. You know they're buried just down the road." She pointed in the direction of Bonaventure. "In the Lumet plot. A real nice statue of Oliver. I walk there sometimes just to say hi and pick up some of the trash people leave."

"I met him. He seemed like a nice kid."

"He came to the kitchen sometimes, looking for cake or a cookie. Everybody loved to hang out in the kitchen. Such a pretty boy. And so polite. A little ornery, which isn't a bad thing."

"That's how I remember him too."

"One of these days there won't be anybody left, nobody to pass the company to."

It was a strange thing to think about.

"People say they see him in the cemetery wandering around at night."

"Oliver?"

"Yep."

A haunted cemetery. Who woulda thunk?

After leaving Anyika's house, I decided to stop at Bonaventure Cemetery since I was so close. The location brought back a wave of memories, good and bad. This was a poorer area, or at least it used to be. Many houses had been restored, some probably turned into vacation rentals, but the remaining shacks still gave the meandering back roads a historical old-world charm and mystery. The cemetery grounds themselves were some of the most beautiful in the world, with oak trees and Spanish moss, dirt roads lined with red camellias, towering statuary framing the languid and placid Wilmington River.

My mother had brought me to the tucked-away burial gardens a few times. We'd walked around and admired the graves of people like Johnny Mercer, one of Savannah's most famous residents. But her darker connection was a sex scene she'd filmed that had the unintended consequence of couples flocking to the cemetery in order to reenact the scene and do their own desecrating. That resulted in a locked gate and a caretaker who patrolled the grounds at all hours. I didn't know if that level of security was still in effect. If so, it would probably have more to do with vandals, since my mother no longer generated that kind of fervor.

She claimed to feel bad about the whole thing and blamed the production company. The city and the Lumets hadn't been happy about it. Me either, because a few of my classmates bragged about partaking in a reenactment. My mother ended up being banned from the cemetery for life, something she thought was hilarious.

Guess I can never die, she'd said. *Even the dead don't want me.*

The tall wrought-iron gates were open, and there was a hand-painted sign that said all visitors must be out by five p.m. I spotted several people, many obviously tourists, wandering around with cell phones, taking selfies in front of the more well-known graves. Some of them were probably there to visit loved ones.

It took me about ten minutes to find the Lumet plot. It was off in a sheltered corner, near the water, in the deep shade of Spanish moss and surrounded by blooming camellias. Anyika had been right. There was an impressive life-size statue of Oliver. He was sitting on a tree stump, holding a beagle puppy on his lap, a look of sweet affection on his face. I got out my 35mm camera and took several photos.

Piled on top of the tombstone were small rocks, coins, and little ceramic figurines of things like angels and animals. There were also several chess pieces. That triggered a memory of seeing Oliver at a few extracurricular events involving chess and band.

There was also a vase of fresh cuttings, mostly giant sunflowers, along with some cheerful white daisies. Off to one side was a small grave with a blank tombstone. It must have belonged to the baby girl.

I caught a hint of movement and, with a start, realized I wasn't alone. Someone was sitting on a bench, hidden by one of the flowering shrubs. I moved slightly, peeking around the bush, and spotted Phaedra. Seeing her here felt out of context, but it was her family plot, and I shouldn't have been surprised.

She saw me.

I was embarrassed to have been caught interrupting such a private moment. "I'm sorry."

"Don't be silly!" She stood up and walked gracefully toward me. She wore a flowing sundress and sandals. Big black glasses she slipped on top of her head like a headband. "It's a public place and I'm really glad to see you. I try to stop by at least once a week to pick up trash and put out fresh flowers." With one knuckle, she wiped at a tear. "People come out here chasing the folklore. They bring their ghost-hunting equipment and their candles and their photos. They leave a mess. Some of it's sweet, like the chess pieces. Oliver loved chess. But some of it's just vandalism."

Our conversation made me thankful that my mother had been cremated and that no grave existed for strangers to defile. I vaguely recalled the cremation decision being made due to my dad's concern about fans digging up her body. But then again, ashes could tell no tales.

"What about the locked gate?" I asked.

"They climb it. And some come by boat, if you can believe it."

Wordlessly, we shifted back to the bench and sat down side by side. She took a deep breath and looked around. "It's so lovely here. So peaceful."

"That statue is amazing," I said. "That's how I remember him."

"I usually toast him when I come." She pulled out a flask with the initials *OEL* on it and offered it to me. "Would you like to join me?"

I shook my head.

She took a long swallow, then screwed the cap back on. "He was the sweetest boy."

"What about the beagle?" I set my camera aside. "Was it his pet?"

"He was scared of dogs, poor thing. He had a bad experience as a very young child. But this dear puppy got him over it." The memory made her tear up again.

"I'll leave you alone."

She grabbed my hand and held on tight. "Don't go. Please. I need company right now."

I could feel the sorrow emanating from her and wanted to find a way to help lessen her pain. "I remember him from a couple of school events," I said. "I think it was band competitions."

She released my hand. "He played the flute."

"Even though he was older, he'd stop and say hi to me."

"That was Oliver. And he was involved in a lot of activities because he had to stay busy or he got into trouble. He couldn't sit still for a minute."

"That's how kids are." I really didn't know, but it seemed right.

"This isn't going to be in your story, is it?"

"No. Absolutely not. This is just two friends talking."

"Thank you." She made a little sound of despair and turned away. "It's hard. To let them go. All of them."

I decided she was talking about the baby and her brother too. She offered the flask again. This time I accepted and took a timid swallow. It was water. And I realized the initials were for Oliver Edward Lumet.

At my surprised expression, she laughed. "We have to keep up appearances, don't we?"

21

"Do you remember the cop who found Chesterfield in the turret?" I asked.

It was late afternoon, exactly forty-two minutes after my arrival at the death house, the visit so new that my suitcase was still near the front door in case I changed my mind. Max and I were standing in the kitchen, waiting for the latte machine to spew out some brew.

I could easily recall the number of times I'd been inside the house since my mother's death. Two. One had been when my father was in the hospital and I had to grab something for him. The next was returning him to the house from the hospital and helping him get settled. That was it. Two times in twenty years. And in those two times, I'd never been there long enough for my heart to stop racing and for my body's high-alert signal to stop clanging, telling me to run.

My father poured some milky froth and handed me a cup. The mug had been made by a local potter. I recognized the stamp near the bottom. Max was just finishing creating his own latte when rain came out of nowhere, roaring down. I closed the window above the sink, shaking water from my arms as thunder rattled every pane of glass in the house. There was really nothing equal to a Georgia rainstorm.

"Young guy," my dad said and took a sip of his drink.

I nodded. "Yeah."

"What a tough first day on the job. We don't think about how a murder impacts so many people. Even the neighbors moved away. Some kind of liked it at first, but eventually almost all of them left."

"People don't want that constant reminder," I said.

"Guess not."

"And yet you stay," I gently pointed out. Max, for the most part, seemed to live an unexamined life, so it might not have been that hard for him to stay in the death house, guarding it as if he were guarding my mother herself, keeping its secrets, which might have been few. Or many. I hoped to find out.

"I don't want anybody turning this place into a freak attraction," he said.

It looked the same, but also different. Darker, more cluttered. Smelled like mildew and old sweat. Beyond the kitchen was the backyard, which I couldn't even look at through the window, much less step out the door and enter.

My father was a hoarder. He kept the dishes washed, and I think he vacuumed a few times a year, but everything was covered in dust. Thick haunted-house cobwebs hung from the ceiling, sticking to you if you brushed up against them. I'd been overwhelmed by the idea of being in the house itself, but now, standing inside it, looking at the years of neglect, I felt overwhelmed in a different way.

"Just sell the place and move," I said. "You could even leave Georgia. You don't have to stay here." I looked around while trying to remove a sticky strand of cobweb from the front of my T-shirt. Another blast of thunder rattled the windows, and I felt a small thrill. "All these bad memories."

"I can't outrun bad memories, sweetheart. All I have to do is close my eyes and there they are."

"Yeah, but you don't have to slap yourself in the face with them every day."

I was killing his buzz. He was happy to have me here. Excited. I could tell. Smiling, looking at me, smiling again with a smile that had nothing to do with the conversation. A father just glad to have his daughter home.

I walked through the French doors that led to the living room, passing the office on the way, noting that the desk was the same one he'd had at the old place. In hopes of letting in some light and seeing what was going on outside, I opened the shutters. Dust drifted in the air. Even with the shutters open, the room was dark, in part due to the storm, but also due to windows that probably hadn't been washed in twenty years.

Most of the furniture was the same. The walls were the same color, something off-white. My mother had been fond of minimalism. Funny thinking about that while standing in the center of my father's clutter. The view from the living room windows faced West McDonough Street. If you went out the front door and walked two blocks, you'd end up at Orleans Square. If you went the other direction, you'd find Chippewa Square, where Forrest Gump sat and waited for the bus, holding his box of chocolates.

Locals liked to point out an error in the movie. The streets around Chippewa Square were one-way, and the bus should have been moving the other direction. I don't know why the indignation about the traffic amused me, but it did. It made no difference. The movie, a wonderful movie, was fiction, but people in the South loved their history and loved their cities, especially Savannah.

I mentally took myself back to the *before* days to pull up memories of a house that had been bright and airy, with sunshine falling through tall windows, creating rectangles of light on wooden floors. Marie's cat, Blanche, could often be found in that sunshine, sleeping or grooming, one leg stretched ridiculously high.

But now, even though it was the same house, it almost seemed to have taken on its own cloak of misery. The stacks of random belongings— some furniture, some supplies, some just the kind of stuff that built up when never dealt with, like books and magazines. Boxes of photo paper and even a box of developer in the corner from his photography days.

Did he still have a darkroom somewhere, or had this been dumped here after her death, when he moved from our place in the suburbs? And how many of those black bags were trash? It was like everything, every piece of uselessness, was sucking the light and the life from the room. I spotted the ornate silver urn of ashes on a shelf in the corner, almost hidden by an archaeological dig site's worth of junk.

He saw where I was looking, and said, "We put her back together for you. Do you remember that? You kept screaming that they needed to put her back, so the funeral home did the best they could. And we went to see her before the cremation."

"No we didn't." Why was he telling me that? "They just cremated her."

"You were worried they would cremate one body part at a time. I found you crying about it. I promised she'd be whole first."

"We never went to the funeral home."

"We did."

Why was he lying? Or *had* it really happened? I had no memory of it. None. Usually, with a little prompting, I could find a faint thread, but I had nothing. I thought about Chesterfield's and Ian's accounts of events that didn't mesh. Human memory was flawed.

"But really, Jupe," he said, changing the subject like a pro, "it doesn't bother me to be here. In fact, it makes me feel better."

But was it healthy?

Lightning illuminated the sky, reflecting on the bricks of the wet street. Night storms were exciting, but there was something about a storm that could turn day to night that gave me an extra thrill. Maybe because it was almost an aberration of nature.

"Get back from the window," Max said.

I wanted to stay there and watch, but I stepped away so he wouldn't worry. I heard a loud crash and saw a flash that backlit a steeple silhouette in the far distance. That was followed by the beep of the microwave as the power went out.

"About time we had one of these storms," my dad said. Then, "Why don't you settle in?"

He seemed anxious to have me unpack, to commit, probably because he couldn't believe I was actually going to stay. He retrieved my suitcase, and we walked up stairs that were wide, with one turn before reaching the second floor. Even the steps were stacked with things. Baskets of clothing, shopping bags, shoes, books, folded and unfolded towels, going or coming. I probably would have been trying to explain the mess, but he didn't seem to notice.

We went straight to my room.

Like everything else in the house, it was a time capsule.

I'd never really *lived* at the house, since my dad and I had the other place, so it didn't contain my full sixteen-year-old personality. I'd stayed there quite a bit, but it had never felt like enough. It was somewhat impersonal, kind of fake, but I knew I would find drawers of my old belongings, mostly from my goth phase. Some of my skull earrings were still hanging on a little earring tree on the dresser.

I put my laptop down on the desk and pulled an earring off the tree and stuck it through a hole in my ear.

We both laughed.

It looked as if my father had actually cleaned this room. A sweet gesture. No dust on the wooden floors, at least none that I could see in the dim light. Same queen bed with a down comforter. Same pink walls that were so pale they were almost white.

We were one level closer to the roof, and the sound of the rain was louder here.

My dad must have had the same thought, because he said, "It's really coming down." He patted the pockets of his jeans. "I left my phone in the kitchen. Someone has probably already called it in, but I should contact the power company just in case. You get settled."

He left me alone.

I opened the two sets of almost theater-quality curtains complete with gold tassels. I think my mother had actually hired someone to make them. They'd done the whole house. My room also overlooked McDonough. I saw headlights moving slowly. Far off toward Whitaker it looked like the traffic lights were out too. The houses and buildings were dark.

I decided to check the closet. All the wood was dark and original. Not thinking, acting on habit, I tugged the ceiling chain, then tugged again so the light wouldn't come on when the power returned. In the murky darkness, I passed my phone flashlight around, illuminating a small stack of boxes, some shoes, and a few dresses and T-shirts, all of which should be tossed or given to Goodwill. I reached up to the shelf above the hangers and found a couple of black hats, along with a latex mask I remembered wearing one Halloween. Edward Scissorhands. I put it back.

There were two bedrooms on this floor and another on the third. The one down the hall had belonged to my mother. I left my room and walked there now, stopping at the closed door. Without giving myself time to change my mind, I turned the glass knob. The door almost seemed to open by itself with one long creak.

I stood there, heart pounding.

Waited a moment, then stepped inside, heart pounding.

Walked around the room, heart pounding.

"Don't ever become an actor," she'd told me one night.

We were lying on the bed watching some old movie, maybe *Jaws* or something else that was also one of her favorites. At the time, I never really thought about how our lives revolved around hers. We watched her movies and listened to her music. Went to her favorite places. My dad and I were her satellites, circling her.

She and I used to spend whole evenings together, a mother and daughter thing. Not on any specific night, due to her packed schedule, but she'd carve out time for me, just us time. My dad might be puttering around downstairs, cooking because Marie didn't cook. Maybe that was because cooking was doing and creating for someone else. But at the time, it was something I just took for granted. This was how she was. This was what we did. And she was always so charming and such a joy to be near. That was enough. That was all we needed. But she used to tell me not to become an actor.

"Everybody wants a piece of you," she'd said that night, pausing the movie. "They take little nibbles of your soul until there's nothing left. Then they puke you up and eat that too."

"That's disgusting."

But we laughed.

"I might go into acting," I confessed, lying beside her on the bed. "I'm thinking about it."

"Well, if you do, you have to protect yourself. You have to be careful of strangers. You never know what they might want, or how much of a threat they might be to you. Even the ones who seem harmless."

She warned me about handsome guys. "You can't trust a handsome man or pretty boy," she said. "Handsome men and pretty boys are spoiled and selfish and narcissistic."

"Like you?" I asked, then quickly realized that wasn't something a kid should say to her mother.

She didn't care. She tossed back her head and roared with laughter.

When she stopped, I asked, "What about ugly boys?"

"They can be messed up in another way. How often does a person see a story about some blindingly handsome man kidnapping a woman to make her his own? It just doesn't happen. Girls don't give the ugly ones enough attention, and that makes them mean and resentful. So you want somebody like your father."

"But he's handsome."

"Of course he is." She winked as if we had our own shared secret. "The truth is, he didn't make it in the movies because the camera didn't want to linger on him. And that's a shame, because he's a good actor, an excellent actor. But the poor man simply isn't good looking enough for the big screen, and not even enough for the small."

She un-paused the movie, but I'd always wished I'd asked her to elaborate on her comments. She was such a drama queen that I'd just chalked it up to that. But now I wondered if something weird had been going on that she hadn't told us about.

I heard my dad talking to someone downstairs. Not on the phone, but in person, maybe a neighbor or friend. Two men, discussing the power outage.

I opened one of her dresser drawers, and a scent hit me hard.

The Lumets had made a special perfume just for her. Not anything they sold. It came in an ornate purple bottle, practically small enough to fit in your palm, something she got refilled whenever she ran low. I think the container had been one of the originals used in the very first products ever made by the company. Either that, or it had been a good copy. She'd pull out the stopper and dab it behind her ears. Sometimes she'd run it up her arms, touch it to her wrists, and rub them together.

The scent was wild and woodsy, not overly floral, almost masculine.

"This is me," she'd once said. "They captured me."

It was true. They absolutely had. The perfume was my mother. Her life in beautiful glass. And it was the scent I'd noticed in my dad's car the day her body was found.

Where was the bottle now? I could smell it but didn't see it in the drawer.

I'd been involved in investigations of famous people and been horrified to hear tales of how emergency crews and police would grab souvenirs. I suspected the same might have happened to my mother's belongings. My dad and I had certainly been in no shape to stand guard.

I dug around and found a journal. It felt stiff and unused. When I opened it, I saw there were hardly any entries. Marie didn't seem like a journal person. She was too much of a show-off for that. It had probably been a gift, and she'd probably made a small, short-lived effort.

Her writing was very recognizable because she'd printed with a style so precise it looked like it hadn't been done by a human hand.

I don't have ordinary days. I refuse to have ordinary days. I'm not evil. I'm not a bitch, although I do stand up for myself and won't take any shit. I have had sexual relationships with people other than my husband, because what actress hasn't? I would have preferred an open marriage, but Max isn't into the idea. But what I can say is that I love my daughter Jupiter with all my heart, and I love my husband almost as much, no matter the things he says to me or does out of jealousy. No matter his nasty threats and his drinking and abusive behavior.

People say I lie. Again, I'm an actress. We spend our days lying, so sometimes it's hard to shut it off. But I'm not someone who lies for the sake of lying. I've told and stuck with a few whoppers in my life, many that came with a wink, and a few that were justifiable, like stealing a dog from an abusive owner and saying I found it. Most of my lies have purpose. Like telling a costar we simply must keep in touch after the show wraps. Or telling Max I'm not having someone over.

Those are just the lies that make life move smoothly and are cloaked in what I call misguided thoughtfulness. Those lies are an odd combination of kindness and cowardice. But the truth of all truths is that I love my daughter with all my heart and soul and bones. I'd even die for her.

I couldn't read more, and maybe those words were enough, all I needed. I stood there a long time, listening to the rain, hugging the journal to my chest, then I placed it carefully back in the drawer, this time spotting a container, but not her special one. I lifted it out and noticed the faded logo. Very vintage, a silhouette of an elegant woman with her hair piled on top of her head, a hand near her face, a take on the Gibson Girl design that had been the rage then. The silhouette seemed ready to apply the magical potion to her face.

I was pretty sure it was the same logo I'd seen at the mansion, in the basement, when Oliver had taken me into the tunnels. I thought

151

about how we'd snuck into the storage room and how we'd drawn on our faces. Was this the same product? I wasn't sure. Seemed doubtful because why would it be here?

Like most actresses, my mother had been concerned about the lines appearing on her face and the shadows under her eyes. She'd done peels and Botox and fillers and talked about having to go under the knife at some point.

It was stupid of me, but I couldn't stop myself. I opened the lid and looked inside. I was surprised to see there was still a small amount of the cream at the bottom. With my heart pounding, I replaced the lid, pulled out my phone, and took a photo of the jar. Then I returned it to the dresser.

I needed to get my hands on a Geiger counter. I'd order one from Amazon later. If it was human fat, which I suspected, and not radium, there would be no response from the machine.

"Jupe!" my dad shouted. "There's somebody here who says he's an old friend of yours!"

I realized it was still raining, but it was a gentle rain now, and the thunder and lightning seemed to have abated.

I went downstairs. Standing at the bottom of the steps, watching me descend, smiling up at me, were my father and Quint Dupont, the guy I'd gone to homecoming with.

The replay was eerie, and it made the hair on the back of my neck move slightly. Me walking down the steps, Dupont looking up at me, a wistful half smile on his face.

My mother had been right about the handsome boys. He was someone who'd ingratiated himself because he'd wanted to meet her. And that smile? As he'd looked up at me? That lovesick boy's grin? It hadn't been for me at all, but had instead been for my mother, standing on the landing. She'd been a little drunk, dressed in silk pajamas, no makeup yet—that would be applied at the Lumet party she was attending later—an Art Deco comb in her hair that I'd given her. But she'd been one of those people who was just as amazing, maybe more amazing, without makeup.

I'd glanced over my shoulder, seen her looking more beautiful than any person should look, and I'd felt a rage. Like, why couldn't she have given me this one night? But no. She always had to be the center of attention.

She'd breezed down the stairs, pushed me aside, shook his hand, and flirted, while I stood there watching.

"How old are you?" she'd asked him. "You look a lot older than sixteen."

"Nineteen."

"But still in high school?"

"Senior."

"Did you flunk?"

He laughed. "I have a late birthday, so I started school a year later than some kids."

This was why I never went home. This kind of silly bullshit. Whoever said you couldn't go home again was right. Had it been Thomas Wolfe? Memories that still hurt all these years later. Dupont meant nothing anymore. Maybe he'd read about me and wanted to bask in my light now, what little light I had.

He sure wasn't as pretty as he used to be. That made me want to laugh. Back then, he'd been one of those guys who, if a camera lens turned on him, would be the only thing in sharp focus, the rest of the world blurry. Because nothing else mattered. He was prettier than life. Quint Dupont had the face of a movie star and the body of an athlete and the charm of someone less handsome. And at that time, I hadn't cared about my mother's warning.

"I stopped by hoping I could talk you into going for a drink," he said right now, present day, in real time in the now world, a world that didn't seem as vivid as my memory.

My father was grinning, and I could see he already had us married with a family, residing in a home in Savannah, preferably within walking distance of his place.

"Sure," I said with a shrug. Anything to get out of the death house.

22

Despite what Bennett had noted about southern names, I felt my old homecoming date's handle could seem uncool if bestowed upon a lesser human. But on him, the name became part of the allure attached to the coolest kid in school. *Quint Dupont* just rolled off your tongue, especially if you had a southern accent. It was like saying the name of one of the biggest actors you could think of. So it was funny that now, twenty years later, when I didn't care about such nonsense and he was no longer a beautiful boy, we were finally going to hang out for real.

Most of the people I'd associated with in high school had moved away. My best friend was a doctor in Atlanta last I'd heard, but we'd all lost touch long ago. It was hard to keep up old relationships when things weren't weird, but add murder to the mix and it was almost impossible.

Quint and I ended up at a bar not far from my dad's house. I hadn't intended to *drink* drink, just maybe some sweet tea, but when we got there and were cozied up in a booth, I ordered a beer.

I had to admit he still had the charisma, and his looks weren't *that* bad. He was now only above average rather than radiant. Due to my antidepressants, I had a one-drink limit, so I nursed my beer slowly as he ordered more for himself.

"Would you have slept with me the night of homecoming?" he asked. "If your mother hadn't warned me off?"

"I didn't see a warning, just a blatant flirtation. Pretty hard to miss that."

"Oh, she took me aside and told me I had to get you home on time or she'd come after me herself."

Would I have slept with him? Maybe. Let's be honest. Yeah.

"Do you want to go somewhere?" he asked at some point. "My wife and I have an agreement."

That was what they all said.

All the married men.

"Oh, come on," he said with a smile, leaning back in the wooden booth. He had all of his teeth, and they looked in good shape. "You're one of the only cool girls in school I didn't sleep with." He presented this statement as something that could go either way. A joke or a brag.

"Was that your goal? To sleep with everybody?"

"Yep."

"That's disgusting."

Once I'd made my reaction clear, he pivoted.

"I'm not proud of it," he said. "I'll be the first to admit I was a creep."

And then he got less attractive and had to learn how to navigate the world like the rest of us. I thought about actually saying this aloud, but I couldn't be so mean.

"Are you sure you don't want to go somewhere?" he pressed.

While part of me considered losing myself in that kind of moment, I didn't need the stress right now, or the confusion. "I'm going through a loss," I explained. "Someone close to me."

He'd surely heard the news, and I was not going to elaborate on who that person was. Let him think it was someone other than Salvador. And the truth was that I was afraid all men would be compared to Salvador now. He'd been someone bigger than life. He'd carried a light inside him that very few people had. He and my mother would have been quite a pair. Would he have fallen for her too, suddenly aware of how inferior I was by comparison? I felt a flare of rage thinking about it.

I vaguely wondered what Quint did for a living and where he lived and how many kids he had and who his wife was, but the evening suddenly felt incredibly heavy, and it had lasted way too long already, and I might even have a headache in the morning from one beer. I didn't want to draw out the night any longer.

"I've got to go," I said, sliding across the wooden seat.

That was the thing about drinking. It not only got you through something but could shift your view until you were actually having fun and actually, at least temporarily, enjoying the people around you. I didn't have enough booze in me for that.

"I have an early morning tomorrow." I almost laughed at my choice of words.

He wasn't done with his beer, but he moved to get up. "I'll drive you."

"That's okay. Finish your drink. I can walk."

He was probably surprised by my quick exit, but I felt an overwhelming need to get away from him and the memories.

The walk home from the bar cleared my head, and when I got back to the house, I logged on to Amazon and searched for Geiger counters. Maybe I still had a buzz, because I chose one that had next-day delivery. I'd probably feel silly when it arrived. Then I took a shower and slipped into yoga pants and a T-shirt and went to bed. At four o'clock I woke as I often did. Most nights I was asleep again in thirty minutes.

There was some argument about what really constituted witching hour, but I liked to say it was four a.m. At this time thoughts were the bleakest and the darkness of life could weigh you down. My trick was to tell myself it wouldn't last, that the hands of the clock would move forward and the witching hour would end. The sun would break over the horizon, and the light itself would illuminate the corners and wash away the dark thoughts.

While I waited for dawn, I pulled my laptop close and searched *witching hour*. Definitions were all over the place, ranging from midnight to four a.m. But now that I thought about it, maybe the witching hour, whatever time a person chose, was good for sleuthing.

I got out of bed.

I didn't know how deeply my father slept now. He was old enough that I could see a change in him. Subtle signs of frailties. Not as much energy as someone who used to have a huge amount. I didn't know what a decline in his health meant for our future, my future. I could see a time when I might have to take care of him, which would mean I'd have to reconcile my resentments. Maybe not forgive, but move past them.

When I thought about the old days, the *before* time, at my mother's house, I didn't have many memories of being there. And yet I'd had my own room, and I did recall one Christmas with a tree and turkey and the whole thing. But now as I tiptoed down the stairs, wearing the headlamp I used for camping, muscle memory came into play, and my feet seemed to know which steps to avoid. Evidence of more time spent there than I really remembered and evidence of sneaking around at night. I placed a bare foot to one side, then the other, avoiding that dangerous center where the step bowed and tended to creak more.

The house had always felt spooky to me even as a teenager. In the dark, it almost seemed alive, breathing, watching, holding on to secrets that would never be revealed. But despite all of that, I loved the way the railing was worn and smooth from so many hands touching it over the years. My mother's hand, for one, had added to that polished patina. And it could have been my imagination, but I thought I'd caught a hint of the perfume the Lumets had made for her in areas other than her room, near her dresser.

I reached my father's office and stopped in the doorway as a sense of dread washed over and through me. I didn't want to do this, but I'd put it off long enough.

The office was located off the living room, not far from the kitchen. I could hear the refrigerator running, that heartbeat of a home. I forced myself to move forward, into the room. The office floor had a lime-green shag rug and a wooden office chair on wheels. A photo of my mother was propped on the desktop, near a lamp with an orange shade. The picture had been taken in front of the house, maybe the day she bought it. She'd paid cash with the money made from the show.

I didn't have any photos of her on display in my condo, but I had photos on my phone. I wanted to turn the frame over but was concerned I might forget to set it back up, so I just tried to avoid looking at it.

The chair was big and heavy, with a leather seat. I pushed it slightly out of the way and reached for the first drawer. It was packed and crammed and jammed. I had to shove papers down to get it open all the way. My heart was slamming, and my mouth was dry. I reminded myself of my goal. To find the photos. And, if caught, I'd blame it on sleepwalking. The old sleepwalking defense.

I forced myself to do what I needed to do—remove personal involvement, step away from my own pain and sorrow and fear, and do the job. I adjusted the headlamp beam, and I searched through all the drawers twice. No packet.

Had he disposed of them? Hidden them someplace more secure? Had they really existed? Was it a false memory? I had the feeling my brain was full of those. I actually felt relieved to have failed at my sleuthing. I was getting ready to close the last drawer for the final time when the beam of light illuminated the brown corner of a manila envelope taped to the wood above the open drawer.

What a cliché. I couldn't believe I'd almost missed it.

I untaped the envelope, pulled it out, opened it, and looked inside. And there they were. Glossy eight-by-ten color photos.

With a numb heart, I sat cross-legged on the floor and spread them out in front of me, ten in all. I examined them carefully, one at a time, marveling at the steadiness of my hands and the distance of my soul.

Marie had been a natural brunette, but her hair had been dyed a deep beet red for television. Before *Divination*'s launch, doubters said paranormal shows were over and people wanted reality or comedy. But they hadn't accounted for her star power. She could have made anything a success. When you broke the show down, it was just a predictable plot with some stilted and corny dialogue, and a lot of hot sex. My mother had bitched about the dialogue, but not the sex.

They should give me writing credit, she'd said. *For fixing some of that crap.*

Maybe if the show itself had been a little less tacky, the Lumet family would have been less upset. But they'd hired a wholesome girl who ended up in a series where she took off her clothes every week. Even back then, it had been no secret that Phaedra's parents hadn't been happy with the face of their product.

It might have been the abject horror of the photos that lent them a grindhouse quality. At the same time, I was aware of being very removed, very distant, a clinical observer. There were some full backyard shots, then two of the torso and head, arms and legs, then close-ups, one so near it revealed the small tattoo on her inner wrist with my name. *Jupiter.* Before getting it, she'd laughed, telling me it would say *Found Object,* but when she'd come home, it said *Jupiter,* with two small red hearts. I'd been thrilled, but I would have been thrilled about either name.

I took photos of the pictures with my phone. I checked the backs for any writing or stamps. Like painters, like Salvador, photographers often left their mark on images. Maybe a small gold seal, maybe a stamp, maybe even a signature. I didn't find anything. I scooped them up into a pile. I grabbed the envelope I'd tossed aside.

I'd been so absorbed that I'd paid little heed to the sounds outside the room. Even when a light from the hallway fell across the carpet, it didn't register that my dad was there until he let out a gasp. He stood in the doorway, wearing pajama pants I swear he'd owned back in the *before* and a white T-shirt that advertised a music shop that no longer existed.

"What on earth are you doing!"

Any excuses I might have deployed dissolved. Instead of pretense, I held the photos high. "Where did you get these?"

He lunged into the room, grabbed them and the envelope, stuffed them back inside without glancing at them, as if he couldn't bear to allow his gaze to fall on the images. "You shouldn't be looking at these!" His voice was high, and he was shaking.

I turned off my headlamp and got to my feet. "Are they actual crime-scene photos?" Some police departments had special photographers to document scenes, especially homicides. Photos were often the thing that could push a conviction through, and, as one could imagine, the quality of the photos was extremely important.

"They're good, but not from the police department," he said. "Not that professional."

"Paparazzi?"

"Yes."

"Here." I put out my hand. He was so upset. I didn't want him to pass out, or worse. "I'll put them back."

He handed the envelope to me.

"I bought them," he said. "Paid a ridiculous amount."

"Why?" But I already knew.

"So they wouldn't sell them and they wouldn't end up in tabloids. So you'd never see them. And now here you are, looking at them!"

Only a few photos of the scene had ever been leaked, and those had been taken from a distance, maybe even from a helicopter. These weren't those.

"Bastards," I said.

"I think if it hadn't happened right after she was killed I would have handled it differently, but I just paid the money, and the photos were dropped off."

He was upset that I'd seen them, but he didn't seem upset about my snooping through his stuff. "You realize someone probably has copies or negatives," I said.

"Stupid, I know. And I don't even know why I kept them. I can't explain it. I think I thought I might need them if they tried to get more money from me. Like I could maybe beat them at their own game."

I was returning the packet to the desk. With my back to my father, something slipped from the envelope and landed on my bare foot. I glanced down and spotted an SD card on the floor. It was the kind you used in a camera.

I picked it up and was about to drop it in the envelope when I changed my mind. The card was larger than the ones used now, not anything my laptop could read, but it wasn't so big that I couldn't hide it in my hand while I went about replacing the envelope and closing the drawer.

"How about some hot chocolate?" I asked, hoping to redirect his attention away from pics of a mutilated body to one of his favorite comfort drinks.

I could feel the sharp edge of the SD card jabbing into my palm. I was going to guess it contained digital images of the originals. But then why hadn't he mentioned it when I mentioned the negatives? Instead, we could drink hot chocolate and pretend all was well for a little while. I stuck the card in the side pocket of my yoga pants.

"That sounds good." His voice wasn't as high, and he was calming down.

In the kitchen, while he heated the water for cocoa in a kettle, I sat at the counter and went through the pics I'd taken, careful not to let him see my screen.

I stopped on the photo of the head. It wasn't on the ground. It was sitting carefully balanced in the birdbath, staring at the photographer.

In the birdbath, as Ian had said.

And Ian had been first on the scene.

If all of that were true, which might or might not be the case, it meant whoever had taken the photos had done so before Ian arrived. The head was on the ground, a few feet from the birdbath when I got there. And the ground was where Chesterfield said he left it. The memory of that conversation was seared into my brain.

While I was looking at the photos and thinking all of this, I was also thinking that I couldn't believe I was staring at a photo of my mother's decapitated head while my dad made hot chocolate. Maybe the surreal aspect of the whole thing actually helped. Nothing seemed real. But I guess nothing had seemed real for a long time.

"Here you go." He put a cup in front of me, then shook a can of whipped cream and gave the top of my chocolate a blast.

I tucked my phone away.

"What did the whipped cream say to the hot chocolate?" he asked.

I shrugged.

"I'm sweet on you," he said.

"How about whip it," I said. "Whip it good."

He laughed. "I was never sure about those Devo lyrics. Like were they talking bondage?"

"Oddly enough, the origin was a song of encouragement for Jimmy Carter," I said. "The equivalent of *Go, team.*"

"Interesting. I didn't know that."

"I come upon weird stuff while doing research."

I was joking with him while my mind remained on the mystery. Who had taken the photos? The most likely person seemed the killer. But Chesterfield was adamant that he'd left her head on the ground.

The photos had looked somewhat professional. Even the paper they'd been printed on. I tried to remember how the paper felt, to see any discerning feature in my mind's eye. My dad was a decent photographer. He'd had a darkroom. *Jack-of-all-trades, master of none.*

We lifted our cups.

"Cheers," I said, giving him a half-assed smile, wondering if he could see through it.

We told some more silly jokes, and we drank our drinks.

"I'm so glad you're here," he said.

"Me too."

I glanced up at the clock. Five a.m. Witching hour, no matter which one, was over. "I'm going to drive to the beach and go for a run," I said.

"Now?"

"I want to catch the sunrise. Haven't seen a Georgia sunrise in a long time."

"I'm going back to bed," he announced.

I put together things that would support my lie, like running shoes. Then I left and drove straight to Ian's cottage on the marsh.

23

At Ian's, I parked next to the curb, under a streetlamp, pulled out my phone, and sent him a text. Waited. No response. Sent another one. No response. Checked my watch. Five thirty a.m. I got out of the van and closed the door gently. The sound still managed to reverberate like a gunshot. I sometimes imagined the world as man-made, something akin to a movie stage, where sounds echoed off the invisible barriers that surrounded the set.

I stood in the road, hands on my hips, and looked at the house. So tiny. So cute. I loved the beach colors of the South. Houses in the Midwest were rarely bright and would, quite honestly, have looked odd if they were. One of the upstairs windows had been designated a child's room by the use of a rescue decal called a Tot Finder. It alerted firefighters to the presence of a youngster in case of fire.

I looked around, scooped up some pebbles so small they could qualify as sand, and tossed them gently at the other window. I didn't have to wait long for a light, then a curtain to be pulled aside.

I waved. "It's me," I whispered loudly, moving closer so he could see my face in the glow of the streetlamp.

The window opened, and Ian stuck his head out. "Who's me?"

"Jupiter. I tried to text you."

"I had my phone on Do Not Disturb."

"You're a cop. You shouldn't do that."

"I'm an officer, but I'll ignore the slang."

"Constable on patrol."

"I don't think that's the origin. But anyway, anybody who needs me knows to call twice."

"I didn't know."

"I highly suspect this is just a dream." He stepped back and raised his arms as if to close the window and return to bed.

"No, it's real. Come downstairs." I was still whispering, but aware that my voice was probably too loud.

His head reappeared. "Have you ever noticed in your dreams, whenever you need to get somewhere fast, obstacles pop up?" he asked. "And you never get there. Like the more you want to, the harder it gets."

"Oh, for Scooby's sake. Just come downstairs."

"Pretty sure there will be obstacles."

A light came on next door. I glanced at the house, then back at the window and Ian. "This is not a dream," I hissed.

"Pretty sure it is."

"Oh, bless your heart. Just get down here. You can do it without any obstacles except for maybe a Lego."

A woman's voice joined in from next door. "Shut up or I'll call the cops." There was a pause, then, "Just kidding."

Everybody in the South was a comic.

Ian laughed. "Sorry, Joan."

He vanished from the window again. Thirty seconds later, he opened the screen door with a creak, and I slipped inside the enclosed porch. He was barefoot, tugging on a blue hoodie, zipping it. "What brings you here at this inhumane hour?"

"I told my dad I was going for a sunrise jog, which I still might do so I'm not a liar, but I wanted to show you something."

There were two rocking chairs on the porch. I sat down in one and waited. He finally joined me. He didn't seem to wake up quickly. And here's something weird about me. I found that charming.

"Poppy had a joke I was supposed to tell you if I saw you again. 'What did the ocean say to the beach?'"

"I don't know."

"Nothing. It just waved."

I laughed. "I like that one."

"Me too."

"Do you know the last thing my grandfather said to me before he kicked the bucket?" I asked.

"What?"

"How far do you think I can kick this bucket?"

He chuckled.

"Not as good as Poppy's."

"That's hard to beat."

I pulled out my phone and scrolled through my photos, pausing on the one of the head. I passed the phone to him.

He recoiled at the graphic image, then stared hard, the screen illuminating his face. He used two fingers to enlarge the shot, then he dragged it around as he checked out various areas in the scene.

"There are more," I said. "Keep swiping."

He did. When he reached the end, he passed the phone back.

"You were first on the scene, right?" I asked.

"Yes. Someone called in a tip. It was just me and my partner. We weren't even sure the tip was real. She went to the front door, and I went into the backyard. This was what I saw."

"So did you take the photos?"

He was silent, as if trying to make sense of it, then finally said, "No."

Now he was up to speed. Someone had to have been there before Ian. "Exactly. You told me you compromised the scene by moving the head from the birdbath, then tossing it."

Seeing that the horrific nature of my words upset him, I assumed he was uncomfortable because I was talking about my mother. I reassured him. "That's okay. We have to talk about it. So if someone came later, crime-scene photographers or paparazzi, they would have pictures of her head near the birdbath, where it was when I arrived. Which means somebody was there before you and took these photos. Are you sure you were first on the scene? What about your partner?"

"Like I said, she stayed in front while I went around back. Where did you get this?"

I told him my dad's story. "So now of course I wonder if my dad took the photos. Or was it someone else?"

"Chesterfield might have taken them. That's my guess. Maybe someone else found them, had access to them . . . I dunno."

"But Chesterfield insisted the head was on the ground. He was very clear about it. In fact, it was the only thing he didn't blame on meth."

Ian seemed to be thinking. Maybe he was trying to replay his own conversation with Chesterfield.

"You said yourself that he was an unreliable witness, that he'd run upstairs to hide," I said.

"We never actually verified that he was the caller. Because of the circumstances, a confession, I don't think anybody looked into it."

"Could have been the 911 caller who took the photos."

A sound came from inside the house. The door opened, and a sleepyhead with tousled hair peeked out. "What are you guys doing?"

Ian got to his feet. "We're gonna go watch a sunrise."

"I like sunsets."

"Sunrises are good too. And we're on the East Coast. That makes them even better. Go to the bathroom, and get your shoes and blanket."

She ran off and returned a couple of minutes later.

We all left the porch. I was heading for Maude when Ian stopped me. "No need to take two vehicles. Aren't you coming with us?"

"Yeah, aren't you coming?" Poppy asked.

He was carrying her, and she had her head on his shoulder, her feet, in sneakers, dangling.

He was a good man. I'd known a few good men in my life, Bennett for one, if I really wanted to give him credit where it was deserved. But Ian would have been my mother's perfect guy. Not too handsome and not ugly. His body was not the body of an athlete, somewhat soft but not too soft. He was the kind of person a child trusted, and he was the kind of person a mother trusted to take care of her child for months while she was gone.

I found myself wanting to spend more time with them both. "Yeah." I nodded. "I'd like that." Must have been the hot chocolate talking.

24

It had taken a little convincing, but Jupiter rode in Ian's car. She sat in the passenger seat, Poppy in back, falling asleep and waking up to jump into the conversation before conking out again. Ian had heard it was odd for a kid to dislike getting up early, but Poppy wasn't a morning person. She liked to sleep late, which worked out great for him.

The beach was ten minutes from his sister's house. He and Poppy sometimes rode bikes there. When they pulled up to the parking lot behind the sand dune, the sky was beginning to lighten in the east, but the sun hadn't broken the horizon. Ian grabbed a blanket, and they hurried down the wooden plankway, then into the soft sand.

He spread out the blanket, and he and Jupiter sat down while Poppy stood nearby, clutching Mr. Darcy tight, holding him up so he could see the sunrise too. It made Ian happy to see she was acting like a kid rather than a small worried adult.

"She's nice for a little alien," Jupiter said.

He laughed. "She's great."

"I never thought I even liked kids, but she could change my mind."

Some people might have been offended by her comment, but Ian liked how straightforward Jupiter was, how she said what she was thinking. "They are kind of like aliens," he said. "You think things are going one direction, and they flip it. All the time. I can never predict what she's going to do." He was glad that Liz would be returning soon. He wanted her out of danger, but . . . He let out a sigh and spoke some honesty of his own, voicing something he'd been worrying about. "I'm going to miss Poppy when her mother comes back. Liz is talking about moving to DC, but she might stay here."

"Journalism is a tough gig even if you don't have kids," Jupiter said. "It would be good for Poppy if you were nearby to provide some stability."

He didn't think about being someone who really had much influence in her life, but what Jupiter said might be true. His mind shifted to the reason for her visit this morning, back to the photos she'd shown him. Was his memory correct? He'd been terrified that day, and terror could distort and impact memory. Rewrite it sometimes. But she'd said she recalled it differently too, that the head had been on the ground, not in the birdbath. And yet they had a confession.

He should go to the prison and talk to Chesterfield, get an updated account if possible. But if he'd hung on to his story this long, he probably wasn't going to budge. And if he hadn't done it, he still might think he was the killer. Maybe he'd taken the photos, but someone else had found them. Maybe found the camera.

If the murderer wasn't sitting in prison, then it meant the killer was probably loose. He had to consider the father, who'd always been a suspect in Ian's mind. And then there was Jupiter herself. She comes back and suddenly here's some evidence. But Poppy liked her, and Poppy had an uncanny instinct about people. Kind of her curse.

The waves were roaring, and Poppy was several yards away, closer to the shore.

"It's coming!" Poppy shouted. "I see it!"

The sun was rising, large and orange, seeming to take up the entire landscape. His heart almost cracked at the beauty of seeing the silhouette of his niece standing in front of the shimmering orange glow, waves crashing, birds calling their morning songs, sandpipers running, and the smell of the salt water, the feel of the breeze against his arms.

Poppy let out a squeal of excitement and started running toward the packed wet sand. Waves hit, and the water rushed the shoreline.

Ian didn't understand the sequence of events, the how or why, but suddenly Jupiter was on her feet, racing toward the child.

"Come back!" Jupiter screamed. "Don't go in the water! Come back!"

Poppy paused and stared at the adult barreling toward her. Ian could see she was trying to figure out what was happening. He wasn't sure either. He didn't know why this person was hurtling across the sand at her.

Jupiter snatched her up, poor Poppy's head bobbing like a doll's as Jupiter clutched her to her chest and ran in the opposite direction, away from the beautiful sunrise they'd come to see.

Mr. Darcy fell, but Jupiter kept running, her stride becoming awkward as she left the packed surface and reached softer sand. Once there, she dropped to her knees with Poppy and kept a hold on the child. Jupiter was crying, sobbing, and Poppy, poor kid, was stroking her hair, trying to comfort her.

Ian caught up, retrieved Mr. Darcy, brushed off wet sand, then turned to Jupiter and Poppy, unsure of what to do.

"Hey, hey, hey," he said awkwardly.

Jupiter looked from Poppy to Ian. Suddenly seeming aghast by her own behavior, she let the child go and turned her back to them both, got to her feet, began running again, this time to the hard sand, where she could get more traction. She was moving parallel to the ocean, and as he and Poppy watched, she just kept going.

"She sure likes to run," Poppy said. Then, "Is she coming back?"

"If she doesn't, we'll go after her."

He'd known a few people who'd gone into undercover work, and they'd said it was the hardest thing they'd ever done. Living a lie. The only officers who were good at it were the sociopaths.

She didn't come back but instead collapsed. When Ian and Poppy reached her, she was lying on the beach, still sobbing. It sounded like something was being ripped from her soul. Ian crouched beside her and, as if she were a child, gently pulled her into his arms. She let him hug her. He'd been told he was a good hugger. Poppy helped too, patting her back.

"Is she crying because it's so beautiful?" Poppy asked.

"It *is* beautiful, but I don't think that's why she's crying. I think she's sad."

Poppy started sobbing while clutching Mr. Darcy tight.

Poppy's sobs seemed to pull Jupiter out of her own despair. She straightened and wiped her face with the back of her hand. Jupiter was on her knees in the sand, her eyes full of tears as she looked at his niece. And Ian thought she was beautiful.

Poppy stopped crying too. She tried to smile, but her mouth trembled.

They all got to their feet. Then the three of them began walking back, to the spot where they'd left the blanket, Poppy skipping ahead.

"I know what happened in Florida had to have been tough," Ian said.

"I fell for him," she told him. "That sounds wild, but despite what he was doing, he was in many ways a good man. He took care of people. He had talent. An amazing skill. I robbed his family and the world of him."

"He did it to himself."

She shook her head. "No, it was me."

"I disagree. Don't put that on yourself."

"I didn't want him to die," Jupiter said.

"Nobody wants anybody to die."

"I dream about him, and in my dreams he's still alive. But when I wake up, I know that's not the case. I saw him walk into the ocean and swim toward the sun."

"They never found a body, right? That's gotta be tough. We all need closure."

"I killed him."

"He killed himself."

"He wouldn't have done it if not for me."

"You didn't put a gun to his head and tell him to swim until he drowned. And he did it in front of you. Sorry, but I kinda hate him for that."

"He wasn't a bad person. He didn't kill anybody. Yes, what he did was wrong, very wrong, but he helped people. He took care of his family, and he raised a lot of money for charity. Millions. He was kind of a Robin Hood."

"Was he? Really?" Ian had read about the guy's lavish lifestyle. He probably gave to charity so he could feel better about what he was doing. "From what I understand, he lived a life of excess."

"That's true, and that was my take on it beforehand. But when I saw how much he loved his family, my opinion of him began to shift."

Her view of family was probably very skewed. Her mother murdered. Her father possibly the killer.

"He wanted to take care of everybody in his orbit, from family to his drivers. He made people feel cared for and loved. Being around him was similar to how I imagined it would feel to be in the presence of someone like Fred Rogers. Well, that's probably a stretch, but a person who made you feel safe and unjudged."

Poppy ran up to them, and they stopped talking about the forger. Ian liked to call him the forger. "I've got to get back to work," he said to Poppy. "And you've got important camp things to do."

"We're making mermaid tails."

"See, that's the kind of important I'm talking about."

"Knock, knock," Poppy said.

"Who's there?" asked Jupiter.

"Keith."

"Keith who?"

"Keith me, my thweet printh."

Jupiter looked at Ian and burst out laughing. Some jokes were funny simply because they were so terrible.

He would have said it had been insensitive to watch the sunrise with her, knowing what he knew about the forger, but a dawn jog had been her plan. He felt bad anyway.

"I'm sorry," he said.

"Never apologize for a sunrise." She sighed and seemed better now. "But can anything be normal again?"

"Was it ever normal to begin with?"

Back where they started, he picked up the blanket and shook out the sand. "I don't think you can hope or even expect that. The best you can do is learn to live with it. And if people can't handle who you are and what you're dealing with, then they aren't the right people for you."

"They belong on your shit list," Poppy said.

"True, darlin'," Ian said. Then to Jupiter, so she wouldn't think he was a bad influence, "I didn't teach her that." He rolled up the blanket and tucked it under his arm like a football, then he held out his hand for Poppy to take. "She got it from her mom."

He was suddenly struck by a similarity between Poppy and Jupiter. On the surface, they seemed to have zero in common, yet they were both heavily influenced by mothers who weren't present in their lives, one absent by geography and one by death.

"Would you like to go to a party?" Jupiter asked him, squinting against the sun. "At the Lumet estate?"

He sure would.

"Ooh, a date," Poppy said.

25

After picking up my car from Ian's house, I called Bennett, told him I had an old SD card I wanted to read, and sent him a photo of it with my hand for scale.

"Overnight it to me," he said.

"I don't know if I feel comfortable doing that. Just mail a reader to me, or tell me which one to order from Amazon." I needed to come clean to Bennett about my own investigation, but I wasn't quite ready. I also wasn't comfortable sending the card through the mail and risking it getting lost.

"That's old technology, and it might take some time to find something that works, but I'll send you a few to try."

"Thanks."

"How you doing?" he asked.

"Okay." Additionally, I wouldn't mention my beach meltdown or the photos I'd found at my dad's. Bennett would tell me to come home because none of this was why I was here. I asked him how he was doing, and he sent a photo of himself standing in a parking lot, a dirty mountain of snow two stories tall behind him. "It's not supposed to get above zero today," he said.

"I don't miss the weather, but I do miss you."

"Be careful."

After ending the call, I swung by a coffee shop on Ellis Square and ordered two lattes and a couple of scones to take back to the house. The sun was long up now, but Dad was an all-day coffee drinker. Meanwhile, I was still trying to shake off my reaction to Poppy's walk to the ocean. I knew I should have been embarrassed, but I wasn't. They'd both been so sweet about it. And they didn't seem like strangers or people I'd just met.

On the front step was an Amazon box with the recognizable happy arrow. The box was small, and when I picked it up, I saw it had my name on it. I'd forgotten I'd ordered anything, and it seemed days ago that I'd gone into my mother's room. But it had been just yesterday.

Dad was in the kitchen and seemed happy that I'd thought to pick up a coffee for him. There was something about coffee and little indulgences that helped a person get through the day.

He glanced at the box in my hand.

"For me." I didn't tell him what was inside. No need to suck him into my paranoia.

Upstairs in my room, I opened it, put the batteries in, and tested it. There was always a certain level of background radiation wherever you were. A flight from coast to coast exposed a person to a little less than a chest X-ray. Smoke detectors had a tiny radioactive device in them. Which was to say I braced myself for a slight reading.

I pointed the meter at the wall and began a slow sweep of the room. The digital readout began picking up a small amount, which, according to the little cheat sheet included with the product, was perfectly normal. I'd probably just wasted money I didn't have to waste.

After another sweep of the space, I shut it off and went down the hall, into my mother's room, where I closed the door behind me and turned the detector back on. Holding it level, I walked carefully, keeping an eye on the numbers, which kept rising. As I approached the dresser, they increased further. The numbers blinked, and that old familiar Geiger counter sound I'd heard in movies went off. A slow crackle. The device had two lights, one green and one red. The green light was still on.

I opened the drawer and pointed the device at the jar of face cream. The numbers rose, and the red light flashed. The crackle intensified. Words appeared on the readout screen: **DANGER. Leave the area immediately.**

Disbelief.

I quickly shut the drawer. I thought about how little product was in the jar. Just one finger scoop. Had it evaporated, or had my mother used most of it? I was relieved to find I didn't have to move far from the dresser for the beeping to stop, the danger warning to vanish, and the light to go from red to green. With the numbers in the safe zone, I told myself to calm down as I moved around, walking over to the bed.

I pulled down the spread and floral sheets. Had they been changed since my mother had slept there more than twenty years ago? The device was registering slight radiation but nothing alarming, and the green light was on, not the red.

I went to the closet, which was still full of her clothes, and I passed the gadget around, scanning from ceiling to floor. Trace amounts. The number was just slightly more than it had been in my room.

Back in the sleeping area, I opened dresser drawers. She hadn't been a big pajama person. She'd slept either in the nude or in an oversized T-shirt. She'd tended to wear her silk pajamas to lounge around the house in. The drawer with the shirts she'd slept in was hot.

I imagined her slathering on the skin product in the evening, then crawling into bed. I tried to remember if she'd had that radioactive glow I'd read about, the reason behind the success of the product in the first place. But I couldn't conjure the memory.

I needed to alert my dad, and we'd have to contact specialists.

I started to leave, then, being a journalist who knew the value of photos and video evidence, I forced myself to return. I opened the drawers and repeated everything I'd done before, this time with the phone's camera on, recording video. Evidence of what, I wasn't even sure. A crime? Foolishness? Oversight?

Had someone been trying to kill my mother before she was actually killed? Had the radiation been too slow? Had someone attempted to disfigure her so she couldn't work? If so, who? A jealous rival? My father, who'd praised her success but also suffered silently as her star rose and his fell? Or was it nothing? No connection, just stupidity?

I had another thought.

Downstairs in the living room, I went to the shelf, found the urn with her ashes, and turned the Geiger counter back on. Nothing. I opened the lid and pointed it inside. The counter began crackling. Nothing like upstairs, but the cremains were hot.

The sound alerted my dad. He appeared from the kitchen. "What's that?"

"Let's go outside and I'll explain." It seemed ridiculous to leave the house. My father had lived beside the urn for twenty years, and we'd been hanging out near it. But suddenly the need to get away was urgent.

We ended up in the backyard.

And holy hell, here I was in the place I'd refused to even glance at—and definitely refused to step into. And once again I had to question why my father was really here, why he'd chosen to live in this horror. I mean, he'd added a deck *right off the back door.* There were lawn chairs and a gas grill, a table with big outdoor candles. Even a gas heater for cold nights. Cheerful lights strung around the deck railing, causing me to mentally question everything all over again.

I needed to step up and get involved. Because either he was one sick bastard who'd killed his own wife and liked to relive it every day, or he was unable to physically move past the horror of it.

The first choice might have been true; it very well might have been true. He kept pictures of the scene in his desk. Did he pull them out at night and drool over them? And what about the night cream? Did he have anything to do with that?

Then we had the second choice, the one that seemed almost as awful to me because I should have made him leave. But a person couldn't force someone to do something they didn't want to do. Maybe having a freakin' radioactive home would do the trick and make him realize he needed to get out of there.

I glanced around, and then I said the dumbest thing ever. "The backyard looks nice." The only thing worse would have been *I really like what you've done to the place.*

The birdbath was still there. Simultaneously innocuous and damning.

"I've been slowly working on it." He sounded proud. "I built the deck myself."

Did he bury evidence under the footings? Were there other bodies? That was where my mind went.

I told my dad about the night cream. I watched his face to see if he looked guilty. It was almost blank. I didn't think he understood what was going on. But then I remembered what my mother had always said about what a great actor he was.

I wasn't sure who a person was supposed to contact in such a situation. I pulled out my phone and called 911.

Cops showed up quickly, and I tried my best to ignore the overwhelming echo of that morning twenty years ago when lights were flashing and people in uniform were wandering around. The officer first on the scene talked to us in the backyard. It took a while for her to grasp the situation, and I have to admit it was confusing, but once she did, she called in the Savannah branch of the EPA. I didn't know they had one.

People arrived and slipped into hazmat suits. A person inside a head-to-toe white outfit pulled a small container behind him, somewhat like wheeled carry-on luggage, but this case was a lead box with radiation warning symbols.

"They'll load up the main contaminants and remove them," the woman in charge told us. "Then they'll scan the house to determine levels and whether it's acceptable for you to go back inside."

As was typical in Savannah, maybe more than other places, people started coming to watch. They placed lawn chairs on the sidewalk across the street and some even added umbrellas. A local news van with satellite dishes mounted on the top parked nearby and began setting up. Stands selling water appeared, and pretty soon it was like a full-blown party.

I didn't mind. At least this time no one had died, and I'd long ago come to terms with the knowledge that my mother's life and death and afterdeath weren't solely mine, and that the memory of her had to be shared with millions of fans, many of whom still worshipped her.

I used to find the reminders hard. The events and posts about her on social media. But as time passed, I began to reluctantly appreciate how they kept her alive. And at times I would even come across photos of her I'd never seen before, and I'd save them on my phone. I had a whole album now.

The person in charge gave me and my father little clip-on detectors and explained how to use them. They constantly monitored exposure and would let us know when we'd reached our maximum for a specified period.

"We aren't picking up anything beyond the typical background radiation anywhere but the bedroom," she assured us. She explained a little more about that particular kind of radiation, radium. It seemed distance and something around the radium could do a lot to block it. Like even a dresser drawer. Or an urn.

She went back inside, and Ian showed up.

I lifted the red dosimeter clipped to my shirt, showing it to him. "These measure your exposure over time. Just a precaution. I don't think it's a big deal." The meter reminded me of the days I used to wear a pedometer.

"You did the right thing." He held a small, wet paper bag toward me. "Boiled peanut?"

Everybody in the South was supposed to love boiled peanuts, but I wasn't a fan. The snack consisted of just what you might think, raw peanuts that had been boiled in salted water for several hours, then scooped out and served warm in a paper bag, somewhat like popcorn. Often the boiling included flavorings like barbecue or red pepper. Some people even ate the shells. The very idea made me shudder.

"Where'd you get those?" I asked.

"Over there." He motioned behind him. "Some guy's selling them."

I reached in and took a couple because they were protein, and I suddenly realized I hadn't eaten anything but a scone in forever.

Ian cracked open a shell. He wasn't in uniform. "What you gonna do?" he asked. "We're in the South. We eat boiled peanuts." He popped one in his mouth, chewed, and added, "I just stopped by to check and make sure you're okay."

I suspected, like most everybody else, he was really there to gawk.

"They're going through the house to see if the levels are anything we should be concerned about. It's possible we can move back in, or we might just have to avoid certain areas. We should know soon, I hope."

My father appeared, and I introduced him to Ian.

Dad winced, then went into acting mode. I could see he was trying to decide if he should acknowledge his awareness of who Ian was, the cop who'd found his murdered wife, or just treat him like a new acquaintance. He chose new acquaintance. He ate a few peanuts, then excused himself to go talk to a neighbor and assure her all was fine.

I pulled Ian aside.

It was hard to find a place where there were no people.

We edged our way past a mob, through the gate, and into the backyard. Once again, especially with Ian there, I was feeling the heavy echo of that other time. I told him more about the night cream. He seemed shocked to learn radium had ever been used in skin products.

"It wasn't that unusual. In the 1930s it was in a ton of things. Toothpaste, condoms, chocolate, water, golf balls, and even dishes that you can still find today. People collect them. But back then, the general public was unaware of the danger, and everybody wanted it. It gave people a lovely glow, and nobody knew it was bad until the watch-dial painters started getting sick." They'd been taught to lick the brushes to a fine point, so every day they were ingesting radium. Some of their jawbones had collapsed.

"Definitely heard of that. Such a sad story. How do you think she ended up with it?" he asked. "Any idea?"

"That's what I need to find out."

"Has the fat thing been disputed?" he asked. "I've certainly heard about *that*, because who hasn't, but always figured it was a myth, possibly even generated by the company itself. Like an early, pre–social media version of clickbait."

"I'm pretty sure it's true. I doubt anybody could get away with it in the US today, but I think human fat is still being used in other countries. It's even sought after. I once did research on gangsters in Peru who were suspected of murdering people in order to sell their body fat to cosmetic companies."

"I'm calling bullshit on that. I mean, with the popularity of liposuction why would they need to kill anybody?"

"I could never confirm the story, so it didn't run."

"Anything for beauty, I guess."

I glanced over my shoulder, making sure nobody was within earshot. I stepped a little closer to Ian, saying, "Now I'm wondering if someone in the Lumet family was trying to kill my mother. Maybe they were behind her death."

"I'm not following the logic here."

"I know it doesn't make sense, but what does? Maybe they wanted to silence her for some reason." Was I latching on to the idea because it would finally exonerate my father, at least in my own mind? "And I know they weren't thrilled about her show."

"They could have done it in a much less violent way than cutting off her head."

"Slow poison could be considered less violent."

He wasn't looking at all convinced or even open to this new speculation. "I'm gonna take off," he said. "I gotta pick up my tux, then start my shift."

He tried to hand me the bag of peanuts. I shook my head.

After Ian left and as the crowd continued to increase, I crawled into my van for privacy. Lying on my back on the bed, pillow under my head, legs crossed at the ankles, curtains closed, I called Phaedra on FaceTime.

She answered immediately, her "Hello" light and lilting. She obviously hadn't heard the latest.

Her makeup was perfect, her hair pulled up on top of her head. It looked like she was moving around her house, because I thought I spotted some familiar furniture in the background.

I rolled to a sitting position, ducking my head a bit so it wouldn't hit the van roof, once again piercingly aware of my sad existence, noting the wrinkled T-shirt and jogging pants I'd put on in the predawn for my fake run. The beach with Ian seemed days ago when it had actually been hours.

"You're going to hear about this soon enough," I warned her, "but I wanted to prepare you." I told her about what I'd found in the house.

"Good Lord."

I was glad I'd used FaceTime for the call, because I could see her surprise and shock. Her reaction seemed genuine, with none of that quick and guarded stuff that could go along with the intake of info, followed by an abrupt bout of overacting.

"The company doesn't need any more bad press," she said. "I don't know if it can withstand another negative hit."

"I'm so sorry." This would at least squelch any thought she had of putting my image on their jars. "I did want to ask if you had any idea how my mother might have ended up with radioactive cream."

At that very moment I remembered the case files and the note I'd come across from Phaedra's brother Atticus to my mother. The wording of his message made it sound as if they'd had a fight and he'd sent her a gift as atonement. Had he given her something potentially lethal?

"I don't, but we didn't start locking the room until after she died. Not that her death had anything to do with it. We just thought it was prudent and had been an oversight on the part of my parents and grandparents."

Right. They'd probably discovered Oliver was hanging out in there.

I didn't tell her I'd been inside the very room twenty years earlier when he'd given me the tour. I might tell her the whole story sometime, about how we painted our faces, but I wasn't ready to let that go just yet, and it might be something she'd find incredibly painful to hear. I might never tell her.

"So during the time your mother was alive, anybody who had access to the basement could have gotten in there." Phaedra dropped heavily on a couch, and the room behind her quit spinning in the frame of my phone. "And she stayed with us sometimes and would have had access to the room herself."

"Are you thinking she might have taken a jar?" I said *a jar*, singular, but I suspected she'd gone through more than one, because I remembered seeing her use it a lot.

"I wonder." She shook her head. "So horrible. It's all so horrible."

"Even if she knew it was radioactive?"

"She might not have known. Oh, I feel so terrible about this." She pressed her lips together, then continued, as if having a new thought. "Even if she *had* known, she might have been willing to take the risk. I can tell you when it comes to beauty aids, a lot of people don't care what's in the products they're using. They only care about results."

"I'd think a person would care about radium."

"People do extreme things to stay youthful. I'm so sorry. But I will say one jar wouldn't have posed much of a health threat, as far as I understand it. The real danger came from frequent use."

"I think she might have applied it frequently," I said. "I remember seeing it on her dresser when I was younger. Pretty sure I tried it myself a few times. The urn containing her ashes was even a little hot."

She started crying, and I considered signing off to give her time to process everything.

"This is such a trigger for me. Oliver played down there," she said, sobbing. "I didn't know it. That's why we locked it up, but by then it was too late. He was already sick."

My suspicions about that were confirmed. "I'm so sorry."

She blinked several times as she made an attempt to pull herself together. "Do you have to leave your house?"

"It's looking like we might be able to go back inside, but I'll know more about that later."

"You can stay with us."

If we had to move out, my father was going to need a place too, and I couldn't imagine him ever setting foot in Camellia Manor again. But the invitation was more than just a frivolous thing now. In a normal world where my mother hadn't been murdered, I would think that her having the product was some horrible oversight, but was there more to it? And if so, did it involve the Lumets?

"Are you still coming to the party tomorrow?" she asked.

"I wasn't sure if you'd still have it." I expected them to be hounded by the press.

"The show must go on. But actually the food is already being prepped, and we've already hired catering staff. You will come, won't you?"

"I'll be there." I could wrap up the Luminescent article and focus on my mother. Maybe even do a little digging while on the property. "I never got a dress."

"We have plenty."

I told her about Ian coming as my guest.

"We'll put his name on the list."

Someone knocked on my van door, and I peeked around the privacy curtain. It was my dad. I opened the sliding door, and he crawled inside, sat down, and closed the door. I told Phaedra I had to go and would see her tomorrow night.

"They've given us the all clear," Dad said, without appearing in any hurry to leave. He looked around. "This is a nice little womb."

We both laughed, sat there a bit, then steeled ourselves and stepped out of the womb and into the world and the bustling street.

The urn and the cream had been removed from the house, the rooms scanned. The bedroom still emitted a level that was slightly more than a background radiation reading, but nothing to be concerned about, we were told.

"You can go back inside, but keep wearing the dosimeters just in case," the radiation specialist told us. "I'd suggest wearing them at least a month. By then we'll know if you're exceeding the yearly limit. I'll check back with you periodically."

So we would return, and we would keep the door to my mother's room closed, just like always. I felt kind of silly to have alerted the EPA, and yet in this situation an overabundance of caution was a good thing, and my action had been the responsible thing to do.

Outside, news crews and pop-up vendors began packing, bummed that the event was over. A few people had scampered off when they'd heard just *why* a fuss was being made at our house, but most of the citizens had been looking forward to some entertainment. Now they were sadly folding their chairs and walking home for dinner.

After leaving the Bellarose house, Ian stopped at a little shop on Broughton to pick up his tux. As he was paying, his hand paused over his open billfold, one he'd had since he was a teenager. Then he pulled out his credit card, paid, and left with his tuxedo. At his car, he hung the garment bag on the hook in the back seat, then slid behind the wheel, opened his billfold again, and unfolded a piece of paper that had once been stiff but was now soft from time and repeated handling. It was a photo of Marie Nova, a promo shot for a movie. She was wearing a long red dress, posing seductively. Down in the lower right-hand corner, handwritten, were the words *To Ian. Love M. Nova.*

26

That night, I got a text from Christopher Crane, the actor who'd been in *Divination* with my mother. He finally had time to talk.

I used FaceTime to call him.

His voice was the same, but that was where the similarity ended.

I think if I hadn't seen him in a few bit parts over the years, I might have been shocked by his appearance, even on the smallest screen possible, my phone. He had the look of someone who drank too much, slept too little, and hadn't had enough money to pay for the best cosmetic surgery.

My unsympathetic thoughts made me uncomfortable, but there it was. I guess I was just as beauty conscious as the rest of the world even though I liked to think I wasn't. But at the same time, I couldn't help but wonder what he'd look like without the extreme work. It all made me sad in an undefined way. And then there was my mother, who had been using the "magic" face cream. I once again recalled the way she'd worried about lines on her face, and recalled how she'd been getting fillers and Botox. Maybe, like Phaedra had suggested, she'd simply been willing to try something more dangerous.

"I'll never forget you were the one person who showed up for us that day," I told him.

"I just couldn't believe it. I still can't." He choked on the last word, and his eyes glistened. Another reminder that I wasn't the only one suffering loss. And her death had destroyed his career. Such strange collateral damage.

He didn't seem that surprised that I was looking beyond the person who was sitting in jail for the crime. I asked him questions I knew he'd been asked many times. "Had there been any signs that someone was stalking her?"

"I don't know about stalking, but she had her share of overzealous fans," he said. "More than her share."

And they were still out there, holding Marie Nova conventions around the world. I'd been invited to a few, which I hadn't attended. But I remembered seeing Christopher's name as a headliner. I guess a person had to make a living somehow.

"I don't understand why she didn't hire a bodyguard," I said.

"We tried to talk her into it more than once."

She might have seen a bodyguard as a sign of weakness.

"They sent her weird stuff," he said. "Like dirty underwear. Do you remember that?"

"Yeah. She laughed about it, so I didn't think it was anything to be taken seriously." Maybe that was another reason she'd moved. To protect us.

Christopher and I talked about how a lot of people had come forward and confessed and were still coming forward.

"It makes me have doubts about Chesterfield, that's for sure," he said. We seemed to be on the same page there.

I didn't ask him about the off-camera relationship he'd had with my mother. I knew it had existed, but I couldn't make myself go there. Near the end of the conversation, I was already mentally moving him lower on my suspect list.

"You look a lot like her," he said.

Maybe he just wanted me to.

"I like to think of her the way she looked one day when we were taking a break from shooting, just sitting in the shade laughing about something. She loved to laugh."

She did. I liked to think about the way she'd looked the day we'd driven to the manor in the red convertible that matched her lipstick.

After the call, I showered, clipped my dosimeter to my T-shirt, and went to bed, but I couldn't sleep. I kept visualizing my mother's journal in the contaminated dresser. I got up, tiptoed to the room, and with the help of my phone flashlight, found the drawer and pulled out the small booklet. My dosimeter chirped, but I needed to read just a little more . . .

> *I often say Max isn't good looking, but that's a lie. He just doesn't photograph well. The camera picks up and exaggerates things it shouldn't, and it completely ignores the things that make him beautiful. He's a good man. A better man than I deserve, and I drive him to do things that go against his nature. I know that.*
>
> *We have the best fights, Richard Burton and Elizabeth Taylor kind of high drama, where I throw something at him, and he dodges it.*
>
> *Has he ever hurt me?*
>
> *I'd have to say yes, but those were times when I hit him first, hard, with a fist, and they could have been considered self-defense on his part. He isn't a person who's quick to anger. I bring that out in him. I wouldn't even blame him if he killed me.*

Wow. I of course remembered the fights, as I'd related to Ian, and I'd always suspected she'd enjoyed tormenting him. Had she pushed him too far that night?

I flipped to another entry.

It's no secret the Lumets disapprove of my show. Sometimes I wonder why I don't just let them buy me out of my contract and break all ties, but an actor never knows when a gig will end and if another will ever begin, and Luminescent is steady income. Also, I'm stubborn. And I like having my face all over the world. I'm going to a party there tonight. I heard the event is going to include wild animals. They know how I hate that kind of thing, and I suspect they are doing it on purpose. Guess I'll just have to get drunk, let the animals loose, and hope I don't see that stupid ghost I suspect is actually Grandpa Lumet.

27

As I drove down the tree-lined lane to Camellia Manor, I briefly forgot about my mission and just let nature soothe me. A dappled pattern of light and shadow moved across the windshield of my van, the darkness hardly broken, the towering, protective canopy dense above my head.

I'd read that trees had intelligence. Not like humans, but they were smart enough to adapt and change to their surroundings. They communicated with each other, both underground and through the air, using chemicals, hormones, and electric signals. More recently, it was discovered that different varieties actually needed one another. Like it wasn't good to plant all pines or all maple. Mix them up. Yes, I loved trees. The lungs of the earth.

I'd spent the day shooing reporters away, not taking calls from press, avoiding Bennett. Now, as I drove toward the mansion, Bennett called again. I answered this time and finally told him I was now following two possibly connected stories, the original one on Luminescent, and my mother's.

"I thought I was sending you on a vacation," he said.

"Did you? Really? To the place where my mother died?"

"Your dad is there."

"Correct."

"And it's warm."

"Also correct."

"I think you should come home. Forget about Luminescent. Forget both stories."

"You know that's not going to happen."

"How about this: What if I catch a flight to Savannah?"

That was how worried he was. "I'm fine," I told him. "But I need to get off the phone. I'm headed to a big party at the Lumet estate."

"Party? Got a date?"

Weird thing for an ex to ask, but I think he honestly wanted to see me settled with a good man.

"I had one, but he couldn't make it." Ian had called that afternoon with the bad news. "He couldn't get a babysitter." I'd invited my dad. He'd turned me down. I'd thought about inviting Quint but decided against it.

"Oh, he's got kids."

"Well, kind of. I'll explain later. Don't worry. Everything's fine."

I pulled into the lot where I'd parked before, and grabbed my small suitcase, plus my laptop and camera. I'd come planning to stay the night, but I was also giving myself permission to bail at any time—because that was pretty much how I rolled. Always looking for the exit. Not a bad way to live, in my opinion. In the distance, I spotted helicopter blades and remembered the heliport.

Phaedra met me at the door wearing a pink dressing gown. No makeup, her face shiny and bare, obviously preparty, her skin a prepped canvas. I was always struck by how some people looked more beautiful without makeup. She wasn't one of them.

She gave me a hug, and I think she was genuinely pleased to see me.

"I'm so glad you decided to come! It wouldn't have been the same without you."

I had to wonder about that sentence. I certainly wasn't the kind of person who could make or break a party. That was my mother, not me.

We took the curved, sweeping stairs to the second floor, our footsteps echoing. I was once again intensely aware of the garish splendor of the mansion. It had a lot of gold trim. Real gold? Probably.

"I have the best makeup artist coming," she said with excitement in her voice. "He'll do your hair, everything."

"I need all the help I can get."

Phaedra laughed.

I meant it. "How many bedrooms are in this place?" I asked as we passed closed doors.

"Twelve. And fourteen bathrooms."

"Wow. Glad I don't have to clean those."

"It's excess, I know. I don't live here all the time. I simply can't. I have to get away from it."

"Where do you go?"

"To the mountains sometimes, northern Georgia. It's beautiful there."

I had a hard time imagining Phaedra in such a setting. She probably didn't rough it.

"And I go to Hawaii and San Francisco, also other countries."

Sorry I'd asked.

As we headed up the stairs, I thought about how my mother had walked these very steps the evening of her death. My mind struggled with wanting to feel exactly what she'd felt, from the hardness of the marble to the smoothly polished handrail. But I also wanted to shut down, maybe run away.

I wasn't even sure what I hoped to achieve by being here. Possibly just some reassurance that the Lumets had in no way played a part in my mother's death. But as far as I was aware, no police or detectives had bothered to trace her steps the night of, or even create a solid timeline. I'd never liked that lack of attention to detail.

The room Phaedra led me to was just what I would have expected when it came to opulence and overdecorating, everything a time capsule, the occupants of the house basically living in a museum. My room had ceilings that were twenty feet tall and windows almost as large, with maroon drapes, the fabric heavy and dark, with large gold tiebacks for those times you might want to let in some light. The walls were papered in navy-blue wallpaper with red flowers, and the floor was an intricate inlaid parquet. It smelled musty, like a space that hadn't been used in years.

Phaedra took my suitcase and placed it on a stool at the foot of the bed. It looked small and pathetic there. I was already having third thoughts about staying the night.

"You have your own bathroom." She reached around a corner and turned on a light to reveal a white room of marble, with gold fixtures and a double sink. "And then over here is the walk-in closet." She opened double doors, the movement triggering motion lights. She laughed as she stepped inside. "I told you we had dresses." She slid hangers so I could see how many, and the variety of the choices. "And, of course, you might have brought something of your own . . ."

I hadn't.

"This blue one would look great with your arm tattoos." She pulled it out and held it up to her. Shiny fabric like the dresses my mother had worn. This one was a deep midnight shade, strapless, tight waist.

I shook my head, and she hung it back on the rack.

"Well, have a look. A lot of the gowns have just accumulated over the years. Some are vintage, some are newer, most of them bought for our theme parties. Tonight is just a *party* party. No theme, so wear whatever you like. My makeup person will be here soon."

With that, she breezed from the room, closing the door behind her.

The closet was as big as an office. Half the clothing, male and female, appeared to be costumes, which made it feel more like a prop room. The other half, dinner attire. There were shelves of hats. The costumes made me wish tonight could have been a theme party.

After my mother died, we quit doing fun things. Anything frivolous and silly, like dressing up for Halloween, had seemed off, not right. But having no fun was not the best way to honor her. That was boring and ordinary and completely unlike her.

I dug and tugged through the dresses and was almost ready to go back to the blue one because that color . . . when I reached the very back of the closet.

And my hand went still.

A red dress.

An off-the-shoulder red dress.

I'd seen a few photos of that night, the dinner party, the 1940s cars lining the curved drive, the jazz band, attendees dressed in white suits and black ties, magical lights hanging from trees, my mother in her red dress.

After a few minutes of thought, I picked it, the one I was fairly certain she'd worn that awful night. I found a full-length mirror. I tucked the padded hanger under my chin. Someone knocked, and I hung the dress on the back of the closet door.

The makeup artist entered with energy and gusto and immediately set about opening his case and lining up products on the countertop in the dressing room. Once I was seated in front of him, I scrolled through my phone, stopping on a photo. "Can you make my hair look like this?"

He bent closer. "Oh, Marie Nova. I get that request quite a bit." He sounded disappointed, as if he'd done it too many times. "No big deal."

Thank goodness he didn't recognize me.

It took about forty minutes. Me with my back to the dressing table mirror so when he finally spun me around, I let out a small gasp.

I was always mentally chastising people for remarking on the extreme similarity I never felt was really there. Now, seeing the uncanny resemblance, I wondered if I'd been going out of the way not to look like her, trying hard to be forgettable.

Using a flat iron, he'd straightened my hair and swept it up high in back, ratted at the crown, some smooth pieces hanging free, framing my face. Dark and heavy eyeliner that went well past my eyes. Lipstick that made my lips appear bigger.

Seeing how much I looked like my mother suddenly made me want to cry. I also had to resist the urge to run to the sink and stick my face under the faucet, rinse it all off. At the same time, I couldn't quit staring. At her. At me. At her.

The makeup artist stood back, elbow resting on one hand. "I've done a lot of Marie Novas, but this is wild. You look just like her. I mean, it's bizarre."

"It is, isn't it?"

He whipped out his phone. "I have to take a picture."

Funny how he'd been bored with the idea of Marie Nova to begin with. Before I could put up my hand to say stop, he took the shot. Then he noticed the time. "Oh dear. She's waiting."

No need to ask who *she* was. Phaedra.

He threw his makeup and tools of the trade in the giant black case, snapped it closed, and left.

I went to the bathroom and wet a washcloth. I looked at my face, her face, in the mirror. I lifted the cloth to wipe her away but stopped myself at the last minute. I set the washcloth aside and walked over to the red dress.

And put it on.

I sent a reminder text to my dad. I probably won't be back tonight.

He replied: Have a good time, as good as a person can have in that hellhole. 😄.

I sent a laugh back, then saw I'd missed a text from Ian.

Found someone to stay with Poppy. She can't be here for another two hours. But I'll be there as soon as I can.

That was a surprise. I wasn't sure how I felt about it now, because I'd already settled into the idea of attending alone. But I sent a thumbs-up.

While I waited for the party to start, I went through some of my old photos, pausing on those of Salvador that I'd been unable to make myself delete. As always, I was struck by how much he reminded me of his namesake, Salvador Dalí. I didn't know if their faces were alike at all, or if he'd managed to cultivate the look extremely well. I suspected a little of both.

This life, this weird life, seemed so far from that weird life, and Salvador himself felt so far away. His death seemed years past, but also very recent. And his sister stopping me outside the hospital. Had that been less than two weeks ago? Was that possible?

I'd been diligent about taking my medication, but in all the radiation drama I'd missed a dose. I took it now.

I suddenly realized I needed shoes, so I began going through shelves of clear boxes, finding sparkly ones and red ones and ones with toes so sharp I wondered how anybody could possibly wear them. I found shoes with heels that were several inches tall, and shoes that were platforms meant to elevate a person.

I tried on several styles, took a few steps, and wished I'd been more into fancy shoes when I was younger. My mother had bought me some, but back then I'd wanted nothing to do with such footwear. I still didn't.

"You're going to have to wear dressy heels in your life," she'd said as if she were talking about a person needing to know how to drive a manual transmission.

Just like that time, I put my boots back on, heaving a sigh of relief. I spotted the dosimeter on the T-shirt I'd removed earlier. I thought about leaving it behind because there was no good place for it on a gown, and why would I need it here? But in the end, I chose to slip it inside the bodice, between my boobs. I hoped I wouldn't lose it.

I got a text from Phaedra, telling me to come downstairs. We're all waiting.

I gave myself one final check in the mirror and noticed the dress was a little short and my brown leather boots were visible. I considered kicking them off and going barefoot but in the end didn't like the vulnerability of bare feet. I should have tried on more shoes.

Showtime.

But as I walked down the sweeping marble staircase, a small group of Lumets below, seeing their stunned faces as they watched me descend, looking more like her, maybe more like an apparition, an echo of another time, my choice for the night suddenly felt cruel.

I spotted Sterling, along with a few people I didn't recognize. One guy had a firm grip on the wheelchair of a person who must have been Phaedra's father. He sat with his bony hands clasped on the blanket across his lap, mouth agape as he stared at me in what looked like horror and disbelief. I knew the elder Lumet was in his late eighties, obviously unwell.

I questioned what I'd hoped to achieve by dressing and looking like my mother tonight. I guess some unscripted response from guests or family, because everything they did felt so thought-out and unspontaneous, the kind of thing you saw in people who had a lot to lose, people who owned multimillion-dollar companies with the eyes of the world on them. I was after a surprised reaction, because in truth I didn't trust any of them, not even Phaedra.

And yet I suddenly wished I could go back upstairs and change into the blue number Phaedra had suggested. Or leave. Wash off the makeup, put on my own clothes, and leave. But I was in the scene. I couldn't stop it now. And I had to face the truth. There would be no do-overs. There never were. WWMD. *What would Marie do?*

Milk it.

I continued my descent. When I reached the foot of the stairs, Sterling, bless his heart, stepped forward, grabbed my hand, and leaned in for an air-kiss. "You look wonderful," he said.

Phaedra did the same. She was radiant and otherworldly in a white gown with a golden sash around the waist. Her hair was piled high, with gold lace threaded throughout.

"Too on the nose?" I asked about my choice for the evening.

"Luckily Justin showed me a photo while he was doing my makeup," she whispered back. "But as far as on the nose, depends on what you were trying to achieve. If you wanted to shock the hell out of everybody, I'd say you succeeded." She tucked my arm under hers. "Come on."

Until that moment, my vision had been narrow and focused. Now I looked beyond the grouping and realized there were no other people in the room. Maybe they were already in the dining hall, but I couldn't hear the roar that went along with a crowd.

"Where's everybody else?"

"In light of the onslaught of bad press driven by the discovery at your mother's house, we changed our plans," Phaedra said. "It's just going to be the family. Since some things couldn't be cancelled, we thought it would be nice to have a little intimate party anyway."

A change of plans might have made sense. It didn't make sense that Phaedra had failed to mention it.

She must have read my mind, because she laughed and said, "I was afraid you wouldn't come if we told you. And to be honest, you're the one we really wanted to see."

We ended up being the whole remaining clan of Lumets, six in all. An aunt, an uncle, and a nephew.

Sterling passed around a basket, and we put our phones inside. When he'd gathered them all, he carried the container away, to another room.

A lot of people hated the whole phone removal at dinner thing, but I couldn't help but approve of a meal where no one was distracted by an outside conversation.

Phaedra's father was pushed to the long dining table, where he continued to stare at me, his eyes almost glowing. The rest of us sat down, and I was given the unfortunate spot across from him.

Wine was poured, both white and red. I'd heard about the famous wine cellar. It was rumored to contain bottles worth thousands of dollars, and even some once owned by Hitler. I took a sip of the red, hoping it wasn't a Hitler. At the same time, I reminded myself to go easy on the booze, especially since I'd just taken my medication.

"Marie Nova!" the old man shouted.

Oh, had my plan backfired. "I'm not Marie," I said.

"Marie Nova!" And then he really got into his insults. "Harlot!"

I tried to catch the wine spewing from my mouth and mostly failed, the red staining the white tablecloth. I knew people with dementia loved to cuss even if they hadn't cussed in their previous lives. It was strange and something I'd always been curious about. Had they been cussing at life in their minds all along, or did their core personality change?

I leaned across the table, saying, "I'm sorry, Mr. Lumet. I'm not Marie Nova. I'm Marie's daughter."

"Stop lying to me! You're lying. You've always been full of trickery and witchery and evil deeds and sinful ways. Somebody needs to stop you." To the rest of the group: "Somebody stop her!" He pounded a fist on the table, the china rattling. "I don't know why we must endure this woman!" He pointed a shaky finger at me. "I've never had sex with her. She's lying!"

Whoa. Did this level of an unrehearsed reaction count when the person had some form of dementia? Had there really been a sexual encounter between Phaedra's father and my mother? She'd once laughingly said she'd sleep with anybody for the right part, if he was good looking enough. I liked to think she'd been kidding, but it was hard to say, considering her slant toward the bohemian. Sex hadn't been that sacred to her.

"It doesn't matter anymore, Father," Phaedra said. "All of that is over and done with, and right now we're just sitting here together, eating a lovely meal."

Odd choice of words: *It doesn't matter anymore.* But maybe it was easiest not to push back or try to correct him. She was probably well practiced in the best way to handle this kind of situation.

The father looked around, his gaze moving from face to face. "Where's Oliver? Where did Oliver go?"

People shifted in discomfort, and Phaedra seemed unable to let that one go.

"Dad," she said with heavy sorrow in her voice. "Oliver is dead."

Someone, I think it was Phaedra's nephew, if I'd gotten the introductions right, got up and gave the elderly man a pill and a glass of water. The distraction of the medication was enough to redirect his attention. He calmed down and seemed to forget about me and Oliver.

Everybody relaxed.

Phaedra patted her father's arm. "Everything's fine," she said.

Next to each of our plates was a list of courses. Twelve in all. I guess I was lucky it wasn't fifty.

There were hors d'oeuvres, soup, and salads of various kinds, from plain old greens to more exotic stuffed shellfish, all served on glass plates. There were cheeses and sorbet and stuffed lamb, but my eyes went to the desserts, three in all. I particularly noted the flourless chocolate cake with sweet port wine. I didn't care about much else. Really, give me a piece of jerky and a cookie and I was good for hours. But in the end, I had to admit the food was quite something.

Things were going smoothly, or so I thought, but then everything went to hell before the main course arrived. I started to sweat; my vision became blurry, my arms weak, my tongue thick.

I was proud of myself because even in my messed-up state, I was confused about the situation for only perhaps a minute or two. At first, I thought I'd ingested something that hadn't agreed with me, or it was my medication combined with the wine. I started going through other possibilities, wondering if I might have just at that moment developed an allergy to the shellfish in the salad. But I wasn't that far gone yet, and as I looked around the table, everybody was watching me with expectation.

I remembered how I'd felt checking out of the hospital a short time ago. How my body had been heavy and how my mind had wandered. I damn well knew a strong sedative when I experienced it. That noodle-spine, not-give-a-shit thing.

I wondered if I'd been slipped the same thing they'd given Phaedra's father. Looked like the drugs hit us both about the same time. His head was hanging forward, chin to his chest, mouth open as he snored loudly.

I think I said something about salad with a side of drugs before I melted down the chair like some cartoon character. The person sitting next to me, good ol' Phaedra, was kind enough to help me to the floor and keep my head from cracking against the polished marble.

"I'm ready for the flourless chocolate cake with the sweet port wine," I mumbled. "Where's the cake?"

Everybody laughed.

"We had a business meeting while you were getting your makeup done," Phaedra said. "To be honest, it wasn't unanimous, but the vote was clear. We have to protect the company. It's nothing personal. It wasn't personal back when your mother was alive either."

"You killed her?"

"Nobody said that. Like now, we were very upset with the negative press surrounding her. All those nude scenes. It took a long time for the company to dig its way out after she died. Our stock plummeted to almost nothing. We can't take another blow of that magnitude."

"The radiation thing . . . happened years ago. B-been covered by the press."

"Yes, but what else do you know? You have suspicions, we're sure of that. We can tell by the questions you've been asking. Things are just happening too fast. We haven't had enough time to figure out what to do about you. Or figure out what you know."

I was still on the floor, but sitting up now. Had Phaedra helped me? "I know nothin'. But I can guess. I have a lot of guesses in me."

Just when I thought Pop was out for the night, he let out a snuffle and came around a little, lifted his head, looked at me, and said, "Strumpet! Whore! Slut!"

I pulled myself together enough to say, "Tell me how you really feel."

Everybody laughed again.

"Thank you," I mumbled, eyes closed, one hand waving languidly in the air. "I'll be here all night." I wasn't scared or worried. I just felt warm and calm. I was enjoying myself. *And a good time was had by all,* including me.

Until Phaedra brought up Salvador.

"We are not bad people," she insisted. "And I meant it when I said you and I should be friends. I like you. You're smart. You're funny. You could have been the face of our product. We would have loved that. Well, Father wouldn't have."

Everybody laughed at that. They were an affable bunch.

"But given your history of exposing people. I mean, what you did to your own boyfriend. He really wasn't doing anything to hurt anybody, and you turned on him. You lived with him and slept with him, and yet you turned on him. Not only did you turn on him, you killed him."

"No. Uh-uh."

"Might as well have. You took down an empire, and you'd do the same with us. That's just who you are. No loyalty. No friendship. You are untrustworthy."

Her father blasted me one final time: "Harlot!"

28

"What do you think?" Ian asked.

He was standing near the front door, ready to leave for the Lumet party. He hadn't worn a tux since . . . Well, bad memories, but since his wedding. That outfit had been a weird shade of purple, and no tails. His bride's choice to have him dress in such a garish shade should have been a tip-off. This time he'd opted for the whole thing, cummerbund and tails, all black. *Dignified.*

Poppy clapped, and not in a sarcastic way. "You look so pretty!"

"Thank you."

The sitter had bailed on him, but a neighbor was on her way and would arrive any second. He'd be late for the dinner, but maybe not for dessert and the band and dancing. He'd heard about the Lumet parties. Who hadn't?

Headlights moved across the front window, visible through the closed shutters. His phone alerted him to a text. He pulled it out and checked the screen. It was from Jupiter.

I'm sorry, but the party was cancelled! ☹.

Oh, man. He didn't realize until that moment how much he'd been looking forward to it. He'd imagined the event in his mind, and he might have been reading too much into the invitation, knowing how Jupiter was going as a journalist and looking for clues on what he felt was the deadest of dead ends. Which had given him ample room to turn it into something more in his head.

A date.

"Bummer," he said aloud.

"What?" Poppy asked.

"The party was cancelled."

"Oh no! Does she need to hear a joke?"

Poppy wants to know if you need to hear a joke.

No reply to his question, just I'm going home.

The neighbor came to the door, and he let her in.

"Uncle Ian's been stood up," Poppy announced.

"I have not." Then, to the neighbor, "Well, maybe." But he wasn't going to waste a good tux. Jupiter was going to at least see him in it. He told the neighbor what time Poppy should go to bed. "Lights out at nine o'clock," he said.

They both smiled at his stern act.

Then he left and drove to the Bellarose house.

29

The sound of a radiation alert sent a stab of fear through my chest, enough to wake me up. I found myself lying on my back in semidarkness, a cold, hard concrete floor beneath me. The screech was coming from the dosimeter I'd tucked in my bra earlier. I switched it to silent mode, but the device still emitted a faint glow. The digital readout was blinking, letting me know I'd surpassed my safe dosage of radiation. It also supplied enough faint light for me to make out shelves and a rectangle that might have been a door.

I remembered riding in the elevator, Phaedra's father yelling *strumpet* the whole time until we were out of earshot. Now, here I was.

I rolled to my knees. With shaky legs I managed to get myself upright.

The wall directly in front of me was glowing. I stared at it for a long time, trying to figure out what I was looking at. A kid's drawing. A man, woman, child, and dog. A family. Most likely painted with joy and radium by poor Oliver.

I found a light switch and flipped it. The caged bulb above my head almost blinded me.

No surprise to find myself in the radium room. The shelves were lined with the same product I'd found in my mother's dresser. I was also pretty sure this was the place Oliver had taken me the day of the party, where he'd opened a jar, drawn on his face, and turned off the light. Poor kid.

And I'd done the same.

Poor me.

What was their plan for me? Radiation sickness could come slow or fast, depending upon the dosage. Still, it seemed poorly thought-out, since it would involve a missing person or a hot body. Radiation hot. What about air? Was the room airtight? If so, how much time did I have? Maybe that was the strategy. For me to die from lack of oxygen.

It was hard to concentrate, hard to come up with a plan. I considered pounding on the door and yelling, but that would attract the wrong people. I was surprised I was functional at all. Had the drugs been in my wine? I'd never been so glad for my one-drink rule. Because of my medication, I'd taken only a few sips, and I'd spewed out some of that.

As I tried to decide what to do next, wondering if I should just write a goodbye in face cream, I heard a sound.

The dead bolt turned, and the door swung slowly.

Standing in the opening was a hideous monster.

30

Her van wasn't there.

Her dad answered the door.

"Is Jupiter here?" Ian asked.

Max frowned, his gaze drifting from Ian's face to the tux, back to his face. "She's at the Luminescent party."

"It was cancelled."

"I didn't hear anything about that. I think she'd have told me. I would have gone with her myself, but I can't stand those people or that place." He thought a second. "She told me you couldn't go."

"I found a sitter."

"I think she mentioned asking Quint Dupont."

"You think she just didn't want to tell me she found someone else?"

Her dad made a pained, sympathetic face. "With Jupiter, you just never know. She can be flaky. But hey." He patted Ian on the shoulder. "I wouldn't take it personally."

"That doesn't sound like Jupiter to me."

"Oh, have you known her a long time?" The question wasn't a question.

"No."

"I love my daughter, don't get me wrong. I'd do anything for her. Anything. But that's different. She's my kid. I can see you're another smitten guy who's been charmed. But she's not someone you want to get involved with. Believe me."

"Okay. Whatever."

"Sorry."

Ian turned and left. On the way to his car, he called Jupiter. It went straight to voicemail.

He didn't have a temper. In fact, it was one of his failings as a cop. Not that cops needed a temper, but they should be able to summon some sense of outrage occasionally. His sister said it was because he was a Libra. He didn't believe that stuff, but it fit. Still, he'd gone to a lot of work to get a sitter, get a tux, get up the nerve to even attend the Lumet party, and she didn't have the decency to tell him the truth, that she'd found someone else to go with, or she'd just changed her mind about inviting him. Seemed like he might not have been her first or even her second choice. But he would have understood *if she'd just told him the truth.*

He got in the car, did a three-point turn in the street, and headed to Camellia Manor.

31

"You need to leave," the monster said. "Right now."

As I looked closer, I realized it wasn't a monster standing in the opening of the radioactive room; it was a man, maybe someone close to my age. Hard to tell because his face was deformed. Not terribly so, but wrong. He had very little or no chin.

Then I remembered what Phaedra's father had asked upstairs, and wondered if it was possible . . . "Are you Oliver?"

"Yeah. I remember you. You were nice to me that time you came to the party. We snuck food and champagne. It was fun. Your mom was cool too. I'll never forget the time she brought her driver as her date. My parents still talk about that." He giggled.

"What do you think they're going to do with me?"

"I'm afraid they might kill you like they did my uncle."

"The uncle who died in a car wreck."

"Yeah. He couldn't keep his mouth shut. That's what I heard."

"And Marie? Did they kill her too?"

"Maybe. I honestly don't know. They wanted to buy her out of her contract, but she knew we were still using human fat in the products, and she leveraged that dirty little secret to remain the face of Luminescent."

Aha.

"I think they might have killed me too if not for Phaedra. But they couldn't let me go out in public once my face started falling apart due to the radium. Not really the best advertisement."

"But nobody used it anymore by then."

"Didn't matter. They knew it would destroy what was left of their business. But you need to go. Run as fast as you can toward the highway. Flag somebody down."

What an elaborate facade. I'd visited his grave. My mind still fuzzy, I couldn't recall the date on the tombstone. But I was certain he'd been dead—my mind put air quotes around *dead*—at least a decade. I thought about how Phaedra had sobbed that day in the cemetery. Maybe not really an act, because she might have been crying for the dark turn her life had taken. Was she behind any of this? Or had she just hidden and lied about her son?

"Come with me," I said. "I'll get you out. I don't want to leave unless you come too."

"I can always leave, or at least I think I can. I've never tried. I went along with my faked death so people would remember the beautiful boy and not the ugly man."

"I'm so sorry."

"It was my fault."

"Did anybody explain the danger to you?"

"A little." He shrugged. "I didn't take it seriously. You know how kids are."

And then I asked a rather ridiculous question: "Do they allow you to vote in their business meetings?"

He smiled a little, as much as he could smile. "I was the only dissenting vote today. But now you really do need to get the hell out of here."

My dosimeter was still blinking red, agreeing with him.

And yet I stayed. "Have you been examined by a surgeon for reconstructive surgery?"

"Once. We were told it wasn't possible."

"You need another opinion. Please, come with me," I begged one final time. "I'll help you. We'll do whatever we need to do."

"I can't." He let out a sob, then pulled himself together. "I can't go out in public. I don't want to be seen."

We heard a whining sound.

"That's the elevator," he said, alarm in his voice. "Hurry. They're going to make it look like an accident, just like my uncle. It'll probably be a fall. They'll say you were drunk and fell from a balcony. Or maybe you went for a swim and drowned." He shoved me forward. "Go. That way." He pointed down the long tunnel to a door with a red exit sign.

I ran.

They'd parked Maude in the middle of the tunnel, probably to hide her from anybody who might come looking for me. I tried the van doors. Locked, so I moved on, away from the elevator, toward the exit.

I slipped through the door. It clanged closed behind me. Even though it was night, there were fairy lights strung in the trees. Maybe party decor or maybe everyday bullshit.

I'd gone only a few yards when I heard security sirens. The door must have triggered an alarm. Oliver hadn't thought of that.

Dogs barked, and floodlights so bright they could have illuminated a ballfield came on, making the parking lot as light as day. I heard the slam of vehicle doors and the roar of an engine, heard tires squealing.

And I ran.

As hard and as fast as I could, down the drive lined with vintage lampposts.

And damn if I didn't laugh at how stupid my life was.

Holding the skirt of the red dress high like some heroine fleeing the castle, I ducked into the deep forest surrounding the property, branches reaching for me. I heard the sharp report of a gun, followed by echoes that bounced off the trees. Someone was shooting at me.

32

After giving his name at the guard booth, Ian drove up the long lane that led to the Lumet estate. He'd never been there before, but he'd seen photos. It was more impressive in real life. The moon flickered in and out of the branches that met overhead, and the beauty of the night soothed him. So much that he slowed the car to a stop in order to ask himself what he was doing and why he was mad.

Because he liked her.

And he'd wanted her to see him in his tux. Pretty funny, now that he thought about it. And juvenile.

He sent a text to the sitter and told her he was coming home and would be there in thirty minutes. He was swinging the car around, headlights doing a sweep of the forest as he executed the maneuver on the narrow road, when he caught a glimpse of something. He turned the steering wheel the opposite direction until the beams were aimed back down the road where he thought he'd spotted movement.

He expected to see an animal, maybe a deer, maybe nothing. Instead, a woman was running down the lane, straight for him.

It was one of those things that made a person question reality. She wore a red gown, clutching it high, legs flashing. He'd heard about the weird parties held at the mansion, a lot of them involving costumes and acting. The gothic aspect of this suggested it was part of the event.

But then things got weirder. She was moving so fast her body slammed into his car as if she intentionally tossed herself on the hood. And she stayed there. And her face was one he recognized.

He was sure it was Marie Nova.

His heart pounded, and his mouth went dry. He remembered the day when he'd lifted that very head from the birdbath.

How could she be here now?

He sensed himself slipping. His hands felt weighted as they dropped from the wheel. His mouth went slack, his head fell back, and his foot pressed heavily against the gas pedal. The car revved forward with Marie Nova on the hood. He thought he heard a gunshot at almost the exact time his windshield shattered. Then he lost consciousness.

33

I clung to the hood of the car as it roared forward. I didn't have time to think or fear for my life. All I could do was hang on as the vehicle shot off the road, bounced over uneven terrain, and crashed into the trunk of a tree, the impact sending me hurtling through the air.

I hit the ground with a loud *oomph*, the breath knocked out of me.

I lay there too long. With a sudden start, I realized the precariousness of the situation. Had to get up. Had to keep running. Was Ian alive? That had been Ian behind the wheel, right? Were they coming? Of course they were coming. The headlights were shining into the sky like twin beacons announcing our location.

I staggered to my knees, pushed myself to my feet.

Adrenaline was full of trickery. For the moment, it didn't seem like I had any serious injuries, but that could all be an illusion. Once upright, I saw it was a good thing I'd been tossed through the air; otherwise, I would have been crushed between the crumpled car and the tree.

Something was hissing. The radiator. Or a tire. Maybe both.

I stumbled to the vehicle, tripped over tangled roots, got back up, reached the driver's door, and wrenched it open.

Yes, Ian.

He moved slightly and let out a groan.

I shut off the headlights, but the Lumets were most assuredly still coming. Maybe the security guard too. We couldn't linger, and I couldn't leave him.

I unlatched his seat belt and whispered with urgency, "Let's go!"

He slumped out and dropped heavily to the ground.

I grabbed his arm, wrapped it around the back of my neck, and tugged. He lurched to his feet.

Together we ran for the woods.

The darkness made it almost impossible. We could be stepping into or off anything. I'd put my phone in that stupid basket. I remembered the glow the dosimeter had provided back in the cellar. In that situation it had helped; out here, it didn't provide enough light.

"Phone." I heard traffic on the highway, not that far off. We just needed to get to it. "Do you have a phone on you?" I asked. "So we can see."

He fumbled around in his pockets, found it, turned on the flashlight, and aimed it at our feet.

I felt the urge to cheer him on by saying *Good boy*, but I remained silent as we moved forward over a carpet of pine needles and oak leaves, each step seeming so loud we might as well have been setting off firecrackers.

Ian was getting stronger, moving on his own now. At one point, he paused long enough to call the police, something I hadn't even considered doing. Sounding surprisingly lucid, he gave them the details, the location, his name, and his badge number and requested a full backup. "Perpetrators are armed and dangerous."

I saw headlights through the trees, and urged him to duck down beside me.

He ended the call.

We took off again, knees bent, heads low.

The trees were too thick for a vehicle to follow. They'd have to come after us on foot. All we had to do was keep from being a visible target, and outrun them. But even on foot, they had the advantage of knowing the layout of the property.

"Gotta stop," Ian said, panting.

I was reaching my own limit.

Wordlessly, we sank to the ground, both gasping for air.

And then I heard something ominous. Ian must have heard it too, because I felt him stiffen beside me.

That deep hollow *thump, thump* of helicopter blades that I could feel in my chest.

The arrival of the aircraft worked like a cattle prod. We scrambled to our feet. With renewed purpose, we continued our sprint to the highway.

The sound of the chopper increased.

Debris swirled through the air and pelted our bodies. A spotlight blinded us. I froze and held up a hand to block the intense beam. The aircraft hovered low enough for me to see the human silhouettes inside. Ian tugged my arm, but it seemed pointless.

The blades were so loud I didn't hear the gunfire, but I saw tree bark explode near my head. I screamed. The shots were enough to give me another burst of adrenaline. I ran.

We suddenly broke through the dense stand of trees. And there was the highway, with that beautiful double yellow line down the center. Even in that moment, I thought of my mother and the story of how she'd found me on a road in Georgia. A sob ripped from my throat, my anguish also buried by the roar above us. Far off in the distance, car lights moved in our direction. Not just car lights. Flashing *red* lights, traveling at high speed.

What would Sterling do now that the police were coming? Because I was sure it must be Sterling behind the controls of the helicopter. Would he pull up? Pretend it had all been a mistake? Would they keep shooting at us, kill us, make up another story to go along with all the other stories? And since they were basically local royalty, the commoners would believe them. Or people would look the other way. *Oh, what a tragedy. Marie Nova's daughter tried to hurt them.* Blah-blah-blah.

As I awaited our fate, the scene changed so rapidly it took my brain time to catch up. You know how they say you should never fly too close to the sun? Well, you could probably say the same thing about flying too close to electric lines. It took me several more beats to truly understand what was happening. I heard snapping.

The spotlight vanished.

Above us, but not directly above us, the craft spun wildly, tangled in the power lines winding around the blades, the blades ripping poles out of the earth like a giant and invisible hand harvesting massive carrots.

Then the helicopter dropped straight down like a broken toy. The earth shuddered with the impact. An explosion split the night, and the area went as bright as an atomic bomb blast. A concussion of pressure waves threw us to the ground and rattled my teeth. Chunks of burning trees shot skyward, then rained around us.

Moments later, back on our feet, we ducked and dodged. Trees shattered so close it was like being in the heart of a war zone. I heard a high-pitched screech of metal against metal and looked up. A mammoth steel transmission tower folded and collapsed, dying a slow fast death, the live lines whipping mindlessly, shooting sparks every direction. In the chaos, I realized flames were moving toward the mansion.

Was Sterling dead? Nobody could have survived that kind of crash and explosion. Where was Phaedra? Hiding in the mansion? I imagined her hunkered down in the art room with her fake or not-fake paintings. Despite what she'd done, I hoped she was found safe. And what about Oliver? The dogs? And—I couldn't believe I was having such a thought—what about Maude?

Fire trucks arrived. Ian and I watched as they raced past to save the mansion, the sky so bright it looked like a sunrise. I flagged down a truck and told the driver there were people in the estate. "Dogs too. And someone might be hiding in the underground tunnels!"

They took off. The whole communication seemed like precious minutes wasted, but it had most likely taken only seconds. Then Ian and I walked away from the fire, down the lane, and under the protective canopy of trees and Spanish moss. I was thinking about both Salvador and my mother. They were somehow caught up in the same story, the same fiery sunrise and sunset of sadness. And yet the overarching feeling was one of relief, of closure.

Ian paused in the lane. "What do you think of my tux?"

I looked at him, *really* looked at him for the first time that night, the condition of his clothing screaming *zombie apocalypse*, his clothing bloody and torn. "I have a feeling you won't get your deposit back."

"Totally worth it." He held out his hand, and I took it.

Down the lane we walked until we reached the entry gates. Police were there too, opening and closing them for vehicles. We slipped out.

Cars lined the road. People had pulled over to watch. Someone shouted my name, and I saw my father, his legs scissoring in front of headlights. I didn't know how he'd managed to get past the roadblocks, but he was here when I most needed him.

I broke away from Ian, ran for my dad, and threw myself into his arms.

He hugged me and let out a sob. "I was afraid you were dead. I thought I'd lost you too."

Cameras flashed, and I mentally braced myself for the onslaught of media coverage to come. And then we got the news that not everyone had died in the crash; one person was alive, but in bad shape. A woman in a white dress. Phaedra.

34

Two days after the event at Camellia Manor, much of Chatham County was still without power, and Savannah residents were being told it could take several more days before it was fully restored to the city. Line workers were arriving from other states. All of my belongings, including my van with its solar battery, had been returned by the police. Utilizing my phone's hotspot, I was able to send my finished story to Bennett.

I'd kept the article's focus off my mother and instead concentrated on the psychology of the Lumets and the business reputation they'd been trying to save at all costs. I certainly didn't sympathize with them, and yet there was something oddly sad about the way time and shifting culture changed the perception of a business established over a hundred years ago. Their flagship product, the very thing that had initially brought Luminescent global fame, a product used by kings and queens and movie stars, the product that had defined them, in the end became something taboo . . . It would have been almost impossible to climb back from that, yet they had. So I had no understanding of why they hadn't moved forward ethically. It might have been money, but maybe it had also been the prestige of providing the world with a near-miracle product, a product with a special and secret ingredient. Human fat.

It was no surprise Bennett ran my story within hours of receiving it. The upload to the paper's site was followed by the expected avalanche of media follow-up and speculation, press everywhere latching on to the hot story of the moment, which would be the old story in another day or two.

Information traveled fast nowadays.

The article resulted in some people dumping their fat-laden products, while others tried to buy and hoard every jar they could find. Shortly after the news hit the internet, people began selling single jars online for thousands of dollars. And people began buying them. The commerce was driven by current customers who wanted to make a buck, old customers who were frantic about losing their source and eager to grab what stock they could, and new customers who wanted to know what all the fuss was about.

The mansion and everyone left in it were saved, the dogs and Oliver found. We weren't sure how much radiation exposure I'd gotten, but I tried to tell myself I hadn't been there much longer after the danger alert on my monitor sounded.

Once the fire was cold, two bodies were found in the charred remains of the helicopter: Sterling and the uncle. Phaedra had been thrown out or had possibly jumped. I might be forever haunted by her words that first day we met, about how Sterling shouldn't have been flying.

The few remaining family members initially claimed ignorance of everything, but Oliver blew up those lies fairly quickly. He told detectives how the Lumets had been behind everything, even the radioactive cream gifted to my mother. They'd wanted her out of the picture because she'd known too much, thanks to his uncle, who'd been sleeping with her. And the death of the uncle—Atticus Lumet—had of course not been an accident.

The remaining Lumets ended up admitting they knew about the human body fat, and they reluctantly backed up Oliver's story about someone giving my mother the radioactive night cream. But nobody pointed a direct finger at my mother's killer, not even Oliver. If Phaedra ever regained consciousness, we might have more answers.

A big surprise was that my father really had sent in audition files, and he had a contract offer for a sitcom to be filmed in Hollywood. He was going to be the older handsome gentleman who lived next to a zany young couple. It didn't really seem like a role for him, but something so far out of his lane might be good. I wasn't sure what I was doing or where I was going. I hadn't seen Ian since that night at the mansion, but I'd gotten a couple of texts from him, along with a bouquet of flowers. Funny, since I'd originally thought to send flowers to him that first day.

In my room, the dosimeter still attached to my shirt, I came across a package that had arrived from Bennett. I'd forgotten about asking him to send a reader for the SD card I'd found in Dad's office. Always thorough, he'd sent four options.

One of them ended up working with my laptop.

The card contained a single video.

My hand hovered over the keyboard. What if it was something personal, like a sex tape? I winced, half closed my eyes, and clicked the mouse.

It was security camera footage, dark and murky. I went full-screen and adjusted the lighting. The date in the bottom right corner was the early morning of the day my mother's body had been found. Timestamp, 2:00 a.m. The point of view was from the front door of her house, facing the street. Why hadn't this been given to the police as evidence? Or had it? Was this a copy? If so, I'd never seen it.

As the footage rolled, headlights appeared in the street and turned into the driveway. I paused the image. It was my father's car, recognizable because of the style and a sticker in the back window advertising the band he'd been in at the time.

My heart began to slam.

The car stopped in front of the garage. The overhead door opened. A moment later the car disappeared inside, and the door closed behind it.

I thought back to that night, the *before* of that night, when Quint Dupont and I had gone to homecoming. He'd taken me home early, to the house we didn't share with my mother, the house outside Savannah. My dad had been watching TV. He went to his room, and Quint left a little before midnight. Then I went to bed. I think I took a sleeping pill.

My father must have left when I was in a deep sleep.

I stopped the footage again and sat there staring at the still frame.

"I'm so sorry you found that."

I swung around.

Max stood in the doorway, his face different now that the secrets had been revealed.

I'd long suspected him, of course. He'd had motive. He and my mother had fought, and it hadn't been a happy marriage. He'd been jealous and sick of the other men in her life. I hated to think she might be dead because of me, because they might have stayed together for me. Now I had a double blow. Her death and my father, the killer. And yet it didn't make sense. What about the Lumets? Where did they fit—or did they? I realized he was talking, explaining things. I tried to dial in, but my brain kept jumping away.

"I started keeping track of mileage," he was saying. "When you and I got in the car the next day, I knew you'd driven it."

What? No.

He moved across the room to a shelf. He pulled out a small box and showed me the contents. "Remember this? Your corsage."

I did. I remembered Quint Dupont putting it on my wrist.

"It was on the kitchen floor that morning. I picked it up and hid it. It wasn't your fault, though. Later we found out it was the medication causing your sleepwalking and sleep-driving. And apparently killing."

"I would have remembered if I'd killed my own mother."

"Would you? You never remembered going into the neighbor's house and eating their food, using their shower. You never remembered driving to Hilton Head Island and back, or roaming around Bonaventure Cemetery. You didn't remember going to the funeral home even though you were the one who wanted her put back together."

Was he gaslighting me? Trying to make me look guilty when it was really him? "You should have given this footage to the police."

"I was protecting you. I knew you were jealous of the way your mother flirted with your date. How could you not be? You would never act on it consciously. But you weren't conscious. You came here in your sleep, and you killed her. I know you loved her, Jupe. I do.

"Let's reset this," he said. "Forget it happened. Give me the security footage, and I'll destroy it. That's what I should have done to begin with."

"It was you. You killed her." But had he? The corsage. My Black Dahlia book. How mad I'd been with her that night. My sleepwalking, sleep-driving. My bloody boots. The holes in my memory.

I ran from the room, my heart breaking even as I questioned everything and denied it all. For a raw moment, I wished I hadn't looked at the video. I wished the world had just gone on. And yet someone was in jail for a crime he didn't commit.

I was suddenly outside, walking down the hot sidewalk, my feet bare. I was crying, and I started running. I wished I could run straight to Salvador, but I'd killed him. I guess I *was* guilty of killing the people I loved.

I finally had to pay attention to my burning lungs. I slowed to a walk and heard the sound of a car moving alongside me. I expected to see my dad, there to coax me back to his house. And dear God, I could feel myself turning it over in my mind, wondering if it could possibly be true. Had I killed my own mother? Had I always known, deep down in my heart of hearts? No wonder he'd kept the place. Just in case there were any secrets to find. He wasn't keeping it to honor her; he was keeping it to cover for me.

I glanced over. White car, guy behind the wheel. Not my dad. At first, I thought it wasn't anybody I knew, then I finally arranged the face until I recognized Quint Dupont.

"You okay?" he asked.

"Do I look okay?" I was still walking.

"No."

I wanted the confusion and pain to stop. Just stop.

If he'd been driving faster, I might have thrown myself in front of the car. If I did that now, I'd probably just get bruised, and that would be stupid and funny.

"Did you get the flowers I sent?" he asked.

The flowers I'd assumed were from Ian. "Yes, yes I did." I was on automatic pilot. "Thank you."

"Let me give you a ride," he said.

"Where?" I couldn't go back there.

I stopped walking, put my hands on my knees, and bent over to catch my breath. I noted distantly that my feet were dirty and bloody. How long had I been running?

With my hands still on my knees and my mouth open, I looked up to see if I recognized anything. I was in an area of town I'd been to before, but I wasn't sure how far I was from my mother's house, or even the direction I needed to go to return to at least get my phone. And call the police. And confess.

I got in the car with Quint.

He put the vehicle in gear, and we moved down the street.

35

I didn't notice where we were going or even how long we'd been in Dupont's car, but suddenly we were in the driveway of a ranch-style home with a sickly palm tree and a neglected yard.

"Come on inside," he said.

"Why?" I couldn't think. At all. My brain felt as if it were collapsing just like the electrical pylons from the other night. Just folding up, sparks flying.

"You need some water. You need your feet tended to."

I looked down. They were bleeding. I might not have gone with him under other circumstances. I wasn't the type of person to follow someone without question, but I was numb and couldn't think for myself.

We entered the house through the side door. From there, we went down a set of stairs to a damp-smelling basement, reminding me of Minnesota. Many houses in Georgia didn't even have basements.

He turned on lights.

I dropped onto a brown couch, sinking deep, while he opened a little apartment fridge, pulled out a bottle of water, and passed it to me.

Did he live down here by himself? No, that wasn't right. Hadn't he said he was married? Man cave, maybe. Like before, I vaguely wondered what he did for a living, but I couldn't drum up enough curiosity to care. I truly and completely understood the phrase *dead inside*.

"I saw the news," he told me, standing in the middle of the room. He was dressed in black slacks and a print shirt, his dark wavy hair swept back. "But I'm still unclear about your mother's homicide," he said, hands in his pockets. "Did one of the Lumets kill her?"

"What?" I'd forgotten about the Lumets. All I could think about was what I'd found on the SD card and what my father had told me. "I thought so, but now I don't know."

"I have to admit I'd wondered about Oliver, back before he supposedly died. We didn't go to the same school, but I ran into him a few times at chess meets. We hung out a little, but he was kind of weird."

"I think Oliver was just an innocent victim like so many others." Like my mother.

I swallowed a sob, took a deep breath, then clutched and opened the water. I needed to talk to somebody. I should call Bennett. Or Ian. But I couldn't face either of them. "I haven't told anyone this yet, but I think I know who the real killer is."

His eyes widened, and he slowly sat down on an office chair, waiting for me to continue.

I considered whether I should or should not, then finally said, "Me."

His mouth dropped open, and he stared at me in disbelief. "You're kidding, right?"

"It's me. Or my dad. Probably me. That's why I was running. I'd just discovered the truth." I raised the water to my mouth, but the thought of swallowing anything, even water, caused my stomach to heave. And then I tasted bile and knew what was about to happen. I set the bottle aside and jumped to my feet. "Bathroom" was the only word I could get out.

He pointed to a door in the corner, and I dashed for it, hand to my mouth. I made it just in time to throw up. Once I was done, I straightened and stepped to the sink to rinse my face.

And my dosimeter went off.

Not loud, but a faint early-warning chirp that meant it was picking up more than background radiation.

There was very little in the small space that looked suspect. Cement floor, toilet, industrial sink. Above it, right in front of me, was a mirrored metal medicine cabinet.

I opened it.

On a glass shelf in the very center, surrounded by items you might expect to find, like a tin of Band-Aids and a tube of toothpaste, was a purple glass bottle. The kind of ornate bottle that hadn't been with my mother's belongings.

Now that the door was open, that woodsy, almost masculine scent filled the air, and the sound of the dosimeter increased. I stared at the bottle, so out of context with what I'd just learned an hour ago. It didn't fit the new story line.

I lifted the small container from the shelf, my fingers remembering the curve of the glass and the way it fit my palm.

This was the missing perfume.

How had Quint come to have it hidden in his bathroom?

I returned the bottle to the cabinet.

Finding him with her special one-of-a-kind scent wouldn't have been as thoroughly incriminating if not for another item on the shelf, sitting next to the perfume: the decorative hair comb she'd been wearing the night of homecoming, the night of the Lumet party, a comb I'd given her as a Christmas gift.

I don't know what was more startling. That he had a bottle of her perfume, or that it had been laced with radium too.

My mind struggled to put together the pieces. In less than an hour, I'd been sure my father was the killer, then me, and now I was absolutely positive it was Quint Dupont. And I'd been in such a hurry that I hadn't taken time to fully close or lock the bathroom. But I doubt a lock would have stopped him. The flimsy door suddenly swung open with a bang, and Quint stood there.

It took me a while to realize he was talking. Had I missed anything important? My brain was full of the realization that I was standing in front of my mother's killer while also feeling an overwhelming sense of relief. Not me. Not my father.

I also felt deep regret for the years I'd spent resenting how he'd sent me away, and I regretted my constant background suspicion of him that had always been there. I could admit that now. Redirected suspicion, because, like my father, I'd suspected myself.

"Why did you come to Savannah now, after all these years?" Quint asked. "You just messed everything up."

I ignored his question. "She was my mother."

"Was she? Really? I heard you weren't her kid. That she just found you and took you home. That's what she always told people."

"She had a flair for the dramatic." For a long time, I'd thought maybe my aunt was my real mother, especially after she'd left everything to me—her condo, her cat, everything. But a simple DNA test had confirmed the thing I'd always known in my heart of hearts: Marie was my biological mother.

She was flawed, my father was flawed, I was flawed, but our love for one another had been strong and real. I truly and finally understood that if our love had been less, I wouldn't have been standing here right now. I would not have come back to Savannah, and I would not have kept in touch with my dad. I would have never spoken to him again. I would have closed that door to my past and never reopened it.

"She was everybody's dream," Dupont said with an almost trancelike voice and expression. "I don't think I knew a guy who didn't fantasize about her. I printed out pictures from the internet and framed them. I had a room that was nothing but photos of her. I went to her events and shouted her name from the other side of the red velvet rope, but she never noticed me."

He wouldn't have been used to that. Women ignoring him.

"But the night I picked you up to take you to homecoming? She noticed me that night. Big time. You and I were standing at the bottom of the stairs, and your mother came gliding down like someone from heaven." He was caught up in the memory, his face now reflective. "She was wearing white silk pajamas that were semitransparent, and the fabric clung to her body. But until then, I hadn't known how she smelled, really smelled, up close and personal. It's a scent that's hard to define."

The dosimeter continued to let out a weak chirp. "Mesquite," I suggested. "And cloves. And sage. And a Georgia forest."

"Yeah. All of that. Thanks. And then I slipped the corsage on your wrist, and at that exact moment Marie Nova and I made eye contact. She'd asked how old I was, and I got what she meant. Do you remember that?"

We were talking like two people having a conversation about a scene in a movie, about characters who weren't real. "That's when I knew you asked me out to be near her," I said. "It was pretty obvious."

He laughed, not denying it, then said, "She was on her way to a party at the Luminescent estate, and I wished I could go there with her instead of to homecoming with you. When you were on the other side of the room, she asked me to bring you home early and come and see her."

"I was a good boy. I took you to homecoming and acted like I enjoyed myself. You seemed disappointed when I had you home on time, even a little early. At your house where you lived with your dad. That place in Richmond Hill."

"That was it."

"He was in the living room. I stayed to watch a movie, and he went to bed. When I left, I picked up his car keys." He mimed the motion of swooping keys from a table. "I'd watched both houses enough to know the routines. I drove from the suburbs to Savannah. I think it was like fifteen miles, maybe twenty. The remote control for the garage was on the visor. I opened the door, drove in, and closed the door behind me. And I just walked into the house and waited for your mother to come home from the Lumet party."

"The corsage?"

"You left it in my car."

I pushed past him to walk woodenly to the sitting area. The chirping of the dosimeter stopped now that I was no longer near the source of radiation. I dropped down on the couch.

Dupont moved to a corner where I spotted a big green safe. With his back to me, I couldn't see what he was doing, but I could hear the spinning of the dial and the creak of the door. When he turned around, he was holding a minicassette recorder in his hand, the kind I'd used before smartphones. It could easily be hidden in a pocket while recording.

"I thought you might enjoy hearing this," Dupont said. "I still listen to it every day." He pressed the play button and lifted the recorder so the tiny speaker faced me.

I heard what sounded like someone running, bare feet slapping the floor. That was followed by a grunt and a scream and a struggle.

He'd recorded the kill.

And he was playing it for me, the victim's daughter.

I sat there frozen as the recording went on and on and on. At times it dragged, probably because it was old, and he'd played it so much. I vaguely thought about trying to call 911 but remembered I'd left my phone at my dad's. I glanced around the room, hoping to spot a landline even though few people used them nowadays. Nothing. I thought of getting up, leaving.

Then I heard a new and even more terrible sound. The death blow.

Smiling in satisfaction and pride but also looking kind of sick, Dupont shut off the recorder and slipped it into his pants pocket.

I finally moved.

Not to run away but to kill him.

I jumped to my feet and lunged for him, grabbing him around the throat, squeezing hard. He somehow smiled at me. Puzzled at first, I soon understood why when I felt something hard pressed to my stomach. I looked down and saw a pistol. He must have retrieved it from the safe along with the recorder.

Maybe it was just a primal response, because I really didn't care if I lived or died right now. I released my hold on him.

He kept grinning. "Bye-bye, Jupiter." His voice sounded strained, his vocal cords suffering from my attack.

From upstairs came the crash of a slamming door. He gave a start of surprise, and his smile vanished.

"I picked up dinner!" a woman shouted.

Footfalls moved across the floor above our heads. He jumped back and hid the weapon in the waistband of his slacks, under his shirt.

Just in time, because a girl came hurrying down the stairs. "We brought you chicken, Daddy!"

Following behind her was a woman, probably in her midthirties, blonde hair, tidy clothes, conservative looking.

She frowned when she saw me. It was the expression of a woman who knew her man was cheating on her. "Who's this?"

"An old high school friend," he said.

She relaxed a little. "Well, I hope you two aren't down here killing people."

Was she in on it? Sometimes couples killed together. Rare, but definitely a thing.

She looked at me and explained. "He loves violent video games. I keep telling him they're bad for him."

I took a few steps closer to the wife. "Can I borrow your phone?" I asked, hand out. "I've misplaced mine, and I need to call a cab."

"Sure." She unlocked the screen and gave her phone to me.

Without looking at Dupont, I called 911. When the operator answered, I said, "I'd like to report a homicide and an attempted murder." I asked the wife for the address. She looked stunned, her face reflecting anger at me as well as confusion. I'd done a long-form journalism piece on the wives of killers and how most of them . . . well, refused to see the signs. Just blinded themselves to it all.

The child spouted the address. I gave the info to the dispatcher, then passed the phone back. "Thanks."

I wanted to leave, but I didn't feel comfortable turning my back on him. No need to worry. He darted past us and raced up the steps, taking them an impressive three at a time. The gun fell from his pants and hit the stairs.

The girl shouted after him. "You dropped your gun, Daddy! And do you want chicken?"

Dupont was almost to the top. I lunged and grabbed him by the ankle. With both hands, I tugged hard.

He tumbled down the stairs, trying to stop himself, flailed for the railing and missed it, finally landing at the bottom of the steps in a heap. I picked up the gun and aimed it at him, legs braced, one arm straight, one bent in support. I didn't own a gun, but I sure as hell knew how to use one.

From outside came the sound of sirens.

"Go upstairs and let them in," I told the wife with a nod of my chin. Then to the girl, "You go too, honey."

"You aren't going to kill my daddy, are you?"

He held up a hand, palm out. "Don't shoot me," he said, sobbing.

It seemed like this moment should have been bigger, like it was too easy, too simple, especially in light of all the years that had passed and all the lives that had been impacted. And then there was the Lumet family tangled up in it, their place almost burning down, my father a suspect, not once but twice. Me. Everything that had gone before. But some things didn't present with a crash of cymbals; they just happened, calmly, quietly, rationally after a lifetime of pain and suffering.

"I'm not going to kill him," I told the girl, even though I wanted to. But that wasn't how this should end. I added, just in case he thought he could try to run again, "Unless I have to."

Somebody pounded on a door above us. That was followed by ringing.

"Go on," I told the mother, the wife, the unnamed collateral emotional damage.

She nodded. Her eyes were glazed, her mouth slack. Stunned, shocked by the whole thing. I would probably feel sorry for her later. I had nothing right now.

With her hand on the railing, she moved up the stairs to answer the door.

36

It took some time for the officers to begin to understand what was going on. I told them about the recorder in Dupont's pocket. One of them pulled it out and played it.

Done.

Dupont was arrested and hauled off. His wife and child were told to leave the house, which was designated a temporary crime scene. They would search for more evidence. Killers tended to save things, obviously.

I went outside and sat down on the curb.

I hugged my knees and looked at my bloody feet. With no phone, I couldn't call anybody. I didn't care. It just felt good to sit there and hold this new truth.

The sun was beginning to sink behind the house across the street. People were standing in their yards, watching and talking among themselves, hands to mouths, eyes full of concern, wondering what was going on. I thought about getting up, maybe hitchhiking home. Seemed like a lot of work. The road had been closed to through traffic. I spotted a man walking toward me. He wasn't in uniform, and it took me a moment to recognize Ian.

I was glad to see him, and I told him so.

"The news hasn't hit the media yet, but someone at the office called me, and I came as fast as I could." He sat down beside me on the curb. "You okay?" People moved back and forth around us.

"I'm fine." Actually better than fine. "He was going to kill me, but his wife came home with a bucket of fried chicken." Suddenly the fried chicken seemed hilarious, and I laughed. It was so absurd. I filled him in on what had happened, starting with the SD card I'd found at my dad's house. He put his arm around me and gave me a good hug.

37

Luc Chesterfield was exonerated and released less than a week later. I drove to the prison so I could support him as he walked out a free man. When I discovered nobody was there to pick him up, I gave him a ride to Savannah. And when I found out he had no money and no place to stay, I set up an account for him. My father put in a generous amount, while I scoped out a place for him to live, at least temporarily. It turned out his mother had died while he was in prison. He had one sibling, a brother in North Carolina, and we would try to get them reconnected.

Samples of current Luminescent products were sent to labs for testing. One of the cousins pointed a finger at a well-known, upscale liposuction chain in California, and there was giddy speculation about the famous celebrities that unsuspecting customers might have smeared on their faces. The chain had already shuttered its clinics and hung "Closed" signs, the CEO refusing to talk to the press. I smelled lawsuits on the horizon from patrons who'd had their fat used without their knowledge.

We still didn't know whether Luminescent had been creating any current products for the general public with trace amounts of radium. I doubted it, and yet Geiger counters were flying off the shelves, and two people had reported getting readings from their night creams. I suspected they were just trying to grab their fifteen minutes of fame, much like the attention seekers who'd come forward to confess to my mother's murder. Or they'd picked up ambient readings and panicked. Or they were hoping to sue.

The use of radium would take the crime to another level, because at least as far as we knew, the human fat had hurt no one. In fact, many customers were at this moment writing rave reviews in defense of their favorite products. It would also be easy to dismiss the radium claims as far-fetched, mustache-twirling drama, because what company would knowingly put customers in such danger while also greatly risking its own reputation? But I'd reported on such horrendous stories over the years, and I knew what some businesses were capable of. And we were obviously dealing with behavior bordering on psychopathic. I'd read that narcissism in young adults was up from 12 percent to 80.

During the days immediately following Dupont's arrest, I couldn't quit watching social media to see what people were saying about my mother. Fans and nonfans couldn't get enough of her before, but this newest addition to the story had blown up in a way even I hadn't expected. And all those armchair sleuths who'd claimed someone else had done it all along were gloating now.

The days after the arrest blurred together, but at one point I dropped my father off at Savannah/Hilton Head International Airport so he could catch a flight to LA, where they were going to start shooting the sitcom pilot.

I got out of the van, and we hugged.

I could tell a difference in the embrace. It was the first time in years that I hugged him and didn't wonder if I was hugging my mother's killer. But some neural pathways could not be rerouted without effort, and I suspected it would take my brain, waking and sleeping, time to truly get the new message that my father was innocent. That I was innocent.

And yet I knew no matter what happened going forward, my life would always be defined by my mother's murder. Finally naming her true killer wouldn't bring her back, but it would right some wrongs and quiet the hum in my head that had always told me things weren't right. That hum that had made me suspect my father all these years. That hum that had made me subconsciously suspect myself and redirect those suspicions to him. That hum that had made me wonder if the wrong man was in prison.

"Let me know when you land at LAX," I said as I got back in the van.

It was ten or twelve miles from the Savannah/Hilton Head International Airport to Savannah, depending on the route you took. I took 21 South and was halfway back to my dad's when I got a call from Bennett. I answered hands-free.

"I've got a gig you might be interested in," he said.

I wasn't sure I could handle that kind of leap. I was still processing everything that had happened. "I think I'm going to take some time off."

My dad and I had talked about turning my mother's place into housing for students attending an acting school in town. We'd talked about turning it into a museum and using the proceeds to fund scholarships, but the idea of a museum seemed morbid. We'd talked about razing it and creating a small park, but that felt a little too much like erasing a big part of Marie Nova's life. We'd both tossed that idea pretty quickly. The one thing we'd decided was to clean it out and clean it up and go from there. I planned to stick around, at least for a while.

"I get it," Bennett said. "But this kind of has your name all over it and is in your neck of the woods too. Northern Florida. A mother who's had three kids go missing over the years."

"Wow. That's not in any way suspicious."

"Right. No conviction. Most suspect filicide, but so far there's no proof because no bodies."

I might have talked about time off, but I was a person who needed to be busy, and work had saved me over the years. I think Bennett understood that more than I did. I loved cases that required deep research and deep digging, that fully occupied my mind every waking moment. Uncovering the truth.

I let out a sigh. Of course I was interested. I thought about Ian. Silly of me to get tangled up with someone new. Maybe leaving was the best thing.

"I even have a title," he said. "'Darkness in the Sunshine State.'"

"Hmm. How about 'Dark Side of the Womb'?"

"I like it."

"I was kidding."

"I still like it."

I laughed.

"So you'll take the job?"

It wasn't that far from Savannah. "You almost had me at *filicide*," I told him. "I'll think about it and let you know."

The conversation shifted. "How's Oliver Lumet doing?"

"I don't know." A plastic surgeon, one of the best in the country, was going to examine him. The doctor felt he could help. No promises of a beautiful face, but he thought Oliver could have an average face, a face nobody would notice in a crowd. Phaedra was still in critical condition and hadn't regained consciousness.

I wondered if Oliver would be indicted. Like the other Lumets, he'd known things and kept quiet. He might have helped me escape, but I wasn't blind to his association. He could be considered an accessory for not reporting what was going on. My guess was that due to what he'd gone through, a jury would go easy on him. I hoped so. He deserved a chance at a somewhat normal life. Dupont, on the other hand, might never see the light of day. So far, he wasn't talking, but duplicates of the secret photos my father had purchased were found in Dupont's safe. Bold and stupid of him to sell copies. He'd not only committed the crime, he'd made money off it too.

As with other types of criminals, killers didn't typically stop, although some had been known to marry and settle down for a while, to put killing aside to have a normal life. Until that normal life got boring and smothering. He might have more to hide than my mother's murder.

Using the surveillance video as reference, Ian and I had been able to put together a timeline of the night she was killed. It was so easy now, once we had the right pieces. Everything fell into place and seemed obvious. Dupont's involvement had always been the missing bit of information that confounded and confused the case. And everybody was hiding something, trying to protect someone. The Lumets, trying to protect their company and their reputation. My father had been protecting me. Max had thought I'd sleepwalk-killed her, and he'd tried to cover for me. Even sending me away and keeping the house had been part of his strategy. I wondered if my aunt had known that full story. Had she taken me in thinking I might have killed her sister?

"And what about you?" Bennett asked. "Are you going to be okay?"

I thought about it. A few weeks ago I would have said no. "Maybe." The thought made me feel like crying. Stupid. "I'm taking Oliver to Atlanta tomorrow to see the surgeon. But I'll let you know about Florida."

"Okay. Be careful. Love you."

"Love you too."

That evening, something different appeared in my feed that had nothing to do with my mother. It was a human-interest report about a recent Van Gogh acquisition by a museum in Gothenburg, Sweden. The never-before-seen painting had been found in a house near Arles, France, the town where Van Gogh had lived and painted. He had been fascinated by the Langlois Bridge and had glorified it more than once. This was supposedly a painting of the bridge no one had ever seen, found tucked in the back of an antique shop. I watched the footage, paused the image of the painting, took a screengrab, and enlarged it.

Just like killers, most criminals, any criminals, didn't stop committing crimes. They just restarted somewhere else.

Down in the lower left corner of the artwork was something that looked like a tiny speck of dust or a place where a minuscule spot of paint had faded or worn off.

I couldn't help but wonder if I was just imagining Salvador's faint signature because I wanted him to still be alive. If he hadn't drowned, his fake death must have been planned down to the smallest detail, a boat with no lights waiting for him past the breakers, where the ocean could sometimes be smooth as glass. Maybe more than one boat, a small and silent inflatable to carry him to the bigger boat, with divers in case he ran into trouble. Yes, that was probably it. And everybody but me had most likely been in on it.

No. Not possible.

That night I stole another quick look at my mother's journal, her final entry.

One of the funniest memories I have of Jupiter is the time we went to a play at a minimum-security prison in California. This was before we moved to Savannah and before I became famous. They stamped her little hand with invisible ink that would only show up under a black light. During the play I realized she was sobbing silently, and when I asked why, she said she was going to have to stay in prison because there was no stamp on her hand. I might have laughed. I probably did, in the way adults often don't take childhood silliness seriously. I think she cried through most of the play, even the funny slapstick parts. At one point, when I realized she was still upset, I pulled her onto my lap and asked her if she wanted to leave. She did, and so we left before the play was over. At the exit, they shined a black light on her hand, and there was the stamp. It was a reindeer. She cried about that too, because she felt she'd ruined the whole night. That's just the kind of soft heart she had. Max and I both tried to reassure her. We didn't care that we missed the end, but she was inconsolable until we got home and tucked her into bed. What a dear and kind soul. I love her so much.

The entry illustrated the fragility and unreliability of memory. There was my story of what had taken place at the prison, and then there was her story. They weren't the same, but they were similar. Along with that, time and self-preservation had whittled away the sharply defined edges of my mother and had left me mostly with the public persona. The journal, although sparse, brought her back, not fully, but as a reminder that a softer Marie Nova had existed.

I flipped to the earlier entry I'd read my first day in the house.

In light of what I now knew, the declaration about how she would die for me took on new meaning, and I realized her flirting so outrageously with Quint Dupont had been to protect me, not steal my gross boyfriend.

One thing about Marie was that she could read people. She hadn't known he was a killer, but she'd seen the evil in him. It was very possible she'd died for me, but I would try hard not to feel guilty. She wouldn't have wanted that. Instead, I would do my best to celebrate her love and her bravery.

38

There was something about being on the road that seemed to beg for open windows. I was driving, and Oliver was beside me in the passenger seat, the wind blowing our hair, his hand out the window, riding the waves as we headed to Atlanta.

Normally it would have taken months to get in, but when the reconstructive surgeon had seen the news and Oliver's face, he'd given up a vacation day for a consult. Everyone was touched by his story, and everyone seemed eager to help however they could, including me. I'd been a little surprised Oliver had been willing to go, since his mother was still in intensive care, but after the role she'd played in his removal from society and maybe even the attempted poisoning of my mother, it wasn't for me to question his behavior. He was still trying to decide if he'd visit her at all, mostly because he didn't want to be seen, I suspected, but maybe because he was also struggling with what Phaedra had done. Yet Oliver hadn't completely avoided the topic of his mother. He'd voiced his concern and asked if I thought she'd wake up. At this point, nobody knew. After that, the conversation had quickly turned to Dupont and our combined puzzlement over how he'd managed to pull off such a horrible crime. He just didn't seem that bright.

"How well did you know him?" I asked.

Oliver leaned forward and turned down the music, then raised his window so we could talk more easily. I did the same.

Even though the outdoor temp was close to eighty, he was wearing a black hoodie, while I wore my typical attire of jeans, T-shirt, boots, and leather belt. I figured the clothing must have brought him comfort, like a security blanket, the hood something he could hide beneath if he needed to.

"I didn't know him at all," he said, seeming baffled by the question.

"He told me you two knew each other and that you hung out some. He mentioned chess meets."

He didn't answer right away; he seemed to be trying to remember. "Pretty sure I never met him. And let's face it, he's probably lied about a lot of things."

True. But it seemed like a weird thing to lie about. It was possible Oliver had just forgotten. I couldn't remember everybody I'd known in high school.

I spotted the exit sign for the falls and eased off the interstate to the hiking and recreational area. Near the parking lot were trails that led through dense forest to a lake and a waterfall. It was a four-hour drive from Savannah to Atlanta, and I'd chosen this place to stop because I thought Oliver might enjoy seeing something different since he hadn't left the estate in years.

We used the restroom and sat down at a picnic table. I finished the coffee I'd been nursing after picking it up at a drive-thru. He drank soda. The day was beautiful, but the mood was somber. From where we sat in a private, grassy area, we could hear the falls but not see them. Oliver kept his hood pulled up and his head low to hide from anybody who might happen past. I wanted to tell him his face wasn't really that bad, and it wasn't, but I also didn't feel I knew him well enough to say anything so personal.

"I'd like to see the falls before we leave," he said.

I was surprised since there might be people there. "Me too."

We threw away our small amount of trash and checked the wooden sign at the trailhead. The falls were not far away, with a path that went high above them, and another at ground level that would take a person to the shoreline. We took the low path, and I was relieved to see we were the only ones there.

I followed Oliver down to the water, where the sand was wet and packed hard. We stood there awhile. I could hear birds singing, but I could also hear the distracting sound of traffic on the interstate, a reminder that we needed to hit the road again. But Oliver seemed in no hurry to leave.

"That must have been awful when you watched your boyfriend drown himself." His eyes were bold, challenging, wide, unblinking.

My breath caught, and I felt myself begin to shut down even as I inwardly recoiled at his words. Was that why he'd wanted to come and see the water? Did he have a twisted and cruel streak, born out of his own strange upbringing? And how challenging it must have been to live such a lie, to allow the whole world to think you were dead when you were really alive. That could mess with somebody's head, so I tried to cut him some slack.

He turned, lifted his face to the sun, and closed his eyes. Even with his deformities, he didn't look that bad. His face was just . . . different. A face that, to someone seeing it in the dark, might look like a mask.

39

"This shouldn't take long," Ian told Poppy as she unpacked her crayons and coloring books and spread them out on the coffee table. There was only one other person in the ICU waiting area, a woman knitting in the corner. She had a heaviness about her that suggested this wasn't her first day.

"That's the man I saw yesterday," Poppy said. "Your friend."

Ian looked at the TV. The correspondent was on the right of the screen, Oliver Lumet's photo on the left. No surprise. The tragic story had pretty much dominated media channels worldwide over the past two days.

"He's ugly," Poppy added.

The woman glanced up, chuckled, and went back to her knitting.

Ian put a finger to his lips in a silent *shhh*, then whispered, "You shouldn't say that. He can't help it." He didn't give much thought to what she'd said about Oliver being his friend. He'd ask her what she meant when he got back.

An hour earlier, on his way to pick up Poppy from school, he'd gotten a call from a nurse at the hospital. Phaedra Lumet had regained consciousness. It was especially good news, because they hadn't been sure she'd wake up at all, although he was a little surprised to find she'd asked for him.

Leaving Poppy with her coloring books, he checked in at the desk and was directed to a sanitizing station, where he washed his hands and put on a blue face mask. Then a nurse led him down a hallway into an intensive care unit, monitors everywhere, tubes everywhere, going in and coming out, the loud sound of oxygen like a monster breathing, electronics beeping in a language he didn't understand. Phaedra still had an intubation tube in her throat. She wouldn't be able to talk. He hadn't expected her to be in such bad shape, especially since she'd requested a visit, and now he could see this was too soon.

But her eyes were alert.

What he knew about her injuries was that there were many. A punctured lung, broken ribs, a shattered leg, and a skull fracture that had required cooling down her body temperature to control the swelling. He introduced himself.

She waved his words away as if to say she knew who he was. Then she wrote something on a pad and held it up for him to see.

OLIVER

"He's fine," Ian assured her. "You don't need to worry. Jupiter is keeping an eye on him. And the dogs are being taken care of by a rescue group."

Annoyance flashed in her eyes. She wrote something else, each stroke on the paper seeming to transmit irritation or impending disaster. The new word was even shorter than the previous one. When she was done, she tapped the pen with impatience and turned the tablet back around. She'd added *it's*, so it read *IT'S OLIVER*.

"It's Oliver?"

She rolled her eyes, started to write more, but the import of her two words quickly sank in. Oliver was behind at least some of what had happened. Or that was what she seemed to be saying. But how trustworthy was she right now? She had a head injury. He was tempted to blow it off but remembered what Poppy had said about seeing Oliver.

He thanked Phaedra. Heart pounding, he walked rapidly down the hall to the waiting room. Poppy wasn't there. In a panic, he shouted her name. The knitting woman pointed, and Ian turned to look as Poppy came sauntering from the restroom. He ran to her, collapsed to his knees, and hung on tight, as if the slightest release might cause her to float away.

"Do you need smelling salts, Uncle Ian?"

He let out a muffled half laugh, half sob and eased his death grip on her. The smelling salt thing was Liz's joke, and he wasn't even sure Poppy understood the reference to Victorian women who fainted from tight corsets. "I'm fine, I'm fine. We're all fine."

He pulled away but retained a light hold on Poppy's arms. "Where did you say you saw that man on TV?"

"He was standing on the sidewalk, looking at our house. He said he was your friend."

Sweet kitty.

Then he remembered Jupiter was supposed to drive Oliver to see a surgeon in Atlanta.

40

I felt a chill even though the sun was warm. My heart seemed to close in denial.

I'd uncovered many unlikely things in my career, enough to know that people tended to fill in the blanks with fears and untruths. But we must never shut our minds to the possible.

The phone in the back pocket of my jeans alerted me to a text. I checked and saw it was from Ian. Thinking it might be news of Phaedra, I read it.

Oliver was somehow involved in your mother's murder. Get away from him.

A second text: Where are you?

That pain in my heart had been real. I felt a mixture of sadness and disbelief as I opened Google Maps and dropped a pin to share my location.

"Is this how he did it?" Oliver asked.

I looked up to see him wading into the lake, the water turning his beige pants dark. I put away my phone as he continued to move forward, hands in the pockets of his sweatshirt. He wobbled, regained his balance, and kept going. To the left of us were the falls, tumbling over boulders to plunge into the blue pool. I could see movement and color along the trail that followed the high ridge. Hikers.

"Yes," I heard myself saying in a conversational tone. "It was like that."

He paused to look at me. "That must have been horrible for you."

"It was. It is."

"I saw my uncle die."

"I didn't know that."

"Nobody does. He was sleeping with your mother. Did you know?"

I could feel messages coming in, but I didn't dare look at my phone. "I guessed as much."

"He was leaving the estate one night, and I was waiting for him along the road. I'd picked the perfect spot. I stepped out and stood there in his headlights." He smiled his crooked smile.

"He drove way too fast in that vintage sports car. My mother was always talking about it. I'll bet he was going eighty on that narrow road. He turned the wheel and slammed on the brakes. He missed me by yards, and the car went flying through the air. I found him pinned behind the steering column. I had to wait maybe thirty minutes for him to die. So I know how you feel."

I doubt it. "Did he realize you weren't really dead all those years?"

He let out a snort. "It was his idea. He didn't want people to associate my face with our products. And everybody just went along with it. But even so, everything was well and good until you showed up. I mean, how is this better? How is it better to know what really happened? Nothing can change. Nothing can bring your mother back."

He bent over and reached into the water as if searching for something. It took me a moment to realize he was picking up rocks. Then he began methodically filling his pockets with them.

"So dramatic, I know," he said. "But I've always loved the pragmatic nature of Virginia Woolf's suicide. Did your boyfriend use rocks as weights?"

"No."

"I guess it's different in the ocean, where you've got riptides. I was kinda hoping we'd be near the ocean, but this works."

"He just swam into the setting sun."

"That's beautiful."

"It was."

I waded into the water up to my thighs. I couldn't believe I was going to witness another water suicide. I couldn't allow it to happen. "He loved sunsets."

"It's a good thing to love."

Oliver was deeper than me. The water was up to his chest and only my waist.

He took another step. And vanished.

Just like Salvador.

I lunged and managed to snag the back of his sweatshirt, gripping it tight, tugging his head out of the water as his arms flailed. I heard voices of alarm in the distance.

He looked at me, and his eyes held something I'd never seen in a human before. It was like the sun was living in there, burning in there, all shiny and bright and fevered. He smiled wider than usual, and I saw his missing teeth, no jawbone to hold them anymore. And I could read the intent in his eyes. Yet even in the moment, I felt sympathy. I felt a wave of sorrow for what had happened to Oliver the child. And I felt sorry for Phaedra for the guilt she must have carried all these years. She hadn't hidden him because of his face. She'd hidden him because he'd killed, first my mother, and then her own brother.

Had Oliver been born evil? Or had what happened to him maimed his mind the way the radium had maimed his body?

He flipped around until he was on top of me, and I was the one under the water.

He'd lured me here. He'd played upon my sympathy and pain. He hadn't planned to kill himself. He planned to kill me.

I opened my eyes and saw the broken faceted diamonds of him as I looked up through the shimmering water's surface. Oliver in the sunlight, me in the darkness below. I felt his hands on my throat, choking me, holding me down. Through the water, I saw the blur that was him look up and away.

His mouth moved, and I heard his muffled words as he sounded a fake cry of alarm, a shout for help. He was calling to nearby people who weren't close enough to save me but were close enough to be able to report that he'd tried to rescue me.

Under the water, I thought of Salvador's signature. Was he really alive? If he'd died, his death had to have been painful. And if he could do it, so could I. The pain for him might have been over, and it would soon be over for me.

I think I smiled. At least I tried to.

But then I thought of Ian and Poppy and my father and my aunt and my mother. Especially my mother. I recalled the photo of the flesh under her nails, and I wondered if that was why Oliver wore long sleeves even on a hot day.

I closed my eyes and intentionally went limp. I fought the involuntary need to take a breath that would fill my burning lungs with water, not air. I thought about the drawing I'd seen in the radiation room at the Lumet estate. And I thought about what Sal had told me about art: it often reflected the soul of the creator—their truth.

The picture wasn't a drawing of a happy family but a record of Oliver's kills, beginning with the puppy, then his baby sister. Now me.

My limpness tricked him. I felt his hold lessen. Not completely, but enough. I lunged skyward. I grabbed his arms. I broke the surface. I pulled in air. I shouted for help.

He pushed me down again. His fingers wrapped around my throat once more as I continued to struggle.

And then suddenly his hands were gone.

Just gone.

I surfaced, sucking in air and water, coughing, trying to swim to where it would be shallow enough to stand. Sloshing toward shore. Someone grabbed me. At first I thought it was Oliver, but no. It was a young woman.

"Thank you," I gasped.

"We were on the trail," she said, horror in her face. "We couldn't believe what we were seeing. I said to my friends, *That son of a bitch is trying to kill her.* And we all ran for you."

Yards away, still in the deeper water, two women and a guy had Oliver's hands pinned behind him and were half walking, half pushing him toward the beach. The rocks in his pockets weighed him down, making it harder. I wanted to laugh about that but didn't have the air.

His sweatshirt was tangled around him, one of his arms bare. He had deep red crevices there, some new, from me, some old, from my mother.

It was curious to think that he was both of the men my mother had warned me about. A pretty one and an ugly one.

Oliver was protesting, telling them to let him go, that he'd been trying to save me. They all just pressed their lips together and held on tighter.

And then I heard sirens.

Ian must have relayed our location to the police.

41

Hours later, as I drove back to Savannah dressed in dry clothes I'd dug out of the van, I talked to my dad on the phone. He said he planned to return home to be with me.

"Stay," I said. "The shoot starts tomorrow. I'm fine. It's all over now." Wasn't it? Damn, I hoped so. I didn't want him to miss this opportunity. It had taken him so long to get back on track, and this could really be something.

"Okay, sweetheart. If you're sure you're okay."

That evening, even though I was exhausted, I went to see Phaedra in the hospital. She had a long recovery ahead, and I didn't know what I would have done in her position. She wasn't well enough to share her story yet, but I hoped she would be soon.

She was unable to talk, and too exhausted for any effort beyond writing two words on a piece of paper. *I'M SORRY.*

I took the paper with me when I left. I didn't know why.

Somewhere between almost dying and visiting Phaedra in the hospital, I decided to take the Florida job. I was packing when I got a text from a strange number.

Unknown: I saw the news. Good job, kiddo.

Me: Who is this?

Unknown: You should come to Peru. I think you'd like it here. The sunsets are amazing.

Salvador.

The doorbell rang. Text conversation still going, I answered the door to see Ian standing there, hands in the front pockets of his jeans.

"I stopped by to see when you're going back to Minnesota," he said. "And to let you know that my sister is on her way home."

"That's fantastic."

Because Ian was most familiar with the case, he'd been given the job of interrogating Oliver. Once he was done, he'd shared what he'd learned with me. We finally knew Oliver had masterminded the homicide. He'd ridden back from the Luminescent party in the trunk of my mother's car, and Dupont had met him at the house. Two killers working in tandem seemed so much more horrific than one. They'd known each other, and they'd plotted it, even using the coincidence of the party being the same night as homecoming.

There were those celebrity killers who killed for fame, and there were the ones who had a need to possess the person they were killing, to completely own them and control them, and the only way they could do so was by ending their life.

After all her warnings to me, it seemed my mother had been especially kind to Oliver, possibly because of his disfigurement. He might have been the ghost that had gone into her room at night, the ghost other guests reported seeing also. But this story was only one distraction, and it was already being replaced by other news that came and went as quickly as it could be consumed. Unlike in my mother's day, when her death had remained in the grocery store checkout lanes for a year.

"I'll be moving out of my sister's house soon," Ian said.

I sensed he wanted to come inside, but I was acutely aware of the text I'd just received and the cell phone that felt as if it were burning a hole in my hand.

"Poppy is upset about that, but I told her we could still ride bikes to the beach and hang out and tell jokes." He looked nervous, like he was considering his next words. "I came across this recently and have been carrying it around to give to you." He unfolded something and passed it to me. "But I wasn't sure you'd want it."

It was a photo signed to him by my mother.

"I was a kid. She was doing publicity at a place downtown. I got an autograph."

"And you kept it all this time?"

"I know it seems weird. I think it was because I'm the one who found her."

"Are you sure you don't want it?"

"I've kept it long enough. Too long."

I got another text from *Unknown*. The message was just a question mark.

"I need to reply to this," I told Ian, motioning toward my phone and walking deeper into the house, leaving him on the porch.

"Sure. I'll go."

"No, stay!"

With my back to Ian, I set the signed photo aside and typed my reply: I might have met someone.

Unknown: That was fast. ☹.

Me: We clicked right away.

But I also knew it might be due to our shared trauma. Trauma bonding. That kind of thing could create a sense of connection, but it wasn't real and wouldn't last. I needed to find out.

Unknown: I just want you to be happy.

What a strange concept. Happiness. It wasn't anything I'd really thought about in years, but here, standing in the place where my mother had been killed, it suddenly seemed like something that could actually happen.

Unknown: Goodbye, love.

Love. It was what he'd always called me. In that moment, I realized Salvador had been the first step in my return to life. During a weird and unguarded existence when I was pretending to be someone I wasn't, he'd broken through. I really wished he and my mother could have met. They would have adored each other.

Me: **Goodbye.**

I tucked my phone away and returned to Ian. I had the feeling he and I would know each other for a long time, and we might or might not become serious. He might even be a person I'd share almost everything with, but maybe not this news. I'd killed Salvador once. I would not risk harming him again.

I told Ian about the case in Florida.

"Sounds interesting," he said, then added, "There's been some talk in the department about making me a detective. They think I'm pretty good at detecting stuff, but I told them it was all you." He shrugged. "I'm going to take some time off and think about it."

"Good idea."

"Maybe you'd be into having someone tag along on the Florida story," he said. "Would you need any help? An assistant, perhaps?"

I couldn't imagine being around anybody twenty-four hours a day, but I might be able to tolerate Ian. Maybe I'd even decide to move to Savannah when I was done with the new case.

When I didn't reply, he changed his tack. "Or how about just a friend?" he suggested. "Or both."

"We do make a pretty good team."

I could feel a shift in me. I was still my mother's found object, still proud of it the way I'd been as a child, but stronger because of the story. It might have been corny, but I got the sense I was finally and truly finding myself, which also meant I might be ready for someone else.

I opened the door wider and let Ian into the house and my life.

ABOUT THE AUTHOR

Photo © 2018 Martha Weir

Anne Frasier is the *New York Times*, #1 Amazon Charts, and *USA Today* bestselling author of the Detective Jude Fontaine Mysteries, the Elise Sandburg series, and the Inland Empire novels. With more than a million copies sold, her award-winning books span the genres of suspense, mystery, thriller, romantic suspense, paranormal, and memoir. *The Body Reader* received the 2017 Thriller Award for Best Original Paperback Novel from International Thriller Writers. Other honors include a RITA for Romantic Suspense and a Daphne du Maurier Award for Paranormal Romantic Mystery/Suspense. Her thrillers have hit the *USA Today* bestseller list and have been featured in Mystery Guild, the Literary Guild, and Book of the Month. Her memoir, *The Orchard*, was an *O, The Oprah Magazine* Fall Pick; a One Book, One Community read; and one of the Librarians' Best Books of 2011. Visit her website at www.annefrasier.com.